Booksellers love *The Annie Year*!

"Set against a backdrop of Iowa farm life and a burgeoning meth industry, *The Annie Year* brings to life a warm and wonderful cast of curmudgeonly characters and proves that friendship can save your life. Stephanie Ash makes a huge splash with this debut novel. *The Annie Year* needs to be on everyone's 2016 reading list."

—Pamela Klinger-Horn, Excelsior Bay Books

"*The Annie Year* is addicting and swiftly pulls you into Tandy's need for disruption in her small town life. Tandy makes many questionable decisions, and Stephanie Ash shows that they are often a necessary part of being alive. Funny and full of keen observations, I loved reading *The Annie Year* much the same way I love reading Judy Blume, James Cain, Tom Drury, and John Irving, other writers with the gift of being able to get us inside a character's motivation. Ash has created a flawed character, not without judgment, yet we stick with her and root for her, as we should for ourselves."

—Steve Salardino, Skylight Books

"Stephanie Ash has the voice. Ash's story is to the Midwest like what Larry McMurtry does with Texas and Carolyn Chute with rural Maine."

—David Unowsky, Subtext Books

The Unnamed Press
P.O. Box 411272
Los Angeles, CA 90041

Published in North America by The Unnamed Press.

3 5 7 9 10 8 6 4 2

ISBN: 978-1-939419-96-5

Library of Congress Control Number: 2016952137

This book is distributed by Publishers Group West

Cover design & typeset by Jaya Nicely

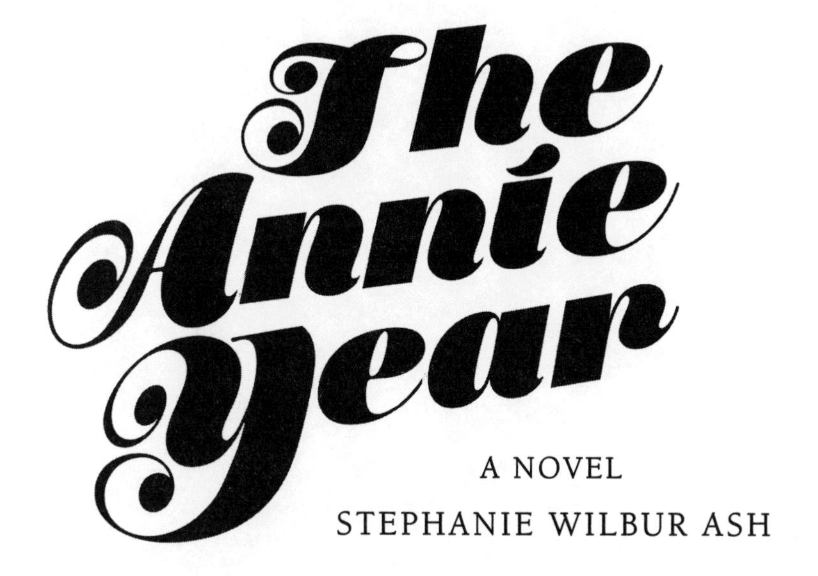

A NOVEL

STEPHANIE WILBUR ASH

The Unnamed Press
Los Angeles, CA

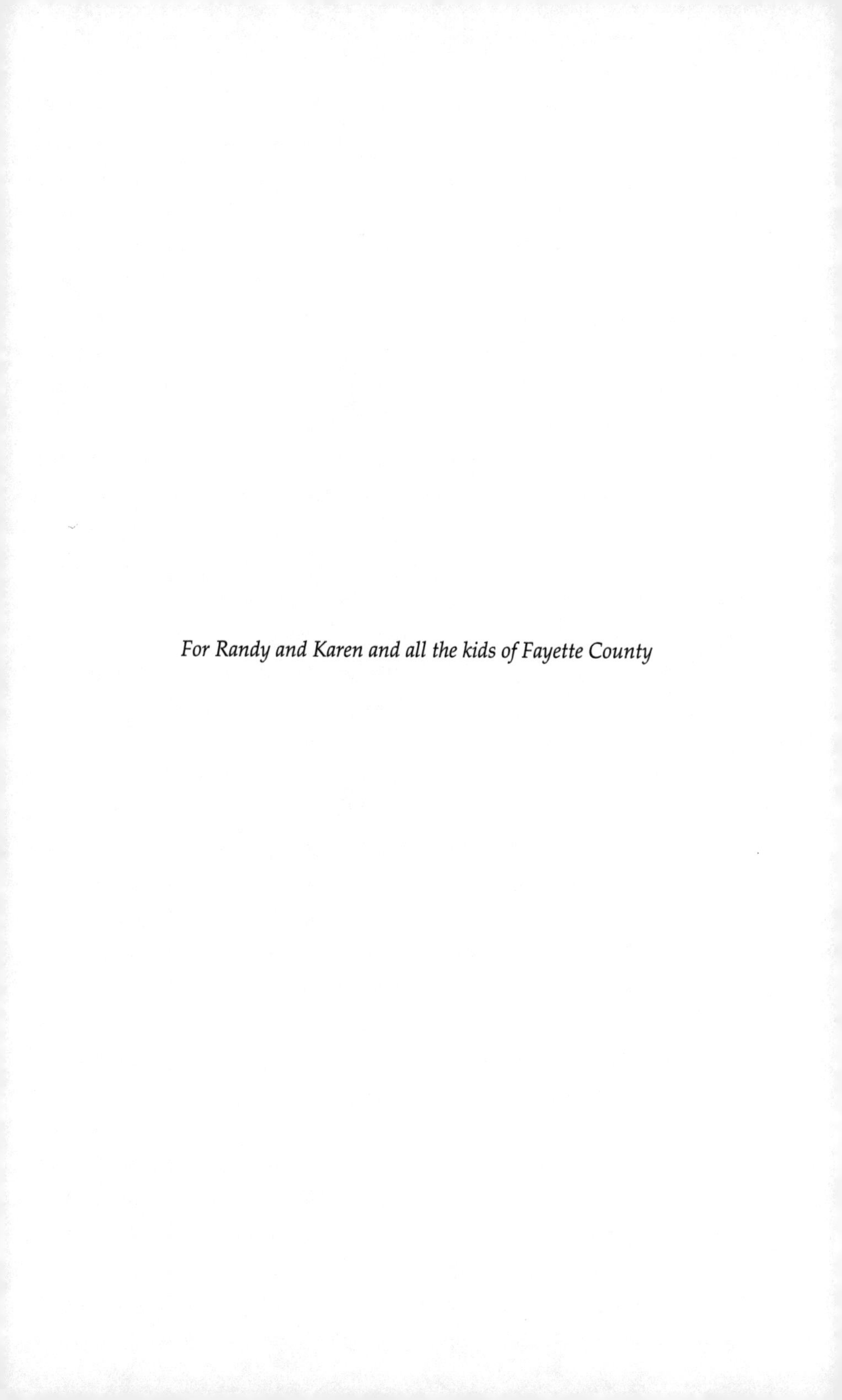

For Randy and Karen and all the kids of Fayette County

In the absence of specific rules, standards, or guidance, or in the face of conflicting opinions, a member should test decisions and deeds by asking: "Am I doing what a person of integrity would do?"

— American Institute of Certified Public Accountants, Code of Professional Conduct, Section 54, Article III: Integrity

Out of her defeats has been born a new quality in woman.
I have a name for it. I call it Tandy.

— Sherwood Anderson, "Tandy," from *Winesburg, Ohio*

I.

A CERTIFIED PUBLIC ACCOUNT

1

The people in this town will try to tell you that the whole mess that was last year started with the new vocational agriculture teacher, but they would be wrong. I was there so I know the truth. In fact, through my own mistakes and failures, the number of which I readily admit to you is plentiful, I caused much of it to happen. Obviously I am in a better position to recount the events than a busybody pastor or a senile doctor or an out-of-work rail worker or an old, crusty farmer who, though immensely wealthy, operates with the social skills of roadkill.

Also, it is my profession to provide accurate accounting based on quantifiable facts. It is a profession I was raised into and have been making a reasonable living at for nearly twenty years. I have spent my entire life correcting the accounting mistakes of those very people I just mentioned. So, ask yourself: Whom among us would you trust?

It did not start with the Vo-Ag teacher, though I had heard there would be a new one, and, in the interest of accuracy, I must say that I was looking forward to meeting him. I was, in fact, curious about him. I had even asked those who had encountered him before me what their impressions of him were. I am a local taxpayer. It is perfectly natural for a taxpayer to be curious about the new public school teacher.

Plus, new people do not often come into this town with the stated intention of sticking around, as the Vo-Ag teacher had flagrantly declared to Silvia Vontrauer. "I will live out the rest of my days here!" he had told her. Such declarations were of great interest to all of us, though I don't expect people like you to understand that.

It started when I purchased that big black sleeping bag of a coat, right before the high school musical and the Thanksgiving holiday, specifically to wear to the quarterly meeting of the Order of the Pessimists, which liked to meet before all the holidays that ask you to drum up renewed happiness for life.

As I was both secretary and treasurer of this organization, I was obligated to go. It was my job to report on the status of the checking account, as well as to write the check at the end of the meeting to cover our expenses. It was also my job to take detailed notes, for posterity, which the members of the Order noted loudly and often—"For posterity!"—before being overcome with laughter, followed by that kind of choking that comes from laughing too hard.

There was no way out of this responsibility that I could see, except death, I suppose. So in the interest of personal enjoyment, and, of course, function, this being the upper American Midwest, I had ordered a new coat off eBay, from a woman called organicsuzee. I paid seventeen dollars for it plus six dollars in shipping, which I thought was a fair price for a hardly worn full-length Lands' End coat filled with goose down.

I fully disclosed this to Doc, the doctor in this town and my father's closest business associate, and Huff, the lawyer in this town and my father's other closest business associate, as they pulled up to me on Main Street in front of the Powerhaus. My father had been dead for a long time, but here were Doc and Huff, every day, still up my ass.

"You paid for *shipping*!" was the first thing Huff shouted, his lips and face going red while he tried to park his golf cart—the only thing the cops in this town let him drive—while also waving a can of beer.

"I am a free and autonomous human being," I said.

"You're a goddamn idiot, Tandy Caide," Doc said, lighting a cigarette. "You could have driven to Walmart for six cents' worth of gas and gotten a coat just as cheap."

"And it's *black*?!" Huff shouted. "It shows so much dirt!"

"How appropriate," I said. "It matches the unclean minds of my company," to which they responded with "Ho! Ho!" and "Oh, *really*, little girl?!"—something they have called me since I was an actual little girl, though today I am in my midthirties and over six feet tall.

It was an unseasonably warm and windless day for November, though a big chill was expected. The sign at First National said 60 degrees and the faint smell of cat pee curled around the air, which meant the farmers were using the still weather to knife anhydrous ammonia into their fields for fall fertilizing. Main Street was unusually thick with cars—six in two blocks. Someone was even forced to parallel park.

Three cars drove past us. The drivers acknowledged our presence with the lifting of the index finger from the steering wheel, as is our town's custom. I recognized each one of them as a client of mine, so I waved back. This is good business. A rusty pickup truck drove by us slowly. The driver had a pocked face. I did not recognize him. A bunch of high school kids were in the bed of the truck, waving cans of beer. One of them I recognized: Hope, the daughter of my best friend, Barb, who is Huff's daughter. I had not spoken to Barb since high school, not counting Barb's yearly income tax appointments or the occasional ask for a coffee refill at the diner across the street from my office. I had not seen Huff speak to her either, except briefly at Christmas when they exchanged pie and bottles of whiskey. I had not spoken to Hope since before she went through puberty. These people, plus Doc—this was my closest family. This is how we do "family" here.

The truck peeled off and the daughter, Hope, threw her beer onto the street.

It was far too warm to be wearing a full-length goose down coat. But what could I do? I can't control the weather.

Once my eyes adjusted to the darkness of the Powerhaus, I could see that Huff was especially jolly. He had been to Winthrop earlier in the day, where he had taken some mutual clients from the Winthrop co-op late-season golfing, with free drinks all around, with the most free drinks going to himself because, as Huff liked to say, "Just because I have a gift with people doesn't mean I shouldn't be paid for it."

Gary Mussman, the laid-off machinist Doc and Huff had put on retainer when the Chicago Great Western railroad operation pulled out of town, was folding a napkin over and over in the back booth because Sylvia Vontrauer, chairwoman of the Theater Boosters, was at the window booth in front with Mr. Henderson, the high school choir teacher. Silvia waved at me with one of the ends of that scarf that looks like piano keys.

She considers me to be a great lover of the theater, though this is not the truth. My father always gave $100 to the Theater Boosters. And so the first week of every September, Silvia Vontrauer—wife of Burt Vontrauer, one of my biggest clients—comes gliding into my office wearing that piano scarf, looking for her $100. "No one loves the theater like you and I do, Tandy," she always says right before she takes my check.

I waved back. That's what a good businesswoman does, even to theater people.

"They're sitting at our table," Doc said as he slid into the back booth next to Gary.

Huff waddled into the booth too, a new drink in each hand. "Of course they are," he said. "People like that always sit in the window. They need to be *seen*."

Gary said, with his trademark stupidity: "Yeah! That's where *we* always sit!"

"They're doing it to fuck with us," Huff said. And so the meeting started.

"Who's here? Just us four? Figures," Doc said.

"We're the only ones in this organization," I said.

"At least we have a quorum," Gary said.

Doc asked me to stand and deliver the charter. It wasn't my turn, and I reminded everyone of this. "But you're the worst of the bunch," Doc said. "It's your duty. For posterity!"

So I stood next to the table and recited the oath, which goes like this:

This is the meeting of the Order of the Pessimists, founded in 1992 in response to the unjustified optimism that runs rampant in this town. We believe in schadenfreude, we uphold Murphy's Law, and we embrace the slow, sad, inevitable decay of all things. The only things we can be sure of are death and taxes.

"That was terrible," Doc said.

"Just terrible," Gary said.

Then we sat there, contemplating the vague outlines of one another's ugly faces, as was our custom.

But I was wearing a new coat. There was something about that, something not quantifiable.

So I said, "We always do this. Sit here and say nothing like this."

"Why, Tandy!" Doc said. "You're full of piss and vinegar tonight!" He found this hilarious. It wouldn't be later but that night it was.

"And so right she is," Huff said. "We are a sad and pitiful group." Huff raised his glass, and shouted, "To us!"

Mary Ellen came by and we ordered. She was out of bean soup, and Doc and Huff groaned about having to eat potato soup instead.

"It doesn't produce nearly the desired amount of flatulence!" Huff whined.

Doc said, "I want Tandy to put it on the order of business for next time."

I wrote down in the notebook from my Order of the Pessimists file: *Talk about the crime of the Powerhaus being out of bean soup.*

"Why can't we discuss it right now? You always put things off!" Huff said.

"You always have to question my authority!" Doc said.

"You don't *have* any authority!" Huff said.

Gary looked over at me and said, "This is a good meeting."

Doc said, "Do we have anything that needs to be carried over from our last meeting?"

I checked the notebook. Our last meeting had been the day before the new school year. According to my notes, someone had recommended that we discuss what it is we are thankful for at this current meeting, as it would be near Thanksgiving.

Doc frowned. "Who said that?"

I didn't remember and it was not in my notes.

"Figures," Huff snuffed.

"I think it was me," Gary said.

Huff sighed at Gary and swallowed more of his drink. Doc lit a cigarette and said, "Gary, you are a goddamn idiot and always will be." Then he turned to me. "Tandy, you are terrible at notating the accounts of these meetings and you always will be."

"I thought *I* was the idiot," I said, referring to his earlier comments regarding the extravagance of my coat.

"You are an idiot also, and you are terrible at notating the accounts of these meetings."

"Should I write that down?" I asked.

"Yes," Doc said. "Please note for the record that Gary Mussman will remain an idiot in perpetuity, and that Tandy Caide is an idiot as well, and that she is not the World's Greatest Accountant, despite what the trophy in her office says."

My fingers got tingly and then went numb. At the time I thought perhaps this was from dehydration due to my sweating so much in my coat. Later, I would hear that it is the stress of being on the edge of something dangerous that causes this.

"I'm not going to write that down," I said.

They all looked at me.

"Why not?" Gary asked.

I didn't have an answer.

Huff made his face all fake-soft, like he cared about my feelings. "Are you afraid, little girl, that you *aren't* the World's Greatest Accountant?"

"No," I said, though the thought had run through my head more than once.

"Because you're not," he said. "That's not your trophy."

I wrote it down then. I wrote it down exactly the way they said it. I wrote: *Tandy Caide is not the World's Greatest Accountant.*

And then I stared at it, because there it was, in plain language, in my own handwriting even, recorded for posterity in official Order of the Pessimists meeting minutes.

"Maybe we *should* talk about what we are thankful for," Gary said.

I didn't want to talk about what we were thankful for. Something was churning inside me—something new, or maybe not new but something old that suddenly happened to be a lot closer to my mouth. Perhaps I *did* want there to be something to be thankful for.

Doc said, "Okay then. I'll go first." He held up his lit cigarette. He said, "I am thankful for cigarettes. They mean I will suffer less time on this earth than the rest of you fuckers. Huff?"

Huff held up his glass and said, "I am thankful for whiskey. It helps me forget the good things. Gary?"

Gary took a drink of his beer, thought for a moment, and then said, "Friends?"

Doc held his head in his hands and Huff groaned.

Gary quickly found something more suitable. He said, "I'm thankful I never moved out of this piece-of-shit town when I had the chance ten years ago, because then I never had to make any friends with any goddamn optimists."

"Bravo!" Doc and Huff shouted.

Then there was silence. We stared at one another's face outlines.

"Tandy?" Doc asked.

The tingling again, from my elbows to my fingers.

"I'm thankful the women's toilet works in this place," I said, "though it won't by the time I leave." Doc and Huff laughed. I continued. "I'm also thankful for the clients of mine that are still alive, though they won't be much longer." Doc and Huff laughed again and Huff pounded the table with glee.

Our food came, which brought up the status of the checking account. "There is $272.14 in the account," I said. "If our dinner checks remain at the same rate, and we don't incur any more expenses, that's enough for one more quarterly meeting, with $32.14 left over in April for a charitable contribution."

"Where should it go, do you think?" Gary asked.

"How about vocational agriculture and the Future Farmers of America?" Doc asked, and all three of them stared me down yet again.

I was not prepared for that.

Oh, I should have been! This is how it is in our town. It's not like in your towns closer to the river, where your artistic sensibilities allow you the ability to transcend your problems and your close intellectual friends support you and your efforts to make your life worth living!

"I definitely know that Vo-Ag and FFA could use it," I said, though I knew no such thing.

"I imagine you have some special kind of information," Doc said.

"I am privy to that kind of information, yes," I said, though at the time I was not.

"Kids still take Vo-Ag? Kids still participate in FFA?" Gary asked. "Where the hell will they work?"

Doc and Huff stared at Gary. Then Doc said, "Gary, I take back what I said about you being an idiot. You're a goddamn genius. Tandy's the true idiot. Put *that* in the notes, Tandy."

And I did.

For posterity.

That is how it started.

II.

THE VO-AG TEACHER

2

It was the next night that I met the new vocational agriculture teacher. He was standing at the east entrance to the high school auditorium under a big *ANNIE* sign someone had cut from cardboard and glued some glitter to.

When I add up the total sum of that year, it is this particular line item that always gets me: it had to be an *Annie* year.

You see, if there is a talented tall girl at the high school, they do *Hello, Dolly!* If there is a girl who is unusually ugly but funny enough to pull off Snoopy, they do *You're a Good Man, Charlie Brown.* If a lot of boys get suspended from football early in the season for drinking and one of the star players—the quarterback or the lead tackle or whoever—can convince the rest of the team into singing in public, they do *Guys and Dolls.*

They don't do *Annie* that often because *Annie* requires a certain type of extraordinary talent. There must be a girl, usually a small one, with both spunky charm and believable innocence. That just doesn't happen in this town.

Probably there are Annies with spunky-yet-innocent dispositions on every busy street corner in your town. Here, you might get a believable innocence, and it may even come paired with a good strong church voice, but the spunky charm will have been beaten out of that girl before her tenth birthday, as was the case with Dee Dee Scarsdale, our Annie that year, and she had even been given the privilege of years of music lessons because her mother is the town's band teacher.

There are several children with only spunky charm here, though. They act like they invented spunky charm, throwing rocks at the Country Kitchen sign and then laughing obnoxiously while they toss their hair and their body parts around. They lack even a hint of the believable innocence Annie is supposed to have. The children in this town are like that woman sitting on the swing on *Hee Haw*, Kenny Rogers's wife, pretending to be a virgin but with her breasts popping out of a tightly wound corset and the entire audience in on the joke.

I was looking for my husband, Gerald, and so I didn't notice the Vo-Ag teacher at first. I noticed Elmer Griggs, who owns the golf course, pretending to swing a golf club in the corner for Dave Oppegaard, the head volunteer fireman who also manages the grain elevator. They waved when they saw me. I waved back. Cindy from Prairie Lanes was standing behind the snack table, and she waved when she saw me, and then she pointed me out to her best friend, Helen Sweeter, who also waved. I waved back. Howie Claus, the Methodist minister, was complaining to Clive Liestman, one of John Mueller's farmhands, about who knows what, but Clive was looking at me instead of Howie. Mueller, who is my best client, walked out of the bathroom and then Clive pointed at me and soon all three of them were looking at me.

I decided to keep my coat on.

Doc and Huff held up the west wall by the famous picture of Gerald throwing the state-winning shot put in high school, back when he fit into tiny yellow shorts. Huff leaned toward Doc and whispered something to him. I could see Huff's puffy lips flapping, how he bounced from one bowed leg to another. Doc listened with his spindly tobacco arms crossed, staring me down.

Then Dieter Bierbrauer, the high school principal, waved me over. He was standing with the new Vo-Ag teacher under the ANNIE sign.

And there he was: ponytail, bright red work shirt with the sleeves rolled up, tight faded jeans, man clogs, and that belt.

Dieter said, "This is the new Vo-Ag teacher and Future Farmers of America adviser," and said his name too, "Kenny Tischer," and then, "Tandy is a great lover of the theater."

The Vo-Ag teacher said, "Is that right?" and smiled widely. His teeth were very white, like in a commercial for toothpaste. "Do you love all the arts, or just the theater?"

"I give a hundred dollars every year to the Theater Boosters," I said.

Dieter nodded so fast his white-blond combover flapped.

The Vo-Ag teacher said, "Principal Bierbrauer here was asking me about my belt... *Tandy*."

He said my name slowly, in what you might call a deliberate way. It sounded like he thought my name was special, like it was full of potential.

No one had ever said my name like that before.

"It is an unusual belt," Dieter said. He was looking at the Vo-Ag teacher's crotch.

Perhaps this is okay with people like you, for a man to look at another man's crotch, but this was brand new to me. Dieter actually *bent down* to get a closer look. And then, I don't know why—I can't explain it except to say this is the kind of effect the Vo-Ag teacher had on people, because I don't think I could have helped myself, or maybe I was just a weak person then (I'm stronger now)—but *I* bent down to get a closer look.

There I was, thirty seconds into meeting him, bending toward his crotch.

I must say, though, that it was an unusual belt. It was made of cloth, not leather, and it had red, black, and green patterns and a row of tiny shells stitched along one edge. There was no buckle and no holes on the ends of the belt. Each end was stopped up with a tiny fringe, and the Vo-Ag teacher had simply tied these fringed ends together in a knot above his zipper so the ends waved out like some sort of cotton butterfly.

Maybe you see these kinds of belts all the time where you live. I do not.

I said that too. "I have never seen a belt like that before," I said.

I wanted to say, *Why are you here? Why would a person like you with a belt like this and a ponytail like that and man clogs ever come to a place like this?* But I didn't.

The Vo-Ag teacher squinted at me. He said, "I got it while I was serving in the Peace Corps in the country of Benin, in Africa. For the Yoruba people there, shells were once currency *and* art medium. The Yoruba believe art is inseperable from life."

Dieter and I nodded fast and hard like pecking chickens. Dieter's combover flapped like a flag.

The Vo-Ag teacher said, "It's beautiful, isn't it?"

A stranger who tells you how beautiful his own belt is?

I nodded in the direction of his clogs. They were wool. His feet would get very wet this winter, I thought. He should get himself a good pair of boots if he's going to stick around. I had never heard of the Yoruba. I had never even met a person from Africa. I had only been to Des Moines a couple of times.

Dieter sucked in a big breath, put his big white hands on his thick waist, looked over to somewhere else and then walked there.

"So, what do you do... *Tandy*?" The Vo-Ag teacher did that thing with my name again, and that time I heard what was under it. I'm not such a dull tack.

It was a mocking thing.

"I'm a CPA... *Kenny*," I said, and I looked him right in the eye.

He raised his eyebrows nearly to his hairline, like he was overly surprised, like he was in some sort of play himself right then. He chuckled. He said, "Is that right?"

I said, "That's right."

He said, "Well, I'm terrible with money."

"Is that right?"

"That's right."

"Well, I guess we both know what's right then."

He was exhausting. Certainly you can see *that*!

"It must be fascinating to be a CPA in this town," he said. "You must know the money secrets of everyone sitting in this auditorium."

One of the big cafeteria doors swung open but it was not my husband, Gerald, just Jenny Finch, the checkout girl at Hy-Vee with the big boobs.

The Vo-Ag teacher leaned toward me, and I could feel a tickle in my ear from his whisper, "So who's loaded around here? Bierbrauer? That farmer, Mueller? That crazy lawyer, Huff?"

I think that fight-or-flight thing they talk about on Mutual of Omaha's *Wild Kingdom* is true because I almost hit him, but the cafeteria door swung open again and Gerald came barreling in like a semi.

Gerald could be good like that.

I left that Vo-Ag teacher standing alone, doing a little tap dance in his clogs like some sort of hippie elf.

Gerald was too fat to fit in his seat. It used to be that his body fit into that seat the same way ice cream folds over a cone poured by a poorly trained Dairy Queen girl. But not last year, not that *Annie* year. I put my hands on his shoulders and I pushed down as hard as I could but that just made everyone in the auditorium laugh.

"Did these chairs get smaller?!" Gerald said extra loud, for everyone's benefit. Huff piped up from two rows back—"Put him on the stage!"—and of course Dieter did. And of course Gerald walked right up to it and slowly backed himself into it like his ass was a dump truck. And of course everyone cheered him on.

There isn't a single person in this town who did not like Gerald, except perhaps the high school students who rode his school bus that year.

I sat in my usual seat with quiet and normal-sized Bud Sweitzer on my right and Gerald's empty seat on my left. Mueller, who is indeed loaded with money, sat silent behind me. Then the lights faded and Gerald's face dissolved and Mrs. Scarsdale, the band teacher and mother of last year's Annie, counted down *1, 2, 3, 4,* and the high school band blew the first notes of the first song like a trickle, all wobbly, and then somewhere in the dark the voice of Mrs. Scarsdale's ninth-grade daughter, Dee Dee Scarsdale, oozing fake innocence, sang out: *Maybe far away, or maybe real nearby—*

I pinched the skin on my right wrist hard. The stage lights came up, and I thought for a moment that maybe having Gerald onstage would actually be better because I wouldn't have to look at the production itself. But I saw that though Gerald's hands were still latched around his gut, his eyes were closed, and his head had already sunk into his chins.

I closed my eyes too. I tried not to look at our Annie.

And then a bump and a stumble and then hands on my knees and then hands around my shoulders, and I opened my eyes and just above my nose was the colorful cotton butterfly of the Vo-Ag teacher's belt.

Just like that we were together.

He never asked.

He was just there.

Won't you please come get your baby, maybe? she sang.

He smelled like fresh-mowed sage in a green and wet ditch, like a spice I knew from the kitchen of a long-lost relative, like early spring even though it was the beginning of winter.

From what had always been Gerald's seat, the Vo-Ag teacher watched the stage as if it were a miracle and not a bunch of awkward small-town teenagers trying to live up to their makeup. His eyes got big and round, like eggs; his mouth got open, like a pancake—his face looked like a brand-new breakfast. And when, at intermission, he turned toward me, his eyes were wet.

I'd seen grown men cry, certainly, but only at funerals, and even then I'd seen only the shaking of grown men's backs, which can look just like laughing if you don't think about it too hard. But something about his wet eyes, the way he looked right at me with them, as if he had no reason to be ashamed. It dropped my bottom out.

I watched the whole show. Everything. I watched twelve little girls dance around in dingy underwear. I watched the Hendersons' family dog, playing the part of Sandy, run up the aisle next to me to sniff the crotch of Karen Wilson, the speech pathologist at the hospital. I watched Warbucks's staff dance around Annie wringing their hands, singing, *We've never had a little girl! We've never had a little girl!* I watched Punjab karate-chop a Bolshevik, Franklin and Eleanor Roosevelt get their hearts melted by Annie's sunny optimism—"There's a song I used to sing in the orphanage..." she says. "Think of the children!" Eleanor says. I watched Annie, who was really Dee Dee Scarsdale with her good strong church voice trying hard to show spunk, dream of her real folks. I watched her reject Daddy Warbucks in favor of the fake family, which promised to be a real family, but was really just a couple of criminals looking to make some money off her spunky, charming little heart.

I had never actually watched a show. This time, I watched it all. And for that one moment I believed that a little orphan girl *could* find promise in the sun.

Then Hope ruined it. The daughter of my estranged best friend ruined it. It was a tragic surprise, I suppose, and also not. It was the kind of inevitable sadness I had come to expect but kept forgetting to expect, the kind of sadness that continues to snap me back to the true order of things in my life.

Toward the end of the show—right before Annie and Daddy Warbucks have their big finale, right where she should not have been—she staggered onto the stage. She was in the long red nightgown that indicated her role as Ms. Hannigan, the drunken orphanage headmistress. It was split in the chest to nearly her belly button. She is tiny, like her mother, Barb. Her stomach was flat, pulled back to nearly her spine so that she was like a saltine cracker from the side. But all that exposed skin made her look larger. So did the way she swaggered around as the drunken orphanage tyrant Ms. Hannigan. She weaved in and out of that scene that wasn't hers with an empty wine bottle. *"Did I hear singing in here?"* she slurred. It was a line from way back in Act I. She stumbled, and everyone leaned back, like in those old pictures of audiences wearing 3-D glasses in a movie theater when the monster jumps out for the first time.

Everyone but him, of course. The Vo-Ag teacher leaned as forward as he could. He buried his hands in the long brown hair of Andrea Bodinski sitting in the seat in front of him.

Hope swaggered toward Annie, who just stood there, frozen, and with one wide arc of her skinny arm slapped that Annie across the face.

From the side of the stage, we all saw Mr. Henderson step forward and make a slicing motion across his neck. He mouthed, *That's enough.* Hope hoisted that wine bottle into the air and threw it.

It hit him square between the eyes.

Everyone gasped, including me.

Hope bent over into a big belly laugh as all the lights went out.

Then he was laughing too, the only other one in the auditorium. The two of them were laughing while the rest of us sat in the dark. I will never forget that.

Behind me Mueller kicked my chair. Next to me, the Vo-Ag teacher's hot breath was in my ear, saying, "Who is *that*?" He grabbed my arm and put his forehead on my shoulder. His ponytail swished around and grazed my neck. He laughed and laughed, and whispered into my ear, "What kind of a place is this?" while the rest of them, all of them, said, *"Who's that laughing? Who's that laughing?"* with Huff, loudest of all, shouting: "I SEE TANDY CAIDE HAS A NEW FRIEND."

3

Later that night I lay down on the white eyelet comforter that had been on my bed since I was in the fourth grade. I listened to Gerald snoring in his bedroom across the hall. His bedroom is the one that used to belong to my father and mother. This whole cottage, the one on the go-around at the top of the hill on the north side of town, the one right next to Huff's, used to belong to my father and mother. My father bought it in the fourth year of his business, the year I was born. I have been told by Doc and Huff that he painted the shingles shit brown to match the color of his soul. I have also been told by Doc and Huff that the three of them stalked this cottage like a pack of coyotes, and when old Edie Meier's husband, Elmer, died, they convinced her kids that she was better off in the nursing home over in Fayette, where she could play bridge and eat meat every day and not have to shovel snow off the cottage's driveway. Whether this story is true, and whether this was in Edie's best interest, and whether my father's soul was the color of shit, was always dependent on the drunkenness of Huff or the tenderheartedness of Doc. If the topic came up when Huff was drunk and Doc was simultaneously tenderhearted, I invented urgent work to do and left to do it. I would not wish that disagreement on anyone.

So nothing in this little cottage on the go-around has ever truly belonged to Gerald. It belongs to me only on the technicality of my birthright. But still that other bedroom—the one with wallpaper printed with tiny roses and those cherub babies you see on Valentine's Day—is Gerald's. He had been sleeping alone there since the second year of our marriage, when he decided to no longer wear underwear to bed because it crawled up his butt cheeks when he slept. Also, his snoring sounded like drowning.

I got up and opened the small window that faces out toward Doc and Huff's place across the go-around, shingled in the same shit brown. Out there was that sagy smell again, just underneath the cat-pee smell of newly applied anhydrous ammonia. I thought about the Vo-Ag teacher with his colorful belt and the man clogs that would not survive winter. He seemed too good to be in a place like this.

I went back to my bed, and to stop myself from thinking about him I went over the order of the stripes on the wallpaper, timed to Gerald's snoring—thick, thick, thin, thick, thick, thin, thick, thin—which had always worked for me in the past. It didn't work anymore. The smell of sage and cat pee and my sweat mixed up together. It seemed like the smell of something about to happen.

The Vo-Ag teacher reminded me of Bruce Willis, when Bruce Willis was on that big wraparound farmhouse porch in that Seagram's Golden Wine Cooler commercial in the 1980s. In that commercial, the screen door of a farmhouse bursts open and Bruce Willis comes out of the house with a Seagram's Golden Wine Cooler in his hand. He's got tight faded jeans on and a black T-shirt with the sleeves rolled up. There's a band playing on the porch. He puts this bottle of Seagram's Golden Wine Cooler up to his mouth and uses it as a microphone, singing, *Seagram's Golden Wine Coolers. It's wet and it's dry. My, my, my, my.* And everyone has a wonderful time.

My father hated that commercial. Every time it came on he would throw up his hands and yell, "Jesus Christ! What the hell does Bruce Willis know about farmhouse blues?!"

But I always thought, even then, before I had breasts or my full height or a driver's license: *How does my father possibly know the heart and mind of Bruce Willis?*

Finally I went to Gerald's bedroom and I woke him by touching his penis, and eventually we satisfied each other as best as we could, given Gerald's size. I think it had been about seven months since we had done anything resembling that. Afterward, he pressed himself against my back while I stared at the chubby cherub babies on the wallpaper. He was so fat he couldn't reach his arms around me. His top arm could get to only my left breast, so he held that.

But still he was mine, at least by marriage. People like you may or may not understand this, but when it has been hammered into you your whole life that very little of that life is actually yours, a small technicality like marriage can sometimes mean something.

I said, "What if we got a foreign exchange student?"

He said, "From where?"

I said, "Benin, in Africa?" and as soon as I said it I heard how ridiculous I sounded. Maybe even suspect. "I don't know. Anywhere I guess."

Gerald didn't move. Finally he said, "I don't think it's a good idea."

"Why not?"

"Well," he said, "what if this African foreign exchange student walked out to the backyard one night and saw us making love in our hot tub?"

We didn't have a hot tub.

"You tricked me," I said.

He laughed at me like I was a kid throwing a tantrum. "Oh, come on, Candy Cane," he said. He squeezed my breast. He whispered, "It would be easier, with the water, more buoyant."

"It's too expensive," I said.

"Maybe you should look for one on eBay," he said.

Maybe you should disappear, I thought. But I said nothing.

Gerald rolled to his back and fell asleep. I got up and went to my own bed and did the same.

4

That night, a house blew up. It was on the other end of town from the cottage on the go-around, down by the closed Hardee's, across from the closed A&W, and on an entire city block of houses owned by a holding company in Mankato. It was that area of town where railroad employees had once lived, but most of the houses had been carved up into apartments for Section 8 housing now, or abandoned entirely. I had little to do with that part of town anymore, as few people living there had property or businesses or even enough income to necessitate a CPA. While I was walking to my office that morning, Cindy from Prairie Lanes passed me on her way to open the bowling alley and told me the occupants of the house had not been living here for more than a few months. She heard they were nephews of Arnie Utzke, a former client of mine who had once worked for the railroad and now worked in Forest City at the Winnebago factory. But she wasn't entirely sure, and Arnie had moved to Forest City, so no one could ask him. She did say for sure that one of the men who lived there had his face blown off in the explosion. She knew this because Dave Oppegaard, the head volunteer fireman, had told her earlier that morning when she saw him at the Kum & Go. Oppegaard had gone into the burning house and saw him. "His skin was basically melting off his bones," Cindy said. Then she shrugged and asked, "Methheads—what are you going to do?"

But it wasn't really a question.

I wondered briefly if it was the pock-faced man who had driven the rusty pickup I'd seen only a few days earlier. But just as I stood outside my Main Street office, catching a whiff of the cat pee, egg fart, and turpentine smell that hung in the air, the pock-faced man in his rusty pickup truck drove slowly by again. He was alone—no drunken high school students partied in the bed of his truck this time. I watched him and he watched me. I was skeptical of him, as I am skeptical of all new people. I do not know why he was skeptical of me. I had always been here.

I unlocked my office door and, for the first time in my entire life, and probably in my father's life too, I locked the door behind me. Shortly after that, around lunchtime, the Vo-Ag teacher knocked on it.

I opened it. "You don't have an appointment," I said to him from the doorway.

He laughed like a horse. He showed me his white teeth. They were prominent, like a horse's. He seemed to have more teeth than the rest of us.

"Dieter said I can smoke here," he said. He had a pack of cigarettes wedged between his multicolored belt and his too-tight jeans.

It is true. It's one of the special features I offer my clients, and I believed then that it was what kept most of them from driving to Decorah or Dubuque or La Crosse. My biggest client, John Mueller, and I have a joke about it even. I say, "It's not the accounting?" And Mueller says, "A monkey could do the accounting if he had the right software."

"You can smoke in the teachers' lounge," I said.

"Dieter says I can smoke here," he said.

"Dieter running my office now?" I asked.

He laughed again, like this was all some big joke. And then he poked me with his long, bony index finger, right below my belly button.

The people where you live, do they poke each other like that?

"That girl, Hope, the one who threw the bottle, she showed up in my class today."

What was I supposed to say to that? I said nothing.

"It was either Vo-Ag or expulsion," he said. "No other teacher would take her."

"I have an appointment," I said, and closed the door.

It was a lunch appointment with Mueller, though he would never call it lunch. What he would say is "I am coming to town," and I would meet him at Country Kitchen and make damn sure there was a double order of onion rings there, even though a doctor in Waterloo told him he's not supposed to eat onion rings because of some vague evidence discovered during his colonoscopy, a vagueness of which had only strengthened fifty-year-old Mueller's resolve to eat more onion rings.

I never wanted to sit at one of Barb's tables, but Mueller would ask to switch if we didn't. "She's the fastest," he would say. He believed his food would taste better because it would be hotter.

But his logic was flawed. The hotness of the food is related not to the speed of the waitress but to the length of time it sits in the window after the cook has put it on a plate. I have seen Barb stand outside and smoke two entire cigarettes while someone's patty melt got soggy in that window.

But still I sat in one of Barbie's booths and, without speaking to me or even making eye contact, she brought two cups of coffee and a double order of rings.

That is excellent customer service, in case you have never seen it.

Mueller wanted to hear what was happening with Winthrop. He was looking to buy the co-op there. The co-op members didn't have enough money anymore to make it profitable. Mueller did, but he was worried about the tax implications of buying an entire co-op, which he had never done before.

"Well, it won't be a co-op anymore if you own it entirely," I said.

"What if other farmers won't use it because it's not a co-op?" he asked.

"Huff went," I said. Huff, the drunk lawyer who refused to speak to his own daughter—he's the one who handles people problems in this town. In case you are not aware, that is the definition of irony.

"It'd be cheaper for me to pay you to go to law school," Mueller said, shaking his head.

That wasn't true. I had run the numbers on this the last time he had said it. It would cost him an additional $120,000 that wouldn't pay off until after he was dead, even if he managed to live until age seventy-two.

The cheapest option would be for Mueller to develop people skills himself. Even rudimentary ones would be an improvement. But of course I didn't say that. I said, "I'm ready when you are," which made him chuckle, which is always good for business, even if it is ironic.

And that is all the talking we did about it, about anything really. Mueller is not so much for talking. He is for eating. He never gets fatter, though. He is a relatively trim man, save for beefy farmer hands and a barrel chest that has increased only in width and not girth as he has aged. I used to marvel at how he could eat so much at our lunches, but then I realized they were likely his only meals of the day because I paid for them. Mueller has always known how to butter his bread with other people's butter, even though he has plenty of butter.

Suddenly Barb appeared next to Mueller, all one hundred pounds of her. She stared him down. The coffeepot she held was shaking in her hand, her iron forearm strength was wavering. This was something I had never seen before. Mueller just shrugged and stared back, waiting for her to say something. Barb's saying something would have been highly unusual. I stared deep into my coffee, which was almost as black as I could feel Barb's heart to be at that moment.

Then Barb did say something. "This Clive Liestman," she asked Mueller directly. "Is he all right?'

Mueller shrugged. He looked into his onion rings, then picked one up and ate it. He said, "Yeah, I guess he's all right. He shows up for field work. He handles the machinery. He doesn't stir shit up. He's a farmhand. That's the definition of a model employee."

Then she turned to me. "What about you, Tandy? What do you know about this Clive?"

My hands went numb again. My armpits itched. I looked down at the stack of onion rings. The ones Mueller had not eaten were stuck together with batter and oil. I would have to pull them all apart before I could make one mine.

"Not much," I said. "Why do you ask?" It wasn't really a question. If she was unwilling to tell me, I was unwilling to tell her my opinion of him.

"Don't pretend like I don't know all about you," she said.

"Don't pretend that I care," I said back, though I regret it now as I regret all the awful things I have ever said to her or anyone, including Doc and Huff, who, unlike Barb, do not deserve my clemency.

"I'd ask you to not be an asshole but I don't think that's possible," she said.

"I am not in the business of telling people what to think," I said.

It was the longest conversation I'd had with Barbie in more than seventeen years that wasn't about income taxes.

What did I know about this Clive? At the time, he was coming by my office almost every day around three P.M. He would dip his middle into the chair across from my desk usually reserved for clients and then stretch his long body out at both ends. He liked to show off all the time how big he was, but frankly, I always thought it made him look loose, gangly, disconnected at all the important parts. The fingertips of his big hands would touch one wall of my office while his dirty boots rested against the other wall, and every time he splayed himself out like that, I thought that if he weren't working for Mueller I would walk right through his body and out the door.

He would talk for an hour about buying a farm of his own somewhere around here, though I knew he did not have the money and never would. You can't just buy a farm around here anymore unless you inherit a farm from your parents that you can leverage, or you are a famous actor or professional athlete, or you are a corporation. While he talked, I would nod and say, "Mm-hmm," and "Of course," but mostly I watched him touch everything on my desk. He was very lazy about his touching. He touched whatever was nearest him first, and when he was done with that he would reach a little farther away for the next closest thing. Sometimes when I saw him parking his pickup in front of my office, I would quickly move around the items on my desk to see how easy it would be to control the order in which he touched them. It was very easy.

"Next year, I think," he would say. "Next year, when the interest rates fall."

"That is prudent," I would say.

Then I would wait for him to lean over the desk and kiss me. It always took a long time for him to get there, but in his defense I never told him to do it any differently.

The day that Barb broke her silence and asked me about him, I spoke to Clive while I was waiting. "My friend asked about you today."

"You have friends?" he asked. I do not know if he was joking or asking an honest question. Understanding him was never a priority.

"Her name is Barb and she works across the street," I said.

He paused a bit, and the corners of his mouth turned down, and then his hands began to lazily finger the items on my desk again: the stapler, the coffee mug from the bank, the letter opener. "Maybe she wants to take me out on a date," he said. "Unless you have any better ideas."

I did not have any better ideas, which is a sad thing to admit. Still, I knew that eventually his mouth would be on mine, large but hollow, like a wet plastic bag over my face. I waited some more, and then it was there, and then I imagined myself poking through his face with the letter opener.

I kissed Clive until school let out in the hopes that the Vo-Ag teacher would come back and see us there. And when the Vo-Ag teacher didn't, I stopped kissing him and I told him I had to pick up Subway for Gerald, though Gerald could very well pick up his own, and Clive left.

I'm not proud of this. Don't think I am. It's just that these are the facts.

The next day at lunch the Vo-Ag teacher tried to get in my office again.

I said, "I have an appointment," but when I tried to close the door, the Vo-Ag teacher stuck one of his ridiculous man clogs into the doorway, which propped it open wide enough for him to get his bony fingers in. Once he had wrapped his fingers around the door there was nothing I could do.

I've smelled a mowed ditch a million times, and probably you have too. Or maybe not. I don't know what kind of smells you have in the cities where you live. But I'd never smelled something like that on a man's actual body, and twice in one week in November, when there is not supposed to be a freshly mowed ditch smell around here.

It was like a memory. It was like something I inherently understood, but I can't tell you why.

He walked right past me through the waiting area and into the back room where I sit with clients and do my work; I couldn't do anything, I couldn't stop him, I couldn't say, "Would you like some coffee?" or "What can I help you with?" All I could do was wonder: *What kind of a man makes himself smell like a mowed ditch?*

I thought, *An idiot, that's who.*

"Whoa!" he said.

"What?" I asked. It was just my office: a little waiting room in the front, with an olive-green vinyl love seat and some magazines, and my work space in the back where I sit with clients. There is a large desk made from a dark wood and another smaller desk for my computer, plus two chairs. And, of course, the U.S. Tax Code, all twenty volumes of it, bound in green with shiny gold lettering.

Understand that this is not an unusual office. Except for the Tax Code, it's the same as Doc's office up at the hospital, or Huff's law office around the corner, or the home office they share at the shit-shingled house where Doc fell asleep on the living room couch after my father died and still sleeps to this day. And my office is no different from offices of CPAs and lawyers and doctors in Fayette and Independence and even in Postville and Winona and Rochester—pens and pencils in a mug from the bank, a desk pad calendar with circled coffee stains all over it, a letter opener, a stapler, a print of ducks or maybe pheasants.

I myself have a print of a great blue heron, even though they are not normally found around here so far from the river, but my father was fond of them, so it stays, right by the door. I also have a print of a child swinging on a rope into a big pile of hay with an A-series John Deere tractor in the background, even though children here don't do that anymore. I got it at Huff and Doc's garage sale right after I got my CPA license. I paid Huff thirty dollars for it, but Doc put the money in my mailbox a few days later with a note that said, *Keep your mouth shut about it.*

The Vo-Ag teacher said, "Those books. Is that... ?"

"Yes," I said. "That is the U.S. Tax Code."

"Wow," he said. "Makes things pretty tight in here, doesn't it?"

I said, "I just had one of my clients in here yesterday, a very tall man, and he had plenty of space. He stretched out to the point of being nearly horizontal."

I looked directly into the Vo-Ag teacher's face in the hopes that he would get the message.

"Hmm," he said, "that's interesting," though he did not clarify what about it was interesting to him.

He smiled. He was a man who smiled at strange times, times when I knew he could not possibly be happy. He said, "Well, it does make a statement about the state of our world."

"It's the U.S. Tax Code," I said. "It makes statements about taxation."

"Po-TAY-to, po-TAH-to," he said.

I have never heard a single person say *po-TAH-to*.

I decided to treat him like any client. "Have a pen," I said, and gave him one of those pens I had made up with my name on it.

He took it and read it out loud: "Tandy Caide, CPA." Then he said, "Public accountant, private person."

"You don't even know me," I said.

"Everyone around here says so. 'Tandy, now she's a private person.'"

"Who says that?" I asked.

"Dieter," he said, and he smiled again but his eyes went narrow, like he was asking a question when he was making a statement. "And Mrs. Vontrauer."

Of course Silvia Vontrauer would say that! She wears scarves with pianos on them!

The Vo-Ag teacher smiled his big toothy smile. "Dieter also said I could smoke here."

I continued to treat him like a potential client. I said, "Well, there are only two things you can really count on in this life..."

He got excited and said, "Oh, I know this one: death and taxes."

"You seem to know a lot about a lot of things," I said.

He laughed then, and tapped a cigarette on the big desk and asked me for a light.

I pulled a book of matches from the Powerhaus out of a drawer in the big desk and the big red ceramic ashtray off the bookshelf behind me, where I keep it next to the trophy.

Actually, there are two things aside from the Tax Code that distinguish my office from anyone else's. One is the big red ceramic ashtray I also bought ten years ago at Huff and Doc's garage sale. I paid two dollars for it and never got the money back. The other is the trophy. It says: WORLD'S GREATEST ACCOUNTANT. I bought it for my father at Woolworth's a block down from our office more than twenty years ago, back when I was twelve. It was on clearance because the Woolworth's was closing due to the Walmart opening in Independence. I paid fifty cents for it.

The trophy pleased my father. He smiled when I gave it to him. He touched my shoulder. But I didn't know what about it pleased him exactly. I thought it was the price, the good deal I had found. Then I thought perhaps it was the thoughtfulness of the gift. Then I saw him and Doc and Huff bent over and laughing about it. So probably it was the price.

"Can I always count on a light and an ashtray too?" the Vo-Ag teacher asked.

"No. Just death and taxes," I said.

He laughed and smoked and stared at me. There was silence, and something else—something tingly, something electric.

"How can I help you?" I asked him. I ask this of all the people who sit in that chair. It is my business to help them.

"I don't know," he said. "I really don't know." And he laughed a little again.

I knew he would be back the next day.

I suppose, in the interest of clarity, it would be important to tell you that I wanted him back the next day.

I wasn't there, though. Another house blew up, and it was one of Mueller's—the big white rental with the screened-in porch—and so he asked me to go down and look. It was closer to downtown than the other one, within a few blocks of my office. A family who had come from Waterloo lived there. The father had been laid off from John Deere. He was working night shifts at the meatpacking plant for minimum wage and they were Section 8. There was a hole in the roof and smoke was rolling out of it. Some of the men in this town acting as volunteer firemen moved the children's bikes to the next yard over. The whole block smelled like cat pee and battery acid. Dave Oppegaard walked by in his heavy fireman boots and pants and suspenders, which formed arches over his big gut. He asked me for a light and I pulled a book of matches from the Powerhaus from my long black coat.

"Roof blew off this one," he said. "Don't breathe too deep, there's anhydrous everywhere."

Anhydrous ammonia is the main ingredient in homemade meth around here. It may be different where you come from. I don't know how you make your meth, but I hear there are lots of ways to do it. Here, we have giant tanks of anhydrous scattered all throughout our fields, perfect for siphoning if you're in need of some meth. Some of these tanks have motion-sensor cameras on them, until those cameras are broken or stolen. Some of these tanks have locks on them and sometimes this can make a difference for a little while.

"It's kind of ironic that something that increases yield can reduce a person's life," I said.

"Yeah," Oppegaard said. "Maybe Channel 9 will show up."

At lunchtime, the Vo-Ag teacher appeared beside me. "So we blow up our houses here," he said.

Oppegaard just stood there nodding and smoking, his ruddy face getting ruddier. And when he went back to the fire truck he struck up talk with the other volunteer firemen, including Bob Munson and Howie Claus, who raised their eyes to me as soon as Oppegaard opened his mouth.

"Jesus, Tandy," the Vo-Ag teacher whispered into my ear. "What's a nice girl like you doing in a place like this?"

And though it was an inopportune time, standing out there exposed with all those other men I had known my entire life, a switch flipped inside of me. His breath was like a sage lightning bolt. I seemed to rise from the ground, like a current was coursing from a knot in the back of my throat down through my spine and splitting through my legs so that my feet almost lifted off the sidewalk.

Across the street I could see Bob Munson and Howie Claus and Oppegaard all laughing, then Doc and Huff in Huff's golf cart pull up and all of them jabbering. But right then they could not touch me.

I didn't have an answer to the Vo-Ag teacher's question—*What's a nice girl like you doing in a place like this?*—so I said the one thing I know for sure: "I am taking care of the tax needs of my community." But it came out of my mouth small and quiet, like I was speaking from inside a balloon.

The Vo-Ag teacher laughed again, but this time it was a special kind of laugh that gurgled up in his throat and flowed out his mouth. It was like we were sharing some sort of special secret, though I do not know if we were or not. And I can admit to you now that this frightened me.

"I don't like it when you laugh," I said.

He sighed. He said, "None of the girls in this town do." And then he poked me again, right below the belly button, and then, with his arms open wide, he walked backward and away, singing a line from *Annie*: *Bet they collect things, like ashtrays and art!*

I watched that butterfly knot on that multicolored beaded belt from Africa get farther and farther away from me.

Later, after Gerald had eaten his Subway and fallen asleep in his chair, I went back to my office. I turned off all the lights and I locked the door and I closed the dusty little curtains in my waiting room. I sat down at my computer and I clicked my way to eBay and I ordered a multicolored beaded belt exactly like the one the Vo-Ag teacher wore.

I ordered it from a person called africannibal. I paid $5.75 plus $12 in shipping, because I chose the overnight mail option.

The next day when the belt came, I laid it atop my computer monitor, and when clients came in, or the Vo-Ag teacher, or Clive, I hid it in the long skinny drawer of my big desk, the one you are supposed to put pens in.

Then I put my big black coat on and I opened the curtains and stood for a while looking at the lights of the Country Kitchen across the street from my waiting room window. At night the letters of the Country Kitchen sign are lit up, but the kids in this town keep throwing rocks at the *O, R, Y,* and *K* until the bulbs in those letters go out. At night the sign reads: C UNT ITCHEN.

Of course I had laughed about this before. Mueller and I laugh about it all the time, even now. Doc still thinks it is the greatest thing this town has going for it. He wants to print it on a T-shirt and sell it during our town's Fourth of July celebration.

Doc and Huff used to joke in particular about how it is right across the street from my office. *Of all the things you could look at all day long, little girl!*

But this time I laughed about it differently. I don't know if you will understand this or not, but this time it was my kind of laughter.

Inside Cunt Itchen, Barb flew around, coffeepot strong in her hand. Hope sat in a booth at the back, carving something into the table with a butter knife. I waved to Barb to get her attention, but what could she see? Nothing, or at least she didn't look, so instead I said to my stale office air and my dusty waiting room window, "Good night, Barbie. I love you. I am sorry. It looks like I may be leaving soon."

I walked home in the dark, looking in at all the people in their little houses, wondering for the first time if they really were like me, as I had always been led to believe. I had been taught we were mostly the same, some of us just meaner and some of us just stupider, and me and my little village on the go-around just a tiny bit better. Some of the people in this town once had businesses and jobs and land and real estate and history here, but they have lost these things or are about to and they are broken by it. I was hanging on to these things. Was I better, or just lucky? Some of the people in this town never had those things, and some had shown up here recently for reasons unknown to me but were clearly not good ones. Some of these new people were the kind who drank beer with high school kids and gave them hickeys and rides to Kum & Go for cigarettes. Some of the high school kids here were the kind who were waiting for just such opportunities.

And who can blame them? What reason would a young person have to not seize whatever opportunity presented itself? Who among us is in a position to stop young people from seizing opportunity?

But there was something about the way the Vo-Ag teacher liked me, and the way he liked the things I said. He made me think that perhaps I was different, more like him. More, I don't know, special, more above it all. I wanted to believe I was the only one he made feel this way. But this was not the case.

Through their windows that night I could see that the people in this town mostly watched television. But sometimes they made decaf coffee, or played with their babies, or wiped their kitchen counters. Maybe the same things you do, maybe not. I really don't know what you people in your towns closer to the river do in the privacy of your own homes when you're not out in your public spaces winning friends and influencing people. But I can say, without a doubt, that at least, in my perception, the people in this town did look happy doing the small, quiet things they were doing that night.

And this surprised me. I do not exactly understand this yet. But I liked how this surprised me. That night, as I walked home in the dark and looked into the Little Clipper at the corner of Main and Anderson, I was even surprised to see Cathy Claus, Howie Claus's daughter, sitting in the hair-cutting chair she rents from Mandy Lancer. Cathy had her feet on the hair-washing sink and her nose in a *People* magazine and all the lights up, though it was well after seven and she was closed. She was still wearing plastic gloves from setting some perm, but her shoes were off and she wasn't wearing any socks, just stretching her toes with her heels on that sink.

I am capable of surprise. I am capable of seeing interesting things and enjoying those interesting things. And I was suddenly and inexplicably proud of this.

5

Gerald had a hot tub put in the backyard. Gary and some of his out-of-work friends from the railroad pulled a truck up to the backyard and dumped it out. It wasn't one of those nice hot tubs either. It was one of those round, cedar-planked hot tubs that is basically a giant wooden can, kind of like the troughs farmers keep heated for cows in the winter. You had to walk up a little stepstool to get into it. And when you sat in it, the water came right up to your neck. You looked like a disembodied head.

That's what I saw of Gerald for nearly a week. He sat in that hot tub every day after his after-school bus route, right up until Thanksgiving, stewing in his own juices. He stood up only to pee off the side of it, and he got out only to sleep and drive to Subway. The night before Thanksgiving he even ate a footlong meatball sub in the hot tub and then washed the sauce from his face with the water.

"It's okay, Candy Cane," he called to me through the kitchen window. "The chemicals in the water keep it clean."

An hour later he was still calling to me: "Come out! Please?"

What choice did I have?

And besides, I was curious. In the interest of accuracy I can admit that now.

Haven't you ever been curious in your life?

It was very hot. The air was cool. I was naked. We did make love in there. His theory about buoyancy was correct. And yes, I enjoyed it. Certainly I am allowed to enjoy myself occasionally.

But I did not enjoy it later, as I lay with Gerald in his bed. His drowning snore made me feel like I was drowning too. I got up and went to my own bedroom and lay down in my own bed.

But I was still drowning.

I was out the door before Gerald woke up that morning, even though it was Thanksgiving Day.

It was so pleasant! No one was up. No lights were on. There was no movement. I walked downtown. I got a story in my head: if anyone came out of their home and asked me why I was heading to the office on a holiday, I would tell them it was urgent work for Mueller. By the time I got to the office, I had even convinced myself of this story and I sat down and turned on my computer to do it.

I pulled the multicolored beaded belt out of the drawer, but instead of laying it on top of my computer, I threaded it through the belt loops of my black work pants.

Why not? *It's a holiday,* I thought.

I was very productive that morning—I did all of Mueller's payroll for the month, four days ahead of schedule.

At lunch I went to Prairie Lanes, which is always open on Thanksgiving, and I bowled the same way I always do: over the air vent, my first two fingers rubbing together until they make a whisper sound. My fingers into the ball's holes, lifting it out of the ball return. Forward to the foul line, find the center, walk backward five steps. Three large steps forward. Swing the ball behind me, before me, release.

The ball: airborne, then dropping just right of center, which is how I avoid the 7-10 split. Then it rolls straight home, the little engraved 10 on the ball appearing and disappearing with no tilt until the ball hits pins 1 and 3 with a clean smack, followed by all the others.

Almost always. Sometimes the 10 pin is left behind.

That Thanksgiving of that *Annie* year, Cindy came down from behind the shoe counter and shook her finger at me. She said, "You could really be somebody big in bowling if you could put some spin on that thing."

It was something she had said to me dozens of times. I nodded and smiled in the way that's good for business. But I wanted to say, *Why would I ever chase a wild spin, Cindy? If I ever got higher than a 260, you would take my picture with your little pink camera and pass it to Terry at the paper, who would put it in the sports page, which Pat Lancaster would read on the radio. And then Doc and Huff would crack loud jokes about it at the Chamber of Commerce meetings on Wednesdays. Doc might even get Mary Ellen at the Powerhaus to serve me a meat loaf in the shape of a bowling ball. Huff might show it to the whole bar. Clients of mine who weren't even there might talk about how hilarious it was when they bring their receipts to me in January.*

Do you know what would happen if I put a wild spin on the ball and started knocking that 10 pin down?

I would start to think I am something special.

Do you know what they do in this town to anyone who thinks she is something special?

They eat her for lunch.

I walked home after bowling and it was so warm I could smell myself inside my coat. I took off my coat and my blouse was soaked with sweat. As I walked up the rise to the go-around, I could see that someone—Huff probably—had attempted to string Christmas lights on the tree in front of my little cottage, but had got only halfway through the job, as many of the lights were just lying on the grass.

In Huff's house, Doc and Gerald were sitting around the kitchen table drinking Coors Light. Huff had his head in the oven but pulled it out when he heard the door shut behind me. His face was red and sweaty and smiling. He raised his whiskey, in that glass with a mallard on it that was perpetually fleeing a whiskey lake, and said, "Big turkey this year. Like there are two of them." Then he squealed like a hog and pointed to my waist.

Gerald followed Huff's hand. "Well. Isn't that a lovely," he said.

I had forgotten to take off the belt.

The laughter—it seemed to tip over chairs and go on for hours, but not from Gerald. Gerald just sat there, drinking his beer. Waiting.

I walked back down to my office and I cleaned the whole place with Formula 409. I fell asleep, scrunched up on the little green love seat in my waiting room, in sweaty clothes. When I woke up it was dawn and my cheek was stuck to the vinyl. But still I did not go home. I sat in my chair at my office and I waited for whoever would walk through the door.

I was hoping for the Vo-Ag teacher, but in the interest of clarity I can say that if it had been Clive, I would have been all right with that as well.

When the Vo-Ag teacher came, I let him in, and when he sat down across from me in the chair usually reserved for clients, I pulled the red ashtray off the shelf behind me and slid it toward him.

The Vo-Ag teacher put his big man clogs on my big wooden desk. Just like Clive, yes, but more compact, in control. He didn't touch a single thing. He just lit a cigarette and waited.

"Would you like to hear a story?" I asked him.

"I've got all day," he said.

So I told him.

There is a headstone out at the cemetery already engraved with my name. Before he died, my father had the prudence to purchase the plot right next to his.

There is more.

Immediately after my father's funeral, when I was just eighteen years old, I was sitting in Huff's dining room as blank as a new orphan could be. Huff was at the end of the table, cutting the obituary out of the paper and sticking it in a scrapbook with double-sided tape, muttering about how the whole world was going to shit and he was the only one who cared enough to document it. Doc was at the other end, alternating between staring at me and staring at the table, leaving giant drops of wetness on it from his eyes.

At some point, Doc reached into the pocket of his old denim shirt and pulled out his pack of cigarettes. There was one left. He tapped it on the table to set it, but he did it too hard and the cigarette snapped in half.

His face, it was like it melted. Then his body shook so hard the whole table shook, and, consequently, Huff's scrapbook project shook, so Huff threw the double-sided tape at Doc and called him an old jackass and then shook with sobs himself.

I don't know why I did it. Maybe I am just a good and helpful person. Maybe I have a natural inclination toward customer service.

Maybe my father taught it to me. Maybe I will never know. But I picked up the double-sided tape and both ends of the broken cigarette and I taped the cigarette back together. Then I laid it on the table in front of Doc.

Doc looked at it and then he looked up at me with a kind of hopefulness, as if I had made some sort of important promise to him. I looked away to the double-sided tape in my hand. I turned it over and over.

Doc picked up the cigarette. He lit it. He smoked it all the way through the tape, which burned up with the cigarette, turned into smoke, and went up into the air and then into all of us.

"You'll go far in this town," I heard Doc say. I just nodded. I wasn't proud or excited or even upset. I was relieved. It was done. I would go far in this town. This would be the town I would go far in.

I moved back into the little cottage next to Doc and Huff. My father owned it free and clear. I finished college by correspondence so I could work the business. When Gerald graduated high school, I married him because my father had once cheered loudly for him at a track meet. Gerald moved into the cottage and started driving school bus. For five years I did payroll for Mueller and under-the-table CPA work that one of Huff's clients in Decorah signed off on because he owed Huff money, until I got my CPA license.

I never lost one business day, not counting my father's funeral. Last year, the Chamber of Commerce elected me secretary and treasurer, my father's old positions, vacant for almost seventeen years. By then the Chamber was essentially inactive—it was just me and Doc and Huff and Pastor Howie Claus, even though Howie often wasn't invited because his righteousness was so tiresome and his church has tax-exempt status.

Mostly we just ate bean soup together on Wednesdays.

"So that's what a nice girl like you is doing in a place like this," the Vo-Ag teacher said.

"That is why I still live here, yes," I said.

"It doesn't have to be that way," the Vo-Ag teacher said. He was looking at me in a way that showed me he was serious, that he really cared, or at least that's what I believed at the time.

"My husband bought a hot tub," I said. "I will stew here until I die."

6

Then some kid threw a mathematical compass at the back of Gerald's head while he was driving the school bus.

The pointy end of the compass stuck into the back of Gerald's neck, and it continued to be stuck there even as he drove the busload of kids to the hospital. Judy Skody, the nurse on duty, yanked the mathematical compass out of Gerald's neck while he was standing in the hospital lobby. The kids ran off the bus and scattered through town like roaches, eventually ending up at Prairie Lanes, where they tipped over a vending machine and smashed the glass for the candy, until Dusty and Vern from the police department showed up with their police car lights flashing and they all scattered like roaches again.

I heard from Judy later that Gerald had been very mature about it, that he simply said thank you and then sat silent and still on the examining table as Doc stapled the wound closed, that he patiently waited an extra hour for the painkiller prescription to be ready so he wouldn't have to make a special trip back.

Gerald stayed home for a couple of days, watching television, eating all the casseroles my clients brought to my office for him, and making me check his wound every two hours when I was home, even in the middle of the night.

The wound wasn't that bad—just a tiny hole in a soft spot at the base of his neck, no worse than a tick bite.

He took a lot of painkillers. He sat in the hot tub from the time *Oprah* was over until it was time to go to bed.

"Come out and sit with me, Candy Cane," he would call from the hot tub at night, his voice lazier than usual from the painkillers.

"What about your wound?" I would shout from the kitchen window. "It's not supposed to get wet."

"I'll risk it," he said. "Come out and let's just talk." But I knew he didn't want to just talk.

Eventually he went back to work, and then of course all the kids got in on it. They threw whatever they had at him: books, pencils, pocket calculators, their shoes. Two weeks before Christmas, after a shoe hit him in the head, he drove the bus over the curb at the junior high and right into the wall of the school where the band room is.

No one was hurt. It was a brick wall and the bus didn't bust through it.

It made Channel 9, though. Silvia Vontrauer came into my office to tell me a man in a Channel 9 truck had come out and filmed the place on the wall where the bus had hit, even though there wasn't so much as a scuff on it. They showed it that night on the six o'clock news, along with Gerald's school bus driver ID. Client after client stopped by my office to say, "Gerald made the news!"

"No one was hurt," I had to keep telling everyone.

One night, Gerald wanted me to drive him to a bigger hospital, perhaps the Mayo Clinic. "I don't feel right. Maybe I need to go on workmen's comp," he said.

"Well, I can't go on workmen's comp," I said. "I have to go to work."

So he squeezed himself into our little Ford Escort and escorted himself to the Mayo Clinic's La Crosse affiliate. He was gone for three days, and when he came back, he did not speak to me for three more.

Dieter got together a spaghetti supper to honor Gerald's years of service to the school district. The cardboard sign with the sparkly word ANNIE in the high school cafeteria was replaced with a giant poster with various pictures of Gerald glued to it, all taken from the bottom of the school bus steps. It was a timeline of Gerald getting fatter by the year.

The students were not invited. Only the school administration and teachers and staff were there.

Because no students were invited, the choir did not sing. That was the best part about the whole event.

Doc and Huff were not invited either. They showed up anyway, and so I found myself standing with Huff, Doc, and Gerald as the Vo-Ag teacher bowed to them all and said, "I'm Kenny, the new Vo-Ag teacher. I understand you are very close friends of Tandy Caide's?"

"Mistaken on all counts," Huff said, raising a beer he had brought from home.

Dieter gave a speech that thanked Gerald, making mention of his alumni status and his state-winning shot put throw. He said, "It takes the ability to stick to a routine and ignore a lot of noise around you to drive school bus. Gerald brought both to the job, and he did the job as well as anyone could have."

Gerald ate six plates of spaghetti.

Howie Claus, the Methodist minister, said to him, "What are you going to spend all your time on now, Gerald?"

Gerald said, "Wine, women, and song, and the rest I'll just piss away."

Everyone but Howie laughed, including myself and including the Vo-Ag teacher, who laughed so hard he bent over, causing his ponytail to flop down and dangle in the air.

Gerald said loudly so everyone could hear, "I like this guy, Candy Cane."

"That makes one of us," I said. Everyone laughed again, including the Vo-Ag teacher, this time even harder.

I could play that game. In fact, it is probably fair to say that I felt a little proud of myself for playing it. I was clever. *Witty.* I was someone who was not from around here, someone better, someone who could make good-looking strangers laugh. I wanted to make it last forever. I wanted to always feel like that. I wanted to always believe in myself as a person like that.

The feeling wore off by the time we got back home. Gerald immediately removed his clothes and went out to the hot tub. He called out to me. "Come on. You liked it that one time."

My arms went numb. I felt that fight-or-flight feeling.

I guess I couldn't stand it anymore. And I guess I felt like I didn't have to.

I opened the kitchen door and stomped outside and I climbed up the little stepstool next to the hot tub and I looked down on him and I said very loudly, "I will regret that night we made love in this hot tub until the day I die!"

He said nothing, which surprised me, and in some ways was much worse than fighting me. He let his legs float up, and they looked like two hot dogs in a big pot of boiling water, like the last two hot dogs no one wants to eat at a high school football game. Then suddenly he stood up. Water went everywhere. I jumped off the stepstool as he moved toward it. He was coming to catch me.

But he was too fat to do it! He tried moving his foot forward, but he lost his balance and his arms flapped and he almost fell. He had to just sit down on the stepstool and then half slide down it, legs first, like a fat, naked toddler.

Finally he stood there naked on the grass, facing me, steam rising off his giant body.

"They think I should be hospitalized!" he yelled. "For my brain! For my stress! What am I supposed to do?"

I didn't know that about his brain. That was the first I had heard of it. Others will tell you differently, but I assure you this was the first I had heard of it.

I screamed, "How the hell do I know? I'm a CPA, not a doctor!"

Then he got quiet. Then his voice got cold and flat. He said, "I was worried about what you would do without me."

"You don't have to worry about me," I said. "I can take care of myself."

"Don't think I haven't noticed," he said.

He took a deep breath, in and out. Then he leaned back so that he was resting on the side of the hot tub. He stood there, naked and fat, but confident in it, like fat was just who he was. He put his hands on the area that was supposed to be his hips and looked at the stars.

In the morning, he packed some of his things into the Escort and escorted himself to a special place for mentally sick people run by the state and paid for with people's taxes, just a half hour east of here, somewhere along the highway toward Dubuque.

I never asked how long he planned to stay there, but he never asked about a lot of things on my end either.

I guess we both got what we asked for. I can be honest with you now, as I think it is important to set the record straight, plus it is of no consequence to me anymore as the deeds are done: *It was a lie.* I could have taken the day off to drive him to the Mayo Clinic. I just didn't want to. I didn't want to sit next to him in the car for an extended period of time, and then learn about his problems, and then talk to him about his problems, and then help him with his problems. You know—all the things a good wife would do.

Doc came into my office the day Gerald left and said: "You can't drive your own husband to the doctor?"

"Am I supposed to leave my work to do so?" I asked back. "And besides, if he's so bad off, how come he can drive himself?"

"Your father taught you to never answer a question with a question," he said. But that's all he said. He did not have answers to my questions, and so again it felt like a little victory.

But later, when I looked out the window of my office at Cunt Itchen, and I saw Barb buzzing around, working so hard, working until close while everyone else relaxed in booths with pieces of pie and cups of decaf, I got a sick feeling in my stomach, like I had punched an innocent person in the face.

But by the time I got home from work I had somehow forgotten about it. I was alone in the house. There was no snoring. There was no giant naked fat man in the hot tub eating a meatball sub. It was a Friday. I called up the Vo-Ag teacher and I said, "I would like to go bowling with you tomorrow," and he said, "Well, I would like to go bowling with you tomorrow too," and then I lay awake in my bed all night, filled with the kind of delicious, wonderful excitement you see in romantic comedies, excitement of the kind I had never experienced before and probably never will again.

I felt, for the first time, like the person I had always thought I was supposed to feel like.

I felt like all of you.

7

Six people have bowled a perfect game at Prairie Lanes. Their pictures line the hallway to the restrooms. They were taken in La Crosse because in this town if you bowl a perfect game, Cindy makes you go to La Crosse to have a professional take your picture, with your ball held up near your chin, wearing a bowling glove if you wear one.

The people you'd expect to be up there are all up there. Cindy's ex-husband, Mike, and her new husband, Harley, both with big thick black mustaches that look like leeches; Owen Johnson, who has actually bowled a 300 here twice, so there is an additional gold plate underneath his picture; Jeremy Thompson, who just bowls here when he visits his elderly parents; and Andy King, who drank a case of Coors Light before he bowled his 300, vomited in the gutter, and then fell down.

And then there is Doris Mavin. Doris Mavin is the only woman to ever bowl a perfect game in this town.

"She's a fox," the Vo-Ag teacher said. He had just walked in. It was noon—we were lunchtime bowling. His cheeks were red from the cold and his hands were jammed into the pockets of his flimsy gray jacket, which had unnecessary little loops at the shoulders.

The picture of Doris Mavin is fuzzy, like it's supposed to be romantic. She has longish brown hair, parted down the middle and feathered on the sides, like Farrah Fawcett's. She is wearing a blouse with a bow at the neck, sort of modest but in flashy colors, all pink and purple and big streaks of yellow. She's wearing icy-pink lipstick and she might be wearing false eyelashes. Her ball is the fancy kind that women like, blue with light blue swirls, and she's holding the ball up to her tilted chin. On her mouth is just the hint of a smile. It might be fake.

And she is big. You can tell that Doris Mavin is a big woman, even though the picture is just of her upper torso. Her shoulders are broad and her hands are huge and the ball she's holding has a big number 14 on it. Doris Mavin bowled with a fourteen-pounder.

"She looks like you," the Vo-Ag teacher said. And then, "Where can I find this Doris Mavin? I'd like to go home with her."

I had that feeling you get when you are sick from the flu and stand up too fast. I looked around. Cindy was in the back with the fryer and there was no one else in the place.

"She doesn't live here anymore," I said. Sometime in the early 1970s, Doris Mavin moved to this town to be the high school art teacher. She was single. She never went to church. She never took stats for any sports teams or sold concessions or played golf. She never did anything anyone who was planning to stick around would do. But on Saturday, January 17, 1976, at 11:15 in the morning, which was about forty-five minutes after Cindy opened up, Doris Mavin bowled a 300. Cindy was the only one present to witness it.

By the next week she was gone.

"Smart woman, huh?" he asked me.

I sent the ball straight down the lane and left the 10 pin standing. I was waiting at the ball return for my lowly twelve-pounder when he touched my arm. He leaned into me and took his own ball from the rack, and then he sent the ball down the right side of the lane in a wicked spin that curved in a great sweeping arc, zoomed right toward my 10 pin, and struck it on a diagonal with that loud *smack!* you hear on television bowling. The pin flew up, kicked around the back of the lane like it was fighting death, and then fell.

I had never been more attracted to anyone in my entire life. It was like he bowled directly into my ovaries.

I bowled a 225 that day. It was an okay game for me. I had a hard time concentrating after he picked up my 10 pin. He bowled a 258, taking gutters on the last three rolls so Cindy wouldn't try to take his picture. I asked him to do that and he did.

"We are both pretty good at bowling," I said. It was an understatement. We were incredible at bowling.

Later we stood on the sidewalk just outside Prairie Lanes. I couldn't stop staring at his belt, or, rather, the way the white T-shirt he was wearing tucked into his tight jeans, just above his belt. The whole day was spread out before us. I could see us in other interesting situations, sharing other things I had never shared with anyone: ice-cream cones, tartan blankets, picnic baskets in which the picnic supplies are securely strapped inside, each item safely in its place.

I said, "Do you remember that commercial from the eighties where Bruce Willis sings about wine coolers on a big farmhouse porch?"

He did more than remember it. He sang it—*Seagram's Golden Wine Coolers*—just like Bruce Willis had done. The Vo-Ag teacher knew how to act it just like Bruce, using a fake gravelly voice, dancing around with a fake Seagram's. He didn't believe it, of course, I know that now, but it *seemed* like he did.

And it was so beautiful to watch! It made my cheeks burn and my mouth moisten and my legs get weak and ache like I had run a long way to meet him.

"That was very good," I said.

"The best part of that commercial was the end," the Vo-Ag teacher said.

In case you don't know: at the end of the commercial, Bruce Willis sits down on the farmhouse steps and he holds the bottle of Seagram's he's been using as a microphone in front of this shaggy dog. Bruce Willis passes the bottle to the dog like he's expecting the dog to sing into it too, but instead the dog licks the top of the bottle.

"The dog goes and licks it!" The Vo-Ag teacher laughed and bent over his trim waist, giving me a look at his ponytail and the tender part of the back of his neck and the broad expanse of his shoulders underneath his ridiculously light gray jacket.

"Someone probably rubbed a rib eye steak over the top of the bottle to get the dog to lick it," I said.

The Vo-Ag teacher shrugged and said, "Or maybe even shaggy dogs can't resist the sparkling wet and dry taste of Seagram's Golden Wine Coolers." Then he did the thing he had done before—he reached out his finger and poked me in the chest. But instead of pulling his finger back, he kept it planted on my sternum.

I thought right then that maybe it didn't really matter if Bruce Willis's performance was just to sell wine coolers. Maybe it didn't matter if Bruce Willis didn't know anything about life on a farmhouse porch. Maybe it only mattered that he *pretended* he did. And maybe it was okay that the dog didn't really like Seagram's Golden Wine Coolers in his real dog life, because how happy that dog must have been, licking the top of a Seagram's Golden Wine Cooler bottle and finding that it tasted like a rib eye steak—what an amazing surprise for a dog.

I reached up my own hand to the Vo-Ag teacher's, and, not knowing exactly what to do as I had never been in such a situation, I patted it.

He dropped his hand and jammed both of them into his pockets.

This was very disappointing. Never again will I pat a man's hand. Patting a man's hand is the dumbest thing a woman can do.

But then he said, "You should come and talk to the Vo-Ag students. As a guest speaker."

My ovaries were so swollen I could barely remain upright. "I don't like speaking to crowds," I said.

"That's okay. There are only five of them."

I didn't believe him. "When I was in high school, there were at least forty Vo-Ag students," I said. And then it occurred to me exactly what our school board was paying him to do. "You only have five students?"

"I'm also the Future Farmers of America adviser," he said.

I couldn't help myself. "But it's the same five students!"

He became very still. He stared at me. "Certainly your agrarian heritage is important to you, Tandy," he said in a low and very quiet voice.

"Of course," I said, though I had to think a moment about what "agrarian" meant.

"Certainly agrarian practices, policies, and culture are worth teaching in a place built on them, and to anyone who is willing to learn, no matter how many or how few," he said.

"Of course," I said. Though I had never considered it. Not once.

"What would I say to them?" I asked.

"Tell them the truth," he said. "Tell them what a good place this is to be."

I laughed out loud when he said that. It was a terrible thing to do. This is another thing I will regret until the day I die.

He laughed too. But I did not believe it was his laugh, even then. I could see there was a weakness in him that made him laugh when other people laughed, even if he did not find the thing funny.

Oh, what does it matter anyway? We were both laughing, you see? Doesn't that count for something?

"Nice girl like you, place like this?" he asked. "Answer that for them, Tandy."

I said I was available on Wednesday because that is the day I was supposed to attend the Chamber luncheon with Doc, Huff, and Howie Claus, and because that's the kind of asshole I was that year.

I went home alone, where I lay in my bed the rest of the day, thinking about the Vo-Ag teacher and staring out the window across the go-around at Huff's house, where I was pretty sure Doc and Huff were staring back at me. I ordered my wallpaper: thick, thick, thin, thick, thick, thin, thick, thin. Finally I fell asleep, and I dreamed Doris Mavin was making me Toll House cookies in the kitchen of my cottage on the go-around. She served them to me with some Folgers coffee. She said to me, "Little girl, you have too many friends. What are you doing with all these friends?" while outside the window, Bruce Willis danced with abandon and beckoned me with his index finger.

One thing that I have never told anyone is that I am 73 percent sure Doris Mavin is my mother. I never told the Vo-Ag teacher. I never told my father. I never even told Barbie, and Barbie has been my best friend since I became aware of myself as someone with a self. Aside from my father, Barbie was the first person I sensed in the world. She was next to me in the sandbox made from a tractor tire, at the breakfast table sounding out words on a cereal box, in my bed, where she slept most nights until the seventh grade. Barbie, the other motherless child. Barbie, with whom I dreamed of the perfect mother, Bonnie Franklin as Ann Romano in *One Day at a Time,* because she had two daughters and there was no father to deal with, just a harmless handyman whose only job was to fix broken things.

Barbie, with whom I learned to be a woman, of sorts, while fumbling through a world of confused and difficult men.

But I never told her about my Doris Mavin secret, even while we dreamed of Bonnie Franklin as Ann Romano. Perhaps things would have been different if I had. Or perhaps not. Perhaps there is no consequence to keeping our private thoughts private, even from one's own family. Perhaps there is even some advantage to it. Perhaps Barbie keeping her relationship with that boy, Cole, a secret from me was an advantage to her. Perhaps we all need something that doesn't belong in some way to someone else and is just for ourselves.

I had a mother. She died before I could remember a thing about her. According to my father, she was a fine person. That's what he said when I asked about her when I was all jacked up on puberty in the seventh grade. "She was a fine person," he said.

I pressed him. "What did she look like?"

He said, "She had brown hair and she was tall."

I asked, "Do you think I would recognize her if I saw her on the street?"

He said, "You will never see her on the street, so the question is moot."

It may sound strange to you, but I appreciated this information. It was more than Barbie got about her own mother. When she asked Huff about her mother, on the same day I asked my father about my own as we had worked up the nerve together, Huff said, "She left you and you should be grateful because she was a whore."

Barbie ran right across the go-around and into my little cottage, found me on the couch in the living room, and punched me in the mouth. I kicked her in the stomach. That, I suppose, was the beginning of the end. After that day, Barbie stopped sleeping in my bed.

She began to have boyfriends. We continued to be family to each other, and we even enjoyed each other's company once in a while. But we never spoke of our mothers again.

My father married my mother the same day Doris Mavin bowled her 300. My mother died in childbirth with me a little more than nine months later. My father had her cremated, and Doc and Huff threw her ashes into Kennicott Creek so my father would never have to look at her headstone.

But still, when I am bowling, there is very little that holds me back from believing that Doris Mavin is my mother. Only two things hold me back. One is that Cindy says Doris Mavin had a wicked curve, like a meat hook, and I bowl straight, like a broom handle. The other is that Doris Mavin is gone and I still live here.

The next morning at my office, I searched the Internet for where a person might buy some Seagram's Golden Wine Coolers. The answer is nowhere. They stopped making them in 1992, when there was a change in the federal excise tax for wine. Any product with the word "wine" in it became subjected to a quintuple tax increase. Because none of the wine cooler manufacturers could figure out how to get the price points low enough that the typical American consumer would continue to consume them, they just put malt liquor in those kinds of drinks and now sell them as "hard" or whatnot. Malt liquor is cheaper but they charge you the same. That's business.

I searched the Internet for that particular Bruce Willis farmhouse porch commercial too. I came up empty-handed. Despite what you might believe about the Internet, not everything can be found there.

Death.

Taxes.

8

On Wednesday I left messages for Doc and Huff at their offices, alerting them to the fact that I would be unavailable for lunch with the Chamber because I would be occupied with the Vo-Ag teacher. I expressed my deep regret. I promised to follow up with them at their earliest possible convenience.

Then I wrote on notecards some questions I thought the Vo-Ag kids might ask, like "What are some of the best tax incentives offered to farmers at this time?" and "What advice do you have about creating a hassle-free payroll process?" When the time came to leave, I put on my big Lands' End coat and walked down the hill to the high school, and then around the back of it to the dirty temporary construction trailers where Vo-Ag has held class since the old Vo-Ag room became a computer lab twenty years ago.

I knocked on the trailer door, which wasn't a door at all but a piece of plywood cut into the shape of a door and attached to the doorframe with two hinges. I pushed on the door, which had no knob, as hard as I could with my shoulder until it swung open and I stumbled into the room.

I said, "Someone should fix that door."

"Touché," a boy said. He was sitting on top of his desk. He was wearing jeans and cowboy boots and a black T-shirt with something like a zombie on it, something with a melting face. His name was Travis and he was too tall for his body. The other three kids snickered. They were scattered around the room, sitting on top of desks, not in them, as is the intended purpose of a desk. Even the Vo-Ag teacher seemed to be going out of his way to avoid sitting at a desk like a normal person, standing instead next to a tiny one of his own.

"One of us is missing today," he said. "Otherwise, this is it."

"She hardly comes anyway. She doesn't even want to be here," said a girl at the back. Her name was Missy, which is a strange name for a girl in vampire makeup.

"Nice coat," said a boy in a shirt with different kinds of zombies on it from Too-Tall Travis's zombie. It had the word "corn" on it too, but spelled wrong, with a *k*.

"Shut up, Phil," said Missy.

"What?" Korn Phil said to Missy. He put his hand up to his mouth as if he was going to tell her a secret, but in a voice that was intentionally audible to me he said, "That coat is fugly."

"I think you mean ugly," I said. "And I think you mean 'corn' with a *c*."

"Touché," Korn Phil said. "That's French."

"You heard it on a *Tom & Jerry* cartoon," said Too-Tall Travis.

"So clearly it is French," said Korn Phil.

"Touché!" said Too-Tall Travis, and the two laughed, though I don't quite know at what.

"So! Tandy Caide! CPA!" the Vo-Ag teacher said loudly. "What can you tell us about your work as a businesswoman, about the tax needs of a rural community? What are some special tax breaks given to farmers to improve their quality of life? If we were to do a group project for our upcoming Future Farmers of America competition, a project that would benefit this community, what suggestions might you have?"

"Have you seen Hope?" asked the other girl, the one with the blue mascara that made her look like a dolphin. Her name was Beth. "You know who I'm talking about, right? You're friends with her grandpa?"

"Hope is in this class?" I asked. I had not considered this.

"She was supposed to bring her research on heirloom beans today. You know her, right?"

"I suppose so," I said. It was as close to the truth as I could get. I looked down at the floor, which was just some unfinished plywood boards loosely nailed to the trailer's frame. "I have been presented with many difficult questions at once," I said.

"Just answer whichever is most comfortable for you," the Vo-Ag teacher said.

I took off my coat and took the notecards out of the pocket. I put my coat on top of an empty desk near me. I flipped through the notecards until I came to the one about the tax breaks. I said, "There are many ways farmers can save money using special tax incentives..."

Korn Phil raised his hand.

"I would like to continue speaking," I said.

"No biggie," he said. "But you're a CPA, right?"

"Yes," I said.

"So who has the most money in this town?" he asked.

I almost pointed out that the Vo-Ag teacher had asked me that same question on the day we met.

"I am bound by client confidentiality to not answer that question," I replied. I could feel my jaw tighten. My hands began to tingle.

"We won't tell anyone," Vampire Missy said beneath heavy black bangs.

"Who you will and won't tell is moot," I said. "I will never tell you. If I did, you would never trust me again and neither would the person whose financial state I disclosed to you. To be successful in my CPA business, I must be a person of integrity. I must always ask myself, 'Am I doing what a person of integrity would do?' A person of integrity would never tell anyone anything about a client's financial state unless he or she was required to by law or by that client's expressed consent."

"It doesn't matter what kind of person you are. Everyone knows the richest person in this town is Mueller," said Korn Phil.

"Ha! *Mueller*," Too-Tall Travis said, as if he and Mueller were old pals.

"You know John Mueller?" I asked.

"I've been picking up rock for him since I had armpit hair," Too-Tall Travis said. "In case you haven't noticed, Ms. Caide, this is a pretty small town."

"Touché," I said. All four of them smiled at me then. Suddenly I was enjoying myself.

"Armpit hair is Mueller's only job requirement for picking up rock," Korn Phil said.

"You must also have arms," I said. And with that, all of us, including the Vo-Ag teacher, were laughing together.

Korn Phil raised his hand again. "Hey. Are your lunches free? Because I heard that when you work in a business, your company will just pay for any lunch you eat if you're on business."

"There's no such thing as a free lunch," I said. I looked to the Vo-Ag teacher. His eyes were closed and he was nodding and smiling. He seemed to be taking great pleasure in all of this, and this gave me great pleasure. "I own my own company, so every time I eat, I pay for it." I shrugged. "That's business."

"What about when you take a business trip?" asked Vampire Missy. "Do you have to pay for that too?"

"I don't really travel," I said, and then immediately regretted saying it.

"You don't go *anywhere*?" Vampire Missy asked, aghast. "But you're a *businesswoman*."

"My business is wherever my clients are. My clients are here." I looked to the Vo-Ag teacher and he was nodding in agreement.

"So, you've been here this whole time?" asked Vampire Missy. "Right here, in *this town*?"

"Well, I've been to college," I said. It was a dumb road to go down.

Dolphin Beth perked up. "Where?" she asked. "Like, Hawaii? Or Duke?"

"Upper Prairie University," I said.

She blinked her dolphin eyes. "That's not even out of this county."

"You really never go anywhere?" Korn Phil asked. "Not even Dubuque?"

"I go to Dubuque for CPA recertification." I had been recertifying online for several years but I kept that fact to myself.

"There you go," Too-Tall Travis said. "A free trip to Dubuque."

"It's not free. I told you, I own my own business. So I pay for trips like that. Though I can write it off partially as a business expense."

"Well, that's something, I guess," Too-Tall Travis said. "But I still think someone else could be paying you to eat lunch in Dubuque."

I started to argue with him on this again, but the Vo-Ag teacher jumped in. "As a businesswoman, Tandy must be active in the community in which her customers live in order for them to maintain their confidence in her. Isn't that true, Tandy?"

I started to say yes, that other people's confidence in me is all I really have in life, when the plywood door swung open and dramatically, as always, Hope walked in.

She was wearing a black tank top with the straps of her black bra showing through at her shoulders, and tight jeans with holes ripped in so her skin showed through at the knees and thighs. She had a ratty black sweatshirt tied around her waist. Her short black hair was greased back with some kind of shiny oil. She had skulls dangling from her ears. She looked me over as she walked by and said nothing, but the look said she would throw a bottle at me if there was one handy.

The Vo-Ag teacher asked her, "Where were you?"

"The nurse's office," she said, though she did not appear in any way to be sick. She sat down in an empty desk next to him. It faced the rest of the class, as if she were teaching it too.

The Vo-Ag teacher nodded. He didn't say anything else.

"Hello, Tandy," she said.

"What are you doing in Vo-Ag?" I asked. Probably, my mouth was open. Probably, I looked aghast that she was in this class. Probably, it appeared to the rest of them that I thought Hope better than Vo-Ag.

But she was! She was so smart! She was college-bound! She was troubled, yes, but she had so much potential! She was the front-runner for valedictorian!

"This is where they stick you when you get kicked out of the musical," she said.

The Vo-Ag teacher piped in. "We are happy to bring her into our fold!"

Hope said nothing. Her classmates said nothing. They sat quiet, looking at their desks. They did not defend her, nor did they defend themselves. But the Vo-Ag teacher tried. Say what you will about him, but he was always trying. "You walked in at an exciting time, Hope. We were just about to brainstorm with Ms. Caide about possible group projects."

"We're not doing heirloom beans?" Hope asked, and puckered her mouth like she would laugh if she weren't already so far above even her own jokes.

"We could, if you'd done the research you promised," Vampire Missy said.

"You have the Internet too," Hope said.

"I also have integrity, unlike some people," Dolphin Beth said, looking at me earnestly.

"We've moved on to other ideas," the Vo-Ag teacher said to Hope, in a voice that I noticed was different from the voice he used on the others. It was calmer, quieter, a voice you would use in a smaller room with fewer people in it, or with someone you were hoping to gently convince of something.

I should have known then. When I look back on it now, I can see.

"Is Ms. Caide the one who reviews the FFA accounts when we file our taxes?" Hope asked.

"Yes," he said, calmly, quietly.

"You probably know how much money we have," Dolphin Beth said. "We've got, like, thirty-one thousand dollars from selling our test crops."

"I do know," I said. "I'm your CPA."

"We're our own 501(c)3," she said. "That's not the school's money, that's our money." Dolphin Beth was very proud of this money.

"But we still can't buy ourselves a better trailer," Korn Phil said. "Because FFA funds cannot be used for Vo-Ag classroom purposes."

"Rules!" Too-Tall Travis spit.

Hope smiled. It was a distant yet familiar smile. "Well, I was just named secretary of FFA," she said. "It will be nice to work with you—someone I'm already so close to." Though it seemed like a time when a businesswoman who cared about the youth of her town and her customers would smile back, I struggled to do so.

That night, as I lay in my bed ordering the wallpaper, going over the day and what it could all possibly mean, I remembered that distant-yet-familiar smile of Hope's. I recognized it as a smile of Barbie's.

It was the smile Barbie used on me in high school when she wanted something from me but did not want to tell me what it was, lest I say no to giving it to her.

By the summer of our junior year of high school, Barbie had been through every boy at our school. Except for our girlhood, this was our best time together. Huff was allowing her to be only with me. I was Barbie's dutiful keeper, and I had her all to myself. That is, until we met that boy, Cole, at the swimming pool. I could see what was coming the moment he stood before us, dripping pool water, and Barbie moved her foot toward him to catch his drips on her skin.

He was in college up in Minneapolis and was in town only for the summer—his father had bought some old railroad cars, and Cole was helping him clean and move them out. He was not interested in getting to know anyone but Barbie. For the next two weeks I drove to all the secret roads, while they wrestled each other in the back of Huff's Tempo. I would drop them off and come back two hours later, four hours later, the next morning. Then I didn't want to do it anymore. To tell you the truth—a truth I have never told anyone—I was jealous. But instead I said to her, "We are going to get caught."

"Always with the rules!" she cried. "How am I supposed to see him if you won't let me?"

It was my fault, you see. You see how people can make things that aren't your fault seem like your fault when you don't pay attention? Say what you will about the Vo-Ag teacher, but this is something he never did to me. One day she asked me to drive her to the library. She had promised Huff she would research colleges. I dropped her off. I would come back in a few hours. She smiled that smile. It was the smile you give the woman handing you fast food through a window before you run off with it. I knew she was not going to stay at the library. An idiot could see that.

That boy, Cole, disappeared too. Huff had every cop in the county looking for them. Two weeks later, senior year in full swing, she came back. She told no one where she had been, including me, her best friend. Was she in Minneapolis? Was she hitchhiking? Had she been held captive? Had she been drugged? She just smiled that fake smile and said, "I was out living, Tandy."

Shortly after that, she walked by the Powerhaus window while Doc, Huff, my father, and I were sitting in the front booth. We all saw it, how her belly pushed forward and her spine curved away. Huff threw his drink at the window and both the drink and the window shattered and she jumped and she ran.

When Huff caught up to her, hiding alone in an old railcar out on the edge of town, he sent her away to the nuns in Dubuque. Doc and my father felt she would get the best care there and not be a bad influence on me.

I was not allowed to go to her. If I was caught trying to go to her, my father would take away all the money I had earned working for him and I would not be allowed to go to college.

9

A few days later, Gerald sent an e-mail: "Do not expect me for Christmas dinner. Do not expect anything anymore from me."

When your husband leaves you, your arms go numb and, at the same time, someone lifts a 350-pound weight off your chest. You clean your house from top to bottom with Formula 409, and you throw away any paper that has his name on it. You put on your most comfortable shoes and you go jogging, for three miles you go jogging—even though you've never been jogging before and you are wearing a giant black down coat from Lands' End—because you want to clean out the sludge that sits in the bottom of your lungs. And by the time you've run all the way out to the home of your biggest client—a rich, old bachelor farmer with a big white house with a big wraparound porch just like the one Bruce Willis dances around on in that Seagram's Golden Wine Cooler commercial—the sun is up and that farmer client of yours is standing there on that magnificent porch, drinking a steaming cup of strong coffee, which he holds up in salute as you run by, having not yet replied to your husband's e-mail.

School was out for Christmas break. There were entire weeks laid out before the Vo-Ag teacher and I.

My husband was gone. There was nothing to stop us. And he knew that and that is why he brought that sage to my office. It was a small bundle of dried weeds, held together with one of its own. It looked like the old-style haystacks, the way the hay is stacked in the painting in my lobby, but a tinier, browner version, like it was left somewhere for a long time and had shrunk. It was like a shrunken head of hay, from history.

He set it in the big red ashtray. Then he lit it, and it began to smoke, and then he blew it out right away but the smoke continued to come. He said, "Don't be afraid."

Smoke rose from the stack and then fell all around the top of my desk.

"I'm not afraid of smoke," I said, though it was thick.

"Then close your eyes and empty your head," he said, and he sat back and he closed his eyes.

I have no idea if he emptied his head or not—I can't see inside other people's heads—but I do believe he emptied his head, just like he asked me to do.

I leaned back in my chair on the other side of the desk and I too closed my eyes. That mowed-ditch smell was so strong. I did not expect that. Perhaps you will understand this, perhaps you won't. Maybe these kinds of things happen to people like you all the time in your big cities. The strong way that sage smelled made me feel very old and very young at the same time. It made me feel real and also far away. I tried to hold my breath, because the smell was so strong, but then when I breathed, I was actually breathing very deeply. I don't know why. I was thinking about all the smoke, and where it was going, if the room was filling with smoke, but I did not open my eyes to check. I wanted to open the door to my office but I couldn't move from my chair. And then I suddenly stopped thinking about all the smoke and I was thinking about ditches, all the ditches burning in this town, smoke from everywhere, how thick the smoke was in the whole world, how alone a person could feel in that smoke. And the smell seemed to get stronger, and in my head and my heart it became thicker and thicker.

And then I heard a voice behind me saying, "Anything not here for the highest good: be gone!"

I said, "What the hell?" and I opened my eyes.

The sage bundle was not in the ashtray on my desk, and the Vo-Ag teacher was not in the chair in front of me. He was behind me, waving that sage bundle over my head, dangerously close to my hair, and in front of me was just smoke, smoke everywhere, and then suddenly the fire alarm: *Beep! Beep! Beep!*

I spun around in my chair and my knees ran into his knees and he buckled a little bit and fell toward me, and that rainbow belt emerged from the smoke and headed right into my face. I put my arms out to keep him from falling into me, and I pushed a little too hard against his waist because he fell back into my bookshelf. The sage in his hand knocked against the U.S. Tax Code and then a large burning part of the sage dropped from the bundle and onto one of the volumes, *Volume S–Si,* and started burning through the pages.

"What are you doing?!" I shouted.

He said, "I was cleansing your space!"

"I didn't ask you to cleanse this space! This is *my* space!" I tried to blow out the sage chunk on *Volume S–Si* and I accidentally blew it onto the carpet.

"But there's a lot of negative energy in this space!" Understand this: he was not making an apology.

"That is not for you to decide!" I yelled over the sound of the fire alarm. I stamped out that burning sage on the carpet with my shoe.

He stood on the chair so he could reach the fire alarm on the ceiling and fiddled with it until the *beep, beep, beep* stopped.

"I think we both know that this negative energy is not coming from me," he said. A normal person, knowing he had made a mistake, would have left then. He did not.

He kept saying, "I'm sorry. I'm sorry. Sometimes I go too far," until I asked him to leave.

But I knew he would be back.

I locked the door and I pulled all the shades and I turned off the lights and I sat in my little lobby and I stared at the print of the great blue heron.

He knocked. I just stared at the print.

He left again, and still I sat there, staring at the print.

I thought about the only time I had actually seen a great blue heron in real life. I was standing with my father on the deck of the riverboat casino in Dubuque. My father had lost several hundred dollars on blackjack, believing that blackjack was better than slots because at least you have some control in the matter. He saw a great blue heron moving slowly near the riverbank, and he said, "Look, Tandy. Look how that bird has to move her long neck and head backward to get her skinny legs moving forward. If that bird wants to move about this world, she has to go back with her head to go forward with her feet."

I saw that he was right, and then I asked, "But what about when she flies?"

My father did not answer, just shook his head and said, "Great blue heron. How great you are. How blue."

The Vo-Ag teacher came back when it was dark. He said, "Please let me in," and I don't know why but I started to talk. I said through the closed door, "I was larger than everyone in school by a full head, from kindergarten on, even the boys."

"Let me in," he said.

"There wasn't fat on me," I said. "There was some muscle, but not a lot. Mostly it was my bones that were large, my structure. I am big-boned."

"I think you're beautiful," he said.

"During puberty I grew even bigger. At night I would lie in bed and I could feel my body growing. It hurt, especially in the shins and the thighs and the ribs. Sometimes my ribs were growing so fast I couldn't take a deep breath because of the ache. I would walk around, holding my breath. I wanted it to stop."

"Awful," he said. "Open the door."

"I grew even larger. The summer after eighth grade I grew seven inches. My feet went from size seven to size eleven. I went to the first day of ninth grade wearing jeans that had to be specially ordered from the JCPenney catalog for tall women. I could hardly walk, it hurt so much. I wore these tall women's clothes, but I didn't even have my period."

"Tandy," he said.

"They all stared, everyone, even the people who knew me and saw me every day."

"They shouldn't have done that," he said. "I would not have done that. Open the door."

"Then people in this town started to tell me things. Grown-ups told me things, and children. Once Alison Harbinger ran up to me on the street and whispered, 'The man in the house next door shows me his penis in the window.' In high school, the health teacher, Jack Brewer, reached out and grabbed my arm in the hallway one day and said, 'I'm in love with someone who is not my wife.'"

"Let me in."

"When Matthew Eitzen's son died last year and he came to close out the estate with Huff and me, he sat down in one of the chairs and he said, 'My son was drunk, so he deserved it. I can't tell my wife that, or his wife, or the other kids. But that's what I think.' When we stood up to shake hands he was staring at my chest. Huff did nothing. Huff thought it was funny."

"Let me in, Tandy."

"Even Barbie did it. The night before Huff sent her away, she crawled through my bedroom window and sat on my lap like a little girl, even though she's older than me by six months. She was tiny and pregnant and she cried and cried—'Why did my mother leave me, Tandy?! Why?'—and I just sat there, frozen, with her on my lap in that rocking chair, rocking her while she soaked my nightgown through to my big-boned shoulder with her hundreds of thousands of tears."

"Let me in, Tandy."

I asked him, as if he of all people would have an answer, "Why do people tell me these things? Why?"

"I don't know," he said.

"I'm just standing here! I'm not doing anything special! Why are they always looking to me?"

"Honey," he said.

It was the only time he ever called me honey.

"Honey," he said. "I know."

And I guess all I needed was someone to confirm it.

I started laughing, and then he started laughing too, I could hear it through the door, and I was laughing so loud and hard that I had to double myself over and he did the same too, and we each bumped our heads on our sides of the door so that they were separated only by that old door, and then we laughed at that. I said, "The only time I've really spoken to Barbie as a grown woman, I made her refill my coffee for over an hour. Finally she said, 'What do you want?' And I said, 'Remember Jack Brewer, the high school health teacher?' And she said, 'Yeah, so what?' And I said, 'One time, in high school, he told me he was in love with someone who was not his wife.' And Barb said, 'That's what you stuck around here for?' And I said, 'Yes.' And she said, 'That's why you've made me come by five times to fill your coffee?' And I said, 'Yes.' And she said, 'You're a grown woman.' I said, 'It's just been bothering me.' And she said, 'Jesus Christ, Tandy. He said that shit to everybody.'"

The Vo-Ag teacher and I laughed and laughed until there was nothing left inside of either of us.

He said, "Are you going to let me in, Tandy Caide?"

I said no, and then I opened the door.

10

I touched his hand. It was warm and smooth. I didn't know which part to touch next. I wanted to touch his face, the lines around his face, the lines around his mouth. I wanted to touch his ears, to stick my fingers in them. I wanted to put my tongue deep inside his ears and taste his brain. I wanted to put both my hands around his neck and squeeze. I wanted to pull out that stupid black band that held together his ponytail and chew on it and then rip out strands of his hair and then eat them. I wanted to put my hands around his waist; stick my fingers down his throat, my tongue; put my hands inside his shirt and under his arms, deep into his armpits. I wanted to lift him up like a baby. I wanted to knock him down. I wanted him to knock me down. I wanted us to knock each other down and pick each other up and then do it again.

His hand brushed the inside of my palm. Then there were two hands. And then I went forward and then he went forward and then he was all around me and we fell down together and then we got back up and then we did it again and then we got back up again and then his ponytail was undone and my hands were buried deep, deep, deep inside the hair at the base of his neck, and then we were half naked, and then we were half on and half off the vinyl love seat, and then he said, "This isn't about love, not like you might think."

"I know that," I said.

But I didn't. I completely thought it was about love. I just said that in the hopes that we would sleep together.

Interestingly enough, my belief at that time that it was about love was a bold-faced lie too, to justify my desire to be naked with him. So: I lied to him that it *wasn't* about love so that he would make me naked, and I lied to myself that it *was* about love so that he would make me naked.

These thoughts are a circle. I can draw their track with a mathematical compass, but here, one year later, I still cannot find a place in them to land, except to say that yes, we are all basically animals.

It was Christmas Eve, a holiday I had celebrated only with my husband in my adult life, and only with steaks and television. Surely even you can understand this. The Vo-Ag teacher and I spent the night in my office, and we made love three times—on the floor, on the vinyl love seat, which stuck to our bodies and made weird and embarrassing noises we ignored, and on my desk. The third time, the bells of the Methodist church rang out because it was midnight and Christmas Day. It made us jump and then cry out and then laugh and then cry real tears, it was so beautiful. We cried and we kissed each other's tears and we continued to make love as the church bells rang out: *Joy to the world! The Lord is come!*

Around late morning, after we had slept all wrapped up in each other's limbs on the floor of my office, I told him I wanted to take him to the little cottage on the go-around. I wanted him in my own bed, where there were sheets and covers and a soft, springy mattress.

"Your husband... ?" he said.

"No," I said. "He's gone."

Huff and Doc, however, were not. They were expecting me for Christmas lunch. They were standing in the yard of the go-around when we pulled up in the Vo-Ag teacher's little Volkswagen Bug. And of course Barb and Hope were there too, just getting out of Barb's Pontiac, having just arrived for their once-a-year Christmas visit, during which bottles of whiskey and pie would be exchanged and few words spoken. And of course Silvia Vontrauer had parked her Buick behind them, waiting to deliver unto me the Christmas wreath I had purchased from the Theater Boosters and forgotten to pick up. And of course Mr. Henderson, the choir teacher, was sitting in her passenger seat, because that is how things happen around here.

The Vo-Ag teacher said, "I can just drop you off."

"No," I said. For once in my life I wanted everyone to take note of what I had done.

We got out of his car, and I waved to all of them as they stood in the snow with their mouths gaping like wide-open garage doors. Silvia Vontrauer approached me slowly, handed me the wreath, and mumbled, "Merry Christmas from the Theater Boosters." Then she ran back to her Buick and pulled away, with Mr. Henderson in the passenger seat, mouth still agape, staring at us until we all disappeared from each other.

Hope and Barb and Doc and Huff just stood there. And they continued to stand there, saying nothing at all, while I hung the wreath on the nail in my front door that has served wreath-hanging purposes for as long as I have been alive and probably before.

I opened the door of the little cottage and I motioned the Vo-Ag teacher in. As he walked through, I gave his butt a little smack. I bowed to my family. Barb sighed and lowered her head. She turned and walked into Huff's house. In my head, I told Barbie that I was sorry. Then I closed the door and chased the Vo-Ag teacher into my bedroom.

It was time for me to have something for myself.

When we got hungry, he made eggs. When we got thirsty, we drank Mike's Hard Lemonade, which is what people drink now instead of Seagram's Golden Wine Coolers. At least that's what he told me, and he seemed like a person who would know, and anyway, he had a twelve-pack in his car.

When Doc and Huff came pounding on the door of the little cottage, asking, "When are you coming over to open your present, little girl?" which I already knew was a gift certificate to the Powerhaus, because that's what it is every year, I shouted through the door that I was enjoying my best Christmas ever in my own home. The Vo-Ag teacher covered up his snicker with his long, thin fingers that smelled of me. We were half dressed and into our third Mike's when she came to the door.

Hope was standing in the snow, wearing that baggy black sweatshirt with the skulls all over it, sockless in these little Indian moccasins, her short black pixie hair shining blue in parts in the glow of the Christmas lights from the big tree. She was holding two pieces of pie. "They say they are concerned about your nourishment," she said, convincing no one. "You know my mother, always looking out for her family," she added, again convincing no one.

"I know your mother's ways very well," I said. Caretaking was not on the list.

Hope sat down at the kitchen table. She reached for one of the Mike's on the table and popped it open. She took a swig, set it down, and contemplated it. It felt like she was about to deliver unto us a stern talking-to.

"So," she said to the Vo-Ag teacher. "Have you asked her yet?"

"Asked me what?" I was confused.

She took another sip of the Mike's.

"You're too young to be drinking that," I said.

"You're too married to sleep with my Vo-Ag teacher," she said, setting the bottle down anyway.

Touché, I thought. But later I would remember that: *her* Vo-Ag teacher.

She smiled at me with that distant smile of her mother's, that fake smile of yore. Then she turned to the Vo-Ag teacher and was all business. "I need to know if Tandy is in," she said to the Vo-Ag teacher. "I need to know if she is part of our big plan." Then she picked up the Mike's and left.

I turned to the Vo-Ag teacher.

"It's not the right time," he said.

"Now is as good a time as any," I said. "What is the 'big plan'?"

"It's a Future Farmers of America project." He pushed his long hair back behind his ears with his fingers. Then he pushed some of my hair back with his fingers. He put my earlobe between his fingertips and gently squeezed it, like he was giving it a hug. A tiny electric shock went through my body all the way down to my groin.

He said, "The Vo-Ag kids and I need your help so we can build a sod house."

I didn't even know what a sod house was.

11

My father said Upper Prairie University was the most economical option, but really it was the closest.

It was shortly after April 15—Accountant's New Year, the only holiday my father celebrated, and college applications were due. He was not interested in visiting colleges. He was interested in being drunk outdoors. I drove him to a midseason high school track event held on the campus of Luther College, a college I had heard was good. It was almost the end of senior year. There was not much time left.

"Oh, you stupid country kids," he mumbled as our high school boys ran their hearts out.

He was truly awed only by Gerald, who threw a winning shot put of fifty-one feet to qualify for state even though he was just a junior.

"That boy was born to throw heavy objects," my father said. Gerald, he said, was made out of what he called "farm-boy muscle"—something hard held him to the ground, but it was wrapped in soft and pliable flesh. He shouted to the track coaches, "I want him to throw something better than a shot put. A keg of beer! A dining room table! An eight-point buck!"

He said to me, "I like that boy."

"Assholes," he said about Luther College, though.

"Hippies," he said about the University of Iowa. "There will be drugs, people from Chicago. That's worse than Dubuque! Is that what you want?"

I wanted to sit alone in a small room and look out the window at a view different from the other windows I had looked out of, or into, the previous seventeen years of my life. I wanted Barbie to bring her baby to that small room and I wanted us to sit on the floor to play with the baby, and then I wanted us to take the baby for a stroller ride around a campus. I wanted to watch Barbie be a mother, and, in watching her do it, learn all about what it takes to do it, and perhaps give to the baby what I felt like I had missed out on. I also wanted to eat a meal in a restaurant where I could hear bits of the interesting conversations of strangers, and then ask those strangers to pass the salt, and then have those strangers pass the salt and then never see those strangers again.

"Upper Prairie. It's only fourteen miles," he said. "You can drive there."

When he said that, my heart fell like two rocks through my legs, landing in my feet. How would I sit in a small room and look out a window if I continued to live with him in the cottage on the go-around? How could I eat in restaurants with strangers if I ate every day at the Powerhaus?

Upper Prairie was the only place we visited. I drove. He said he wanted me to learn the route, but really he wanted to drink a case of Coors Light.

During the tour, he was silent and stewing and reeking of beer. The boy who gave us the tour was from Waukon, and when he told us that, my father snorted, as if you couldn't find a bigger piece of shit for a town than Waukon.

The boy was good, though. He said to my father, "I see you've been there."

The boy's name was Karl, with a *K*, "The good German way," he said, and nudged my father with his elbow, which almost knocked my father down. He wore a gray T-shirt with the words UPPER PRAIRIE UNIVERSITY in black, and tight jeans, and a leather necklace with a shark's tooth dangling from it. I waited for my father to say, "You're the furthest you can possibly be from an ocean and you wear shark jewelry! Are you some kind of fairy pirate?" but he said nothing.

Karl gave us a tour of the campus. He talked the whole time. He gestured with broad, steady hands.

I liked his curly hair, long all around like Greg Brady's. I liked how when he walked, he was loose in thighs that bulged through his jeans. I could imagine him bouncing from a grain bin to a barn with a twenty-pound bag of feed over his shoulder, and then writing things down in a notebook, fingers flipping fast.

I laughed at all his jokes, but I said nothing because I was saving all my energy to repair whatever terrible thing my father would say.

Despite all of this, the potential was not lost on me. Everywhere I went I saw people I had never seen before, going places I had never been. Some looked vaguely familiar, and I did see some who had left my own high school, and I waved at them, of course. But even they had their own new places to go.

And all of them wore different kinds of clothes from those I had seen before, shirts with funny sayings on them, and interesting jewelry. The girls wore lipstick in natural shades, as if the goal of the lipstick was not to be seen, but to instead make you a better version of yourself.

It was like walking around inside a television.

There were restaurants too. Not as many as I had hoped, but there were restaurants. I wanted to eat in all of them.

When Karl asked if there were any questions, my father finally spoke. "Does she have to live here?"

Karl said, "The college recommends that all freshmen have an authentic college experience."

I held my breath. It was the kind of thing that would set my father off, the kind of thing you might hear on public radio: *authentic college experience*. But my father just nodded—a slight up and down with his chin.

Karl said, "Well, I'll take you up to the dorms now," but my father stopped him.

"We're done here."

"I would like to see the dorms," I said.

"Well, I would not," he replied, and then signaled the end of the conversation by stumbling toward our car.

When, in the car, he cracked a beer and passed out, I had to pour the beer out my window so it wouldn't spill.

When I went down to the office to help my dad finish Mueller's payroll the next day, Doc and Huff were there.

Huff said, "You know they're the Peacocks, right?"

"I know," I said.

"You're going to be an Upper Prairie cock," Huff said.

"I know," I said.

Huff pulled at his hair and looked from my father to Doc and back. "They're just little girls!" he cried.

"I don't have a problem being a cock," I said. There was a hard bump poking me in my throat.

"Well, it makes perfect sense considering your DNA," Doc said to me, looking at my father.

I did live there. It was what the college recommended.

But I came home every day to hand deliver the mail to the post office and work on Mueller's payroll. I had to pay for the dorm room out of my own savings, which came from working for my father anyway, a fact he repeated on a regular basis.

"That's the business's money, not yours," he would say, even though the records I kept clearly indicated otherwise.

I drove there in Huff's Tempo. I paid Huff fifteen dollars for the use of the car on a month-to-month contract. "I've seen young people piss everything away," he said, referring to Barbie. "You're lucky this Tempo has only one tempo: slow."

I moved into a little dorm room on the first floor. I claimed the top bunk as my own. It had access to the only window in the room: a tiny, horizontal window that looked out to a view of the dumpster, yes, but beyond it a small sliver of a bean field—orderly stripes of bean rows—and then a lush and wild woods.

I had a roommate named Melanie. I saw her for seven minutes, mostly on that first day. Her mother cried a little while moving her in, and her father said, "Be good, Mel, study hard," and cried a little too. Then they left. Then so did Mel, because her boyfriend was waiting in the back parking lot in his white Mustang. I saw her once more when I opened the door one afternoon to find them having sex on the floor, both wearing shirts but no pants.

As soon as she left that first day, I sat on my top bunk and looked out at the view for a long time. The woods were dense and thick, beautiful. They were the kind of woods you see in movies.

When it got dark, I walked to one of the restaurants downtown. It was a pizza place called Margie's, full of people I did not know. College boys in red shirts and baseball caps with MARGIE'S printed on them made pizzas from different ingredients kept in small metal containers. I watched a whole pizza being made from dough to slicing.

I ordered a slice of pizza with white sauce. I didn't know what white sauce was. I learned it is delicious.

The salt and pepper were right in front of me so I didn't need to ask for them. But that was okay. All around me people buzzed with talk about things they were going to do, and things other people I didn't know had done, and how wonderful those things were.

I ate at Margie's three times a week for lunch during the fall of 1994—every Monday, Wednesday, and Friday. On Mondays, Karl, who had been my tour guide, ate with me. We had a microeconomics lecture together on those days.

He got that shark's tooth in Jacksonville, Florida, during an FFA exchange trip in high school. He talked about how modern farmers needed to protect themselves from the forces of government. He said diversification was the key to low risk, limited government was the key to market innovation, and conservative spending and debt management was the key to sustainability. He showed me charts. He had a steady hand for graphing data. He said, "Someday we'll figure this all out again."

We went to see a Halloween showing of the horror movie *Children of the Corn* in the student union. He covered his eyes during the scariest parts, but I laughed loudly through the whole thing. The idea that children would worship an evil force in a cornfield was absurd. But the idea that children would murder the members of their community made a certain kind of sense to me.

Karl said, "You're a strange bird, Tandy Caide," and I said, "I cannot disagree with you, Karl," and we left the movie holding hands. And when we got back to my dorm room we did not go in. We walked through the bean field and into the woods. We grabbed at each other in the dark to make each other jump, and then we kissed. His mouth was warm and wonderful. The floor of the woods was covered in leaves that stuck to our bodies. The dirt underneath the leaves smelled good. It was good dirt. We made love on it, the trees bending down toward us, the earth cool on my back, Karl warm all over and inside me.

We never went back to my dorm room. And we never went back to his. I didn't want to see his dorm room. That was his business. Mine was mine. Once we drove east in his Ford Bronco to the banks of the Mississippi River and made love there in the dark with the frogs and the living things singing all around us. We both got As in microeconomics.

Sometime that October I saw Bobby Coyle from my high school at the post office. He told me Barbie had had the baby and it was a girl and she had named the baby Hope, after a character on the soap opera *Days of Our Lives*. He told me she was living with the baby out at Huff's parents' old farm five miles out of town.

I ran back to the office to tell my father I was going to go see her. He rubbed his face, which is what he did when he couldn't think of how to bend me to his will. "It will hurt Huff's feelings," he said finally.

"I don't give a shit about Huff's feelings, and Huff doesn't give a shit about mine," I said. I wanted to see the baby! I had never held a baby!

He said, "Not as long as you live in my house!"

I said, "But see, I don't live at your house. I live at Upper Prairie University."

He rubbed his face some more. I thought he might rub all his skin off. He said, "Do you think you can afford to go to college without this job I provide for you? Do you think Barbie wants you rubbing that college in her face?"

Not going to see her is the real greatest regret of my life. I went to see Gerald instead, who was still in high school. He was drunk from doing beer bongs. I drove him home in Huff's Tempo and I let him lie on top of me in the backseat until we both felt a little better.

By the time I ran into Barbie again, Hope was in preschool, Barbie was working at Cunt Itchen, my father was dead, I was married to Gerald, and what she needed from me was some solid tax advice.

"I'm not here to make your life more pleasant, Tandy," she said.

"Nobody is, Barbie," I said.

She told me to call her Barb.

I told the Vo-Ag teacher everything, even the parts about Gerald. In fact, I can admit to you now—as I have learned through this past year that I am not always perfect and I have begun to accept this about myself—I lingered on the parts about Gerald. I made it known to the Vo-Ag teacher that I was not so enamored with Gerald. And with my skills at logic and storytelling, I led the Vo-Ag teacher to believe that my reasons were justifiable, that I was *right* for not being enamored with my husband. The Vo-Ag teacher nodded and held my hand and smiled kindly and spoke good words in gentle tones of voice.

What a great charmer he was. Or perhaps we shared a particular kind of charm that comes in handy when you need something. Perhaps I wanted him to like me, to tell me the things I wanted to believe about myself and my life were true.

He had been places, foreign countries. He was not from around here. I thought he would know better than me what is and is not good. But I did not tell him the parts about Barbie and the baby Hope. Barbie is my business. You people closer to the river, in your cities of active and sustainable and diverse commerce, certainly you can understand my reasons for this in ways I knew the Vo-Ag teacher, who did not understand anything about business, never would.

The Vo-Ag teacher made Hope his business, true, but that's an easy thing to do—make a beautiful, troubled seventeen-year-old girl your business.

Barbie, who is an acquired taste, is my business. She always has been. And she will remain so until the day I die.

III.

THE SOD HOUSE

12

Everything has gone downhill since 1976.

That was the year our county's portion of the interstate was completed, and, consequently, the last year the railroad operated as a hub here to places like Dubuque, Chicago, Minneapolis, and St. Louis. That was when eight lunch places closed, and three jewelry stores, and a bookstore, and an opera house; when people stopped coming here to see shows and shop and do all the things I imagine people like you do in the exciting places where you live.

That was also the year of my birth.

"It was a nice place to live, back then," Gary said at the annual New Year's Eve celebration of the Order of the Pessimists. As was our custom, Doc, Huff, Gary, and I were eating as red of prime rib as is allowed by Mary Ellen at the Powerhaus, and celebrating the darkness of winter because, as Huff says, "the fewer hours of sunlight there are, the less we have to deal with it." And as usual each member vowed that none of us would make any of the life changes other people swear they will, because we're all doomed to death and taxes anyway.

Gary had already delivered the charter, as it was his turn, and he had done so terribly, as was his custom, so he was trying to redeem himself, though of course there was no reason to, this being the Order of the Pessimists.

"You didn't even have to go to college back then," Gary said. "You could get hired at a union job with the railroad. They would train you. For free! And the pay was pretty good." To make sure we all got the point, he added, "Everyone had a softball team."

"Everything has gone downhill since 1976," Doc said, unbuttoning his pants to make room for the prime rib to move through his system. He lit a cigarette and leaned back into our booth.

I said, "Maybe you just think that because you live at the top of the hill, so everywhere is going downhill for you." Just a block away in my office, the Vo-Ag teacher waited for me to help him ring in the New Year properly—with mutual orgasm.

"I've got to protect myself," Doc said.

"From what?" I asked. "Villagers wielding spatulas they purchased at Walmart?"

It was beautiful, this power I felt. I can admit to you now that I have been humbled by the recent events of my life, but I have also very much enjoyed my power in many of its moments. Even as I am telling this to you now, with all the deeds done, I am enjoying it.

Doc raised his eyebrows and tapped the ash of his cigarette into an ashtray, which signaled to all of us that he would not be arguing. I got up to leave because at this point, unless there was an argument, I would not waste precious lovemaking time.

"You can't leave," Doc said. "We haven't done the accounting."

"I have a lot of work to do."

He narrowed his eyes. "We're conducting a meeting here."

"This meeting is terrible," I said. "It's going nowhere."

"She has a point," Gary said. "Or maybe that is the point."

"We have to talk about how we're going to donate that money to the Vo-Ag kids. Or maybe that's the work you have to do," Doc said.

"Maybe it is," I said, and went back to my office where Doc and Huff could not touch me, where the Vo-Ag teacher and I made love like animals, sweating and humping and grunting and loud.

Did I mention it was January? And I walked to work happy, bundled in my Lands' End coat? Did I mention it was winter, when I do not have to wave at so many people who wonder where I'm going, and if I'm going there at the right time, and, if it's not the right time, why I am so late or so early?

Every winter I ride above all that, fly above the atmosphere in a different world where the earth is far below me. It is a very special kind of alive. And that point in the middle of winter, when it is no longer enjoyable to most people—that is my absolute favorite time of the year. It is at that point when people stop trying to talk to me on the street, stop trying to search my face for answers. Or, at least, when they are searching my face for answers, it is in my office and at a very high hourly rate, because the middle of winter is when I am doing hundreds of income tax returns. I am solving all the tiny problems of all the people in this town using simple mathematical equations found on worksheets provided by the state and federal governments, with rules prescribed to me specifically by a series of books shelved within my fingertips' reach behind my desk, which are also found on the Internet in an easily searchable format. The people in this town bring me their problems in shoe boxes and grocery sacks and giant messy purses, and I file them into perfectly coherent little reports to be read by that giant thing that is the government. All those little problems of all those little people in this town get accounted for, made right, reported on, and stamped as true and unwavering by me: Tandy Caide, CPA.

And that year, the year of *Annie* and the year of the Vo-Ag teacher, the very dead of winter produced in me an even bigger aliveness. I pulled the hood of my big black Lands' End coat over my head and put my head down to the wind. And the only thing that could move me, aside from the warm and explosive feelings within me brought on by my many sexual experiences with the Vo-Ag teacher, was the wind, and all I had to do to avoid it was turn my head. The air outside was bitter and desolate and empty. Inside my coat it was warm, and it smelled very often like the sweat of the Vo-Ag teacher and our sex. On those bright beautiful days when the temperature on the bank's sign flashed negative, and the sky was a colorless white, I would inhale our warm smell—sage and musk and sex and sweat—and when I exhaled, it would fall to the dirt in microscopic ice crystals like a fairy dust.

All of January I took no afternoon appointments, because after he was done with school, the Vo-Ag teacher liked to come to my office and make love on an inflatable mattress. I bought it from eBay right after Christmas, from someone called nascarlarry who bought it for a camping trip. He planned to propose marriage to his girlfriend on the trip, but she broke up with him before he could get her defenseless in the wilderness. The mattress came with its own inflating device that plugs right into a wall outlet, so I didn't even waste my breath blowing it up.

The Vo-Ag teacher didn't ask me to buy the mattress. I did it on my own to surprise him. After we broke it in, I kept it propped against the wall in the back entryway so clients would not see it.

We made love every afternoon on that mattress, and sometimes on the little green vinyl love seat in my lobby, and sometimes on the floor. We made love well into the night, underneath that print of the haystacks and the old John Deere tractor. We did it hundreds of ways that I'm not sure even you people in your towns closer to the river have figured out, despite your pornographic video stores and your easily accessible Internet. We always did it at my office because, the Vo-Ag teacher said, he was sensitive to the energies inside the cottage on the go-around. "Who wants to make love among the ghosts of failure?" he said.

We did it before and after meetings we had with the Vo-Ag students about the sod house. The Vo-Ag kids, under the Vo-Ag teacher's direction, had decided that a sod house would be a perfect "Living to Serve" community project for FFA competition. The Vo-Ag students had researched sod houses and knew all about how the pioneers built them when they first arrived here, how whole families had spent their first homestead winters huddled inside little structures they created entirely from sod bricks they cut right from the ground.

"It will honor the students' *heritage,*" the Vo-Ag teacher said, sitting naked in my office after we had made extremely energetic love. "That's where it *lives to serve,* Tandy. And it's entrepreneurial too."

"How is it entrepreneurial?" I asked.

"People will pay to see it," he said. I laughed, but he truly believed this.

Once, when we made love, we imagined we were doing it in the sod house, the warm dirt covering our bodies. I laughed at all of it. Of course I laughed! You would have too. It was ridiculous. No one builds sod houses anymore, even for educational purposes. We do not have that kind of tallgrass sod around here anymore. The original, untouched tallgrass prairie from the days before the pioneers had roots that ran twenty feet deep, roots so dense you could make bricks out of it. Almost all the tallgrass prairie has been farmed away for a hundred years or more. Today's sod—even the sod that's been seeded back to "native"—doesn't have a system strong enough to hold it together into a brick that would hold up a house. Pull the sod out of the ground now and it crumbles through your fingers.

So the nights slipped away in absurdity, me watching the Vo-Ag teacher get caught up in his beautiful ideas, especially the "big idea" of the sod house; watching him flap his arms and pace around my office naked while he conjured up new and exciting things to say about sod houses; watching him enact vividly imagined scenes that showed the students to be heroic figures, this town to be some sort of movie version of itself, full of good people waiting to be discovered, himself a super savior, an organic-farming Jesus, a Peace Corps Mary Poppins with a ponytail and a flying Volkswagen who blew in to turn our zombie farm kids into winners and subpar sod into some kind of shiny dirt palace that all of America would admire.

Oh, how it pleased me! His vision of himself here in this town, it pleased me so much.

13

The first Wednesday in February, Doc came by with bean soup from the Powerhaus just as I was leaving for the Chamber meeting.

"Don't bother. Huff is refusing to eat with you," he said. "You know why."

We ate the soup at my office instead, and when we were done, Doc pulled a pack of cigarettes out from his shirt pocket. He lit one with a book of matches from the Powerhaus and then pulled the big red ashtray toward himself.

I could feel it coming. It was hanging in the air but moving around slowly like smoke. I braced myself.

"Your father never fucked around," he said.

"What does that have to do with me?" I asked. And I meant it. My father had been dead for a long time. I was becoming my own person.

"And your husband isn't even dead," Doc said.

"Oh, he's dead all right," I said. I was trying to be witty. I picked up Doc's cigarette pack. I pulled one out and lit it.

"So now you smoke," he said.

"Yes. I find it very soothing." I did not. I found it disgusting. It created in my mouth that warm spit that comes before you vomit.

"Well, you'll be gone soon too then. Smoking will kill you."

"You're still here."

"Not without trying," he said. Then he laughed a little bit and then he asked me, "Is that what you're doing? Are you trying to get out of here?"

"Is that what *you're* doing?" I asked.

"Your father taught you to never answer a question with a question."

"My father is dead," I said. "So tell me again, is that what *you're* doing?"

He didn't answer. Instead, he said, "You are no longer in the Chamber. I've put in a motion to remove you, and Huff and Howie Claus have seconded it and now Howie is secretary-treasurer. You are not welcome at the meetings until this thing is done."

"Business is business," I said, though I knew this was not. Howie Claus was a pastor who didn't even own a business. "And besides, I'm going to be busy working with the Vo-Ag teacher and Mueller on a new partnership."

"You're dumber than I thought," Doc said.

And yet he kept bringing me soup. Every Wednesday. Ask yourself: Who was the dumb one?

I told nothing of this to the Vo-Ag teacher. I never even considered telling him. It was my problem. Maybe I should have told him. Maybe it could have been something we shared together, laughed about years later in our old age.

No. I am glad I didn't tell him. Doc and Huff and my work—this was my business. The Vo-Ag teacher could have told me in a thousand different ways that it could be *our* business, but he would have been wrong.

The work was mine, and Doc and Huff were mine.

Also, there were things the Vo-Ag teacher failed to tell me too, important things that would have been very good to know, so I guess we are even.

I did not disrespect the work. Perhaps I was a fool, but I remained a businesswoman.

14

Then the Vo-Ag teacher asked me to go for a drink.

I suppose this is how some people do it. First you have sex. Then you go for a drink.

I refused to go to the Powerhaus for reasons I'm certain are obvious to you, though the Vo-Ag teacher laughed at my refusal, as if it were all a game.

He drove me over to Four Corners, to a bar called the Valkyrie that he had "discovered," though I had known about it my entire life. He wore that silly little jacket with the useless loops at the shoulders. He played a lot of the Steve Miller Band in his little red Volkswagen Beetle, one of those old ones, exactly the kind of car you would imagine an impractical hippie too focused on looks would drive. He sang along to the songs very loudly, especially the one about time that *keeps on slipping, slipping, slipping into the future*. We held hands. I can admit to you that it felt nice, even though his tiny Volkswagen did not take well to County Road 14 in the winter and had no seat belts. It felt like I was riding in one of those toy cars the Kiwanis bring out for the Fourth of July, but at seventy miles an hour and on ice.

"You should get a truck," I said as we slid across the road, and he rewound the future again on his tape deck.

"You think I should?" he asked.

"It would make a lot of sense for the winters here."

"Perhaps I will. If you think I should."

Oh, how he enjoyed these games! How he enjoyed talking about one thing as if it were another!

The Valkyrie was packed. Everyone was smoking, even though you're not allowed to do that in bars and restaurants anymore. The

Valkyrie walls are carpeted from floor to ceiling with red shag, so it was like walking around in a giant red ashtray.

I mentioned that carpeted walls make no functional sense, and the Vo-Ag teacher said, "It's intimate, Tandy," and put his arm around me and kissed my neck and of course I forgot about it. You would have too. Anyone who has ever loved anyone in a sexual way knows how easy it is to forget your concerns when someone is kissing your neck.

We found the bartender and sat down. The Vo-Ag teacher ordered two Mexican sidecars. The bartender looked at him blankly.

"It's tequila, triple sec, and lime juice," the Vo-Ag teacher explained.

"That's a margarita," the bartender said.

"Po-TAY-to, Po-TAH-to," the Vo-Ag teacher said.

"No one says *Po-TAH-to*," the bartender said. But he made the drinks and brought them anyway, because that is his job.

That Mexican sidecar was so strong I nearly spit it out. It tasted like a Mike's but much spicier, like a Mike's with black pepper. It warmed me, like my rib cage was a radiator that had just kicked on.

The Vo-Ag teacher took a big gulp too. Then he couldn't keep his hands off me. He rubbed my hands and arms and my back. He started in on Valkyries, Norwegian goddesses, which he seemed to know a lot about. I suppose it was sexy talk—talk you do to make yourself seem more interesting or virile.

"Contrary to popular opinion, Valkyries didn't ride winged horses," he said. He was rubbing my hands between his own. "The common representation of the Valkyrie is a beautiful, big-breasted Viking woman on a winged horse. But really, they were more like witches. And they rode on wolves."

"Is that so?" I asked. I was pretending to be interested for the sake of the hand massage.

"Yes! Their job was to decide which dead warriors would live on forever in Valhalla and which would go to hell. 'Valkyrie' literally translates into 'choosers of the slain.'"

"Interesting," I said, or something like that. I don't quite remember. My second Mexican sidecar was being refilled.

He said some more things then, about ravens and grog, but I have no clear memory of them. I had never been so drunk before. I liked it very much. I liked it so much, or maybe I was just drunk enough, that I understood what Bruce Willis was so happy about in that Seagram's Golden Wine Cooler commercial. For a moment, I even understood Huff.

I leaned in and whispered to the Vo-Ag teacher, "I like being drunk."

He kissed my neck and then moved his mouth to my ear and whispered back, "I knew you would," as if he had invented alcohol just for me. And then I saw a pair of boots I recognized, and above them some worn and dirty jeans on some long and lanky legs. And then I saw a pair of tiny slippers, little Indian slippers—those Minnesota moccasins—and above them a baggy sweatshirt with skulls on it, and I squinted into the smoke and I saw that it was Clive, and lo and behold it was also Hope.

There it was. Right before me. Right there in the Valkyrie.

"Hello, Tandy. Hello, Mr. Tischer," Hope said. "What a weird surprise." She didn't even try to run. She didn't even look away. She just held my gaze and seemed to enjoy the irony that it was *she* who was the surprise.

"You know Tandy Caide?" Clive asked Hope. Unlike Hope, he did not look me in the eye. He scanned the room instead, in a clockwise and methodical way, the way I sometimes did with my bedroom wallpaper.

"You know Clive?" the Vo-Ag teacher asked me. But he betrayed nothing, at least at that time.

"Oh, she most certainly does," Clive said before I could answer. He scratched hard on the back of his head.

"*You* know Clive?" I asked the Vo-Ag teacher. Clive was not a student at the high school. The Vo-Ag teacher was not a farmer. Where would they have met? I did not understand. The Vo-Ag teacher did not answer and instead turned to the bartender and promptly ordered another Mexican sidecar. He held up his glass and said, "Here's to us."

I wanted to know how he had become acquainted with someone like Clive, but it was Hope who presented the real problem. Despite some of the outrageous behavior that passes for "acceptable" in this town, we do know enough to not let our high school teachers drink Mexican sidecars with their high school students.

At least this town's CPA knew enough. "You need to go home," I said to Hope. "This is not a place for you."

"You're not my mom," Hope said. "And anyway, I'm here with a legal adult." She pointed to Clive, who lifted his chin and winked at me as if I were getting my due. "I'll be eighteen soon."

"But not today. You need to leave. We will drive you home."

Before I could press it any further, Hope walked right by me—it felt as if she walked right through me—and straight to the Vo-Ag teacher. "What were you two talking about?" she asked him.

The Vo-Ag teacher took a big gulp of his sidecar and, without looking at anyone, staring only at a spot behind the bartender's head and directly into the Hamm's beer sign's waterfall, he said, "Valkyries."

"What about them?" Hope said. She was casually leaning against the bar with an elbow on it, posing as a grown-up, acting as if it were perfectly natural for a high school girl to be next to her high school teacher in a bar.

"I don't think it's anything a child should know about," I said quickly, trying to keep everyone's eyes on the road. I gathered my coat as if we were all leaving, though I remained the only person holding a coat.

The Vo-Ag teacher kept his gaze behind the bar. "They were motherless orphans, left behind to become foster daughters of Odin, the Viking god of war."

My stomach began to burn. The sidecar tilted to one side.

"If he was the god of war, why didn't he kill the Valkyries? Why weren't they kidnapped or ransomed?" Hope asked.

The Vo-Ag teacher went on, staring at that spot behind the bar. "They couldn't die. Any maiden who becomes a Valkyrie will stay immortal as long as she stays a virgin."

I've never seen a girl laugh so hard. She laughed so hard tears ran down her cheeks. Her legs buckled and she had to hold herself up with the bar. It was a wicked laughter, laughter from a person who did not believe in anything anymore, who believed nothing important mattered. Coming from a high school girl, it was terrifying. It may seem impossible to you, but I believe her laughter made the lights flicker. It was the kind of laughter that makes you question all of your choices and the choices of all those around you from the beginning to the end.

The Vo-Ag teacher said, "If you see a Valkyrie before a battle, you will *die* in that battle."

"Ooooohhhhh," Hope said, in that same kind of mocking tone the Vo-Ag teacher had once used on me. My stomach seized. Warm spit flooded into my mouth. I put my Mexican sidecar down and I went to the bathroom and I vomited Mexican sidecars into the Valkyrie's filthy women's toilet.

Hope followed me in. And though I was hanging over a dirty public toilet, I could see that all of her grown-up swagger was gone. Suddenly she was a little girl again—the one Barb would bring into my office when her income taxes were due, the little girl who sat quietly on my office floor stapling the ends of blank copier paper together until there was an accordion of paper fifty feet long winding around my desk, Barb shouting at her to stop making a mess so that the little girl's focus turned to shame.

"Don't tell her I was here," she said. "I shouldn't be here."

"No shit," I said. I went to the sink and splashed water on my face.

"Please. Please don't tell her," Hope said again. She was flapping her hands in a panic. It gave me some courage.

"Do you know how lucky you are?" I asked. "To have a mother, a family? You aren't just hanging out there. There are people looking out for you."

Her face darkened suddenly. "Oh yeah? Name one," she said.

"Your mother."

"She is looking out for herself," Hope said.

"That's not true," I said. "She has devoted her life to you."

"I didn't ask for that!" Hope shouted.

"You should be grateful for it!" I shouted back. "And grateful for Huff! And grateful for Doc! And grateful for me!"

"Huff? Ha!" she said. "You? Ha! Doc? He has to care because he's a doctor. He earns a living off of me!"

"Okay," I said. "Well, I am going to do something for you right now. I am going to tell you that you have no business being with a grown man like Clive."

She narrowed her eyes at me. "I have business with whatever person I can, Tandy Caide. Certainly a businesswoman like yourself can understand the need to seek opportunity freely."

"What kind of business could you possibly have with Clive?" I really had no idea.

She paused, and for a brief moment, I thought she was going to tell me. Then she said, "It's not what you think."

"What do I think?" I asked.

"*He*'s not what you think," she said, amending her statement.

"He's nothing I think," I said. "You shouldn't think about him either. You shouldn't think about any of us. You should think about what lies before you after high school, what better future you can look forward to when you leave this town."

She paused, rolling this over in her head. I thought perhaps that hard thing inside of her may have shifted slightly. She turned and fixed her hair in the mirror. "You should think about that too," she said.

That was the last thing I remember before the sobbing in the Vo-Ag teacher's car as he drove me home. It came in big uncontrollable waves, in shrieks and in deep loud moans. It shook the whole front of his tiny Volkswagen. And when we got to my office, I remember that he hoisted me over his shoulder and carried me inside like a big bag of old clothes headed for Goodwill. He made love to me on the inflatable mattress while I continued to sob.

Maybe that sounds odd to you, but it wasn't. I asked him to make love to me, so he made love to me while I sobbed and it didn't seem odd at all. It seemed like a great act of love and it still does.

15

It was unusually warm for early February, and very sunny. There was melt on the road and melt on my boots and melt on the Vo-Ag teacher's clogs. At some point during the pounding haze of that next morning he asked me if I would take him out to Mueller's farm to negotiate a plot of land for the sod house. He also asked me if I would chaperone the FFA trip to regionals so the Vo-Ag kids could present the sod house to a panel of judges for a chance to win a grant to build it. I was hungover for the first time in my life. I said something stupid. "Yes."

It was too warm for my coat, but I wore it anyway. I was especially sweaty. The Vo-Ag teacher wore his dumb gray jacket with the useless little shoulder loops. The birds were out, and you could hear them, but not as much as I could hear the Vo-Ag teacher belting out Steve Miller songs as he drove, because even though there were no seat belts in that little red Volkswagen, there was a tape deck and a massive speaker taking up the entire backseat.

"Why do you have to sing so loud?" I asked him.

"If it's too loud, you're too old!" he shouted.

"It seems like it would be the other way around," I said. "In my experience, older people need things to be louder."

This made him laugh his big snorty horselaugh. "I could eat you!" he shouted.

The idea of eating something turned my stomach, and I suddenly remembered pieces of the night before.

"So," I said in the light of day. "So you know Clive."

There was a pause that seemed to last for years. I prepared in my head what I might say if he asked me how I knew Clive: he was my client. It was quite simple. One good thing about being a businesswoman is how much you can hide behind business. But he did not ask anything about how I knew Clive. Instead, he responded, "I've seen him around. Mostly at the Powerhaus."

It never occurred to me that the Vo-Ag teacher would go to the Powerhaus without me.

"Don't worry. I go there late at night and I never see Doc or Huff," he said.

"Why do you go there?" Why would anyone go there?

"To learn about the community," he said. "To talk to the laborers. To talk to the common man."

I did not know what that meant by "common man."

"You know," he went on. "Those in a socioeconomic system whose labor fuels the system. Those who are most affected by economic change."

"Oh. Of course," I said. Though I knew no such term, I could see that he was describing Clive.

"Well, I know Clive because he is one of my clients," I said, though the Vo-Ag teacher had not asked. Instead he said, "Can you keep a secret?"

Without waiting for a response, he pulled over then, and we got out of the little red Volkswagen. He went to the front of it and lifted the hood. And instead of an engine, which you find under the hoods of all the other running cars here, there was a shoe box.

"What?" I exclaimed.

"Oh," he said. "The engine's in the back of these kinds of cars."

It was a shoe box for a pair of Red Wing work boots. "It's about time you bought a pair," I said.

The Vo-Ag teacher lifted the lid from the box and inside was not a pair of boots. Inside were one hundred or so foil packets filled with cold medicine pills.

"You must feel a big cold coming on," I said, making a joke.

"Hope gave this box to me," he said. "And Clive gave it to her."

Everyone around here knows that if you buy more than two packs of cold medicine, the cashier on the other end will make you write your name down on a list the store is required to keep because the government assumes your aim is to make drugs that go well beyond alleviating the common cold.

"I wondered how Clive could afford a pair of Red Wings," I said, trying another joke.

The Vo-Ag teacher did not laugh. He got deadly serious. There was not a trace of irony around any of his edges. "She asked me to hold them for her because she is afraid of Clive."

I snorted out my nose a little. "Who could ever be afraid of Clive?"

"You should not underestimate him," he said.

I had a flash of anger then. I felt my fingertips prickle. I felt protective of Clive, though there was no clear reason to be. Perhaps, now that I think about it, I did not like the Vo-Ag teacher telling me who among my own people I should and should not underestimate. But I did not argue it. Instead I said, "You should not underestimate Hope."

Something got a hold of him then—his own flash of anger. He started to pace around the front of his car. "Tandy!" he shouted. "What is she supposed to do? What is a young woman of her intelligence and capabilities—what is she supposed to do with all of that potential? What else is there for her but this?!" He pointed to the foil packs of cold medicine in that place in his car where an engine should have been.

I did not know the answer, but I found myself abandoning Clive and suddenly protecting Hope.

"Well, for one she could go to college," I said, unsure of what that meant or if I even meant it.

The Vo-Ag teacher stared at me with his eyes bugged out, as if I were the dumbest person who ever walked the land. "You obviously don't know her mother," he said.

The prickle disappeared from my fingertips. I became calm and deep and solid then, as if I had suddenly leaped over him, and, from a new vantage point on the other side of him, was able to see how small he really was. I said nothing. I just nodded.

And then the regret set in, sad and strong. What had I done? I had aligned myself with a very stupid man, a man in a ponytail and man clogs, who misunderstood everything about my closest family, who most likely could not wait to tell my biggest client all that he was doing wrong. I stared at the empty fields and the jagged, leftover cornstalks peeking out from under the snow. They looked like legs that had been hacked off at the knees.

He noticed this change in me. Say what you will about the relative stupidness of the Vo-Ag teacher as it relates to this town as a whole, he was able to notice subtle changes in my emotional countenance. He was the opposite of clueless on a one-on-one basis. Perhaps he feared that I would discover those things about him that he did not want discovered, and so he was protecting his secrets. Perhaps he deeply cared about me and wanted to protect me from any unpleasantness. Perhaps both were true. It was early, there was still a lot of ground for us to uncover. And it is still early now in my attempts to process all that happened this past year. I am still getting used to the notion that you can have two seemingly conflicting ideas about your life at once, and that they could both be true.

He closed the hood of the Volkswagen that was actually the trunk. He reached out for my hand and held it in his own. "Help me, Tandy," he said. His eyes were soft, his big horse mouth closed and turned down forlornly. He looked like Winnie-the-Pooh's downtrodden donkey friend, Eeyore.

"How can I help you?" I asked for the millionth time in my life.

"Help me build this sod house with the Vo-Ag students. Help me show them there is something worth living for—something more promising than a box of stolen cold medicine."

He wrapped his arms around me then, and it was warm in them, and it smelled like our sex and sage. He smelled like a good and strong and kind man. And when we pulled apart I smelled the fresh wind of a warm winter day and the crackle smell of winter sunlight. I felt that promise he talked about. I felt like maybe something wonderful was coming around the bend for me too. Sometimes there is both promise and fear in the smell of a fresh wind. It seems impossible, but like I said, I am learning that you can have two seemingly different ideas about things at the same time.

We got back on the road. "A sod house is a service to the community, and serving your community is a kind of love," the Vo-Ag teacher said in a way that showed me he was practicing his pitch to Mueller. He wiggled in his seat like he was going to stand up, but then, because he was driving, he just took both hands off the wheel and stretched them out instead. He stuck his left hand out his open window and curved his right hand around my headrest and touched my far cheek. He said, "It is a matter of civic pride!"

The little Volkswagen swerved all over the wet blacktop.

I looked in silence at the half-snowy, half-muddy fields until we got to Mueller's.

Perhaps it *was* a matter of civic pride.

The year before my father died, Mueller planted five acres of native tallgrass prairie—switchgrass and bluestem and the like—along Kennicott Creek. In return for his promise to keep it there for fifteen years, the federal government gave him $7,000 a year. Mueller had exceeded this requirement by three years.

"That's how these things work," Mueller said to the Vo-Ag teacher. He was eyeing him up and down, spending extra time with the rainbow-colored belt and the ponytail.

"I know how these things work," the Vo-Ag teacher said back, which made Mueller look at me with his eyebrows raised all the way past his forehead to the edge of his crew cut. The Vo-Ag teacher went on. "Did you know that today, native prairie covers less than one percent of its former range, which makes it one of the most endangered ecosystems in the world? That's how farming works."

"I know how farming works," Mueller said. His mouth quivered with the tremendous effort of suppressing his laughter.

We stood in that patch of prairie near the creek. The tallgrass was mostly beaten down by the melting snow. Mueller was in a green Pioneer Seed hat and a green quilted Pioneer Seed jacket, open to show his barrel chest and his dirty overalls. He was breaking up clumps of dirt with his boots. I sweated next to him in my big black Lands' End coat. The Vo-Ag teacher bounded away from us and ran around in the grass, ponytail bobbing, toward Kennicott Creek. The creek was running a little bit in some open patches and frozen in others.

"This plot's been grass since even before your dad died," Mueller said to me.

"I don't remember," I said.

The Vo-Ag teacher bounded back and said, "You like Pioneer Seed?"

"I like free things," Mueller said.

The Vo-Ag teacher bounded away again, pulling at the grass and sniffing it.

"He looks like a cocker spaniel," Mueller said, not even in a whisper.

"You're being rude," I said. He may have been my biggest client, and he may have been right—the Vo-Ag teacher did look like a cocker spaniel—but certainly he could modulate his voice.

"Oh, get off your high horse, Tandy," he said. Then he sighed and became wistful, or rather as wistful as Mueller can get. "Eighteen years this has been tallgrass prairie. You were just a kid. You weren't who you are now." Then just as quickly it was back to business.

The Vo-Ag teacher stopped his bounding. "I can't believe you kept it prairie for so long," he said.

"That was the deal," Mueller said.

"I bet it was nice to cash the checks," the Vo-Ag teacher said. I held my breath. The Vo-Ag teacher really knew nothing about business.

"It's always nice to cash a check," Mueller said.

"I bet it was nice not to have to do anything but protect your topsoil from erosion and your water from fertilizer runoff while you cashed a check."

Mueller, on the other hand, knows a lot about business. "You're goddamn right it was nice," Mueller said. He grinned and crossed his arms and rocked back on his boots. "I got to sit back and let the land breathe *and* I got to buy all new windows on the house. That's called a win-win, Mr. Tischer. And certainly you can understand the benefits of improved energy efficiency, or should I have thought more about the arts and used my profits to build a solar-powered stereo?"

The Vo-Ag teacher did that thing with his arms again, encompassed what he believed to be the entirety of Mueller's farm and its many societal wrongs by raising his arms and displaying his giant wingspan. "Seven thousand dollars a year! For eighteen years! It's fantastic! That's like..." He tried to calculate how much Mueller had netted but he couldn't do the math. "That's so much money!" he said.

Mueller's square forehead got creases in it, and his big lips puckered. His dark blue eyes opened real wide and he looked at me as if I were responsible for the fact that the Vo-Ag teacher couldn't figure numbers in his head.

To be clear, the gross yearly profit Mueller earned on the prairie was, on average, about $9,000, considering overhead. That's $162,000 total over the course of eighteen years, with $126,000 of it taxable income. The Vo-Ag teacher gave me a look too—the same look as Mueller's, except the Vo-Ag teacher's mouth was a wide-open garage door. It implied that I was supposed to defend him, though I don't know why he would think that. We were lovers, true. But the Vo-Ag teacher always knew me to be a businesswoman.

But then again, if I was a businesswoman, why was I out there on the Vo-Ag teacher's behalf? I still ask myself that sometimes. I have even searched the Internet, late into the night, for answers to that, except I don't know how to phrase the question. I keep looking up things like "business etiquette and lovers" and "balance work and personal life." Nothing there has been remotely helpful to me regarding my particular situation, and some of it seems to be written in a foreign language. For instance, you probably know what "downtime" is, but I had to look it up.

"What the hell does he want?" Mueller asked me, the Vo-Ag teacher standing right there, listening.

"He wants to use the sod from the grass to build a sod house here," I said.

Mueller looked at the ground and smiled a bit and then began to make sounds in the back of his nose like he was holding in little sneezes.

I went on. "It's for an FFA project, called 'Living to Serve.'"

Mueller's face turned red and he started to shake all over in that way the men around here laugh, that way that could also be crying but isn't if they eventually look up at you to see if you are in on the joke. Mueller looked up, and I tried to be in on the joke. I gave him a little chuckle, as I am accustomed to doing in my business. Mueller rolled his eyes.

"Don't give me that fakey bullshit," Mueller said when he was able to catch his breath. "Doc and Huff were right. You're a goddamn genius, Tandy Caide. And also a goddamn idiot."

That burned me. It was like a little ember of sage fell into my chest and burrowed there. But at least I knew then where Mueller stood. You always know where Mueller stands. That is something very special about him that you cannot say about most people, even myself sometimes.

I said nothing about my relative genius or idiocy. Instead, I asked again, "Can the Vo-Ag teacher and the FFA students build a sod house here?" The Vo-Ag teacher stood next to me, listening and hoping.

"Doesn't FFA have a shit-ton of their own money?" Mueller asked.

"We have to create the project from resources already present in our community, not using the benefit of our own individual or collective resources," the Vo-Ag teacher said.

"What did he just say?" Mueller asked me.

"Everything has to be donated," I said.

Mueller nodded, but he remained unconvinced. "This tallgrass prairie sod has been here awhile, but it takes a couple of hundred years to develop the kind of root system the pioneers had. It won't be the same."

"We know that," the Vo-Ag teacher said. "But we want to try."

Mueller snorted. Then he shrugged.

"So they can build a sod house here?" I asked.

Mueller took a handkerchief out of his pocket and wiped the laughter from his eyes. "How do I know? Do I look like Michael Landon?'

Mueller looked out at the rows of hacked-off cornstalks and frozen dirt spread out before us for miles. He sighed a sigh that was both satisfied and resigned. This does not change my previous assertion that you always know where Mueller stands. For the people in this town, feelings of satisfaction and resignation are often present in the same sigh.

"My, my, Tandy Caide. If your father could see us now. This is one for the books."

"So that's a yes?" the Vo-Ag teacher asked.

"I need to consult privately with my CPA about this," Mueller said.

The Vo-Ag teacher bounded off and I became filled with regret and an impending doom. Without the Vo-Ag teacher standing next to me, I could see myself more clearly—see my current idiot self as something different from my usual business self. My head was pounding from all that had happened the night before. I could feel somewhere deep in my burning-ember heart that this was going to go bad for all of us. I leaned in real close to Mueller and I whispered, "Say no."

It was then that I got the real Mueller, the Mueller I knew from Cunt Itchen and nearly twenty years of payroll and tax consulting. He softened his eyes at me, and it felt like he could see right through to the real me, which he may well be able to do. Everyone in this town can see through to the real me, especially those in close proximity to Doc and Huff and my dead father. He said, "Why don't *you* say no?"

I had an answer but I did not want to say it. I was weak; I was unable to step out from under the all-encompassing wingspan of the Vo-Ag teacher. I was a lonely person who needed to be close to someone who loved me in a different way from how I had ever been loved. How could I admit that to my biggest client? Instead, I dug the toe of my boot into the dirt. The sun beat down on the back of my neck. My big black coat was stuck to it. I said, "People shouldn't answer a question with a question."

"There are lots of things people shouldn't do," Mueller said. "But it is not my business to tell them that."

He is a good person, Mueller. You should know that. Though admittedly my sample size is small, certainly smaller than yours, he is one of the greatest people I have ever known.

Finally I said, "Well, someone's got to keep an eye on the fire."

It was the right thing to say, I guess. Or maybe it was the safe thing. At the very least, it made him laugh again, and it is always prudent to make your biggest client laugh.

Somewhere in the distance, the Vo-Ag teacher pulled at the long prairie grass and dug his hands into the dirt, searching for answers.

Mueller said, "One acre, and I'm going to plant corn around the rest."

"That's fair."

"And I want my taxes done free."

"Income tax? That's fair."

"No. Business too. For the whole year."

"That's more than the acre is worth planted," I said.

"And what is my trouble worth?"

He is a savvy businessman, Mueller. I respect it immensely.

"Not payroll," I said. "I can't eat without the payroll."

We had come to an agreement. In retrospect, I can see that it benefited him in every way and would leave me $5,000 short for the year and on the hook for any of the Vo-Ag teacher's certainly disastrous mistakes.

Though I should note here that Mueller has yet to turn the rest of that prairie over to corn.

"It *is* winter," Mueller said after we shook on it. "And I *am* getting real tired of *Wheel of Fortune*. I guess we're both fucking with him now, huh, Tandy?"

I let him laugh it out. Nearby, the Vo-Ag teacher tried to leap over Kennicott Creek, but ended up with a leg in the water, losing one of his man clogs and soaking his sock clear through. He had to get down on his knees to fish out the clog, and so the knees of his jeans got soaked through too.

Still, to this day, as I recount this all to you now, I don't know why I did not say no to the sod house. There were so many reasons to say no.

But I do know why I said yes. I know why I continued to go along with it.

I did it to please the Vo-Ag teacher. It was the wrong kind of pleasing, but still, that's why.

It didn't work. Later that night, after making love at my office, the Vo-Ag teacher got full-blown wistful, more wistful than I have ever seen anyone except Doc. "Imagine them out here where there was nothing, absolutely nothing, but this... this sod!"

"Who?" I asked.

"The pioneer husband and the pioneer wife!" he replied, as if I should have known. "Two people digging down into the one thing they both have: the sod! Sod filled with millions of bugs and organisms, three feet deep or more, teeming with a life they can't see but *must* believe in—to make their vision real!"

"What vision?" I asked.

"A shared vision! A vision of a *shared life*!" he said. He got excited, and he stood on his side of the inflatable mattress, which redistributed the air so that I almost flipped off. He pulled a shoe box over from the coffee table next to us. This shoe box was for a pair of athletic shoes like what people in shoe commercials wear, not Red Wing work boots. In it was not a whole lot of cold medicine, but rather one small brick of sod he had dug out of Mueller's adolescent prairie.

He picked the square of sod up gently, so it wouldn't fall apart. It looked like a dead person's scalp with hair on it, all dried up. He held it out to me, like it was a present.

I didn't take it. Perhaps I should have. Perhaps I should have gone a little further with him than I did.

He turned that sod around and around in his hands. He acted like he was some sort of dirt scientist whose job it was to show me firsthand all that I had been missing all these years, how uninformed I was about my own life. He explained to me how good it used to be in my town before we all ruined it. "It wasn't like this," he said, pointing to the little square of sod, a few roots woven around in the dirt, but mostly falling apart around the edges. "Back then the sod was dense, the homes heated and cooled themselves!" he said, as if sod houses were marvels of technological advancement.

"They leaked," I said, not enjoying the task of listening to someone tell me how dumb I was. "I'm pretty sure the dirt walls were filled with moles and snakes and bugs."

"Not dirt, Tandy. *Sod,*" he said, and then he insisted we get on the Internet right then so that he could show me "real sod."

You probably already know this, but somewhere in Minneapolis, near the airport and the largest mall in the country and a Hilton hotel and thousands of miles of interstate with cloverleaf exit ramps, there is a twenty-seven-thousand-acre wildlife refuge and interpretive center that specializes in wetland and prairie things. On the Internet, there is a photo of a cross-section of real native prairie sod encased in glass. Unlike the sod the Vo-Ag teacher dug up on Mueller's farmland, this real prairie sod is as old as the Indians and the buffalo and maybe even the dinosaurs. Tallgrass—for instance, bluestem and switchgrass, which is much of what Mueller had planted—can be seven feet tall, but the root system for these grasses are nearly ten feet deep. They are deeper than they are tall, which seems entirely backward until you see a picture of it on the Internet. The roots of these grasses look like a mass of hanging brown hair. They taper down to a point, like the hairs of a paintbrush or a ponytail.

We were cheek to cheek in the dark, the Vo-Ag teacher and I, naked, sharing my work chair, our faces just inches from the computer's screen. He was whispering like we were in church. When his mouth made words, the skin of his cheek slid against the skin of my cheek. "That's what you build a home out of, Tandy. But of course that's pretty much gone."

The Vo-Ag teacher sighed. He lay back down on the inflatable mattress and curled into a naked little ball. I lay down with him. I covered him with my own body. I asked him then, half ironically, half not so, what he had asked me when we first met. "What's a nice guy like *you* doing in a place like this? Why aren't you in Minneapolis, at this center studying prairie grass and things?"

He turned his head and stared at me, and in the blue glow of the computer screen, I could see that he was looking at me as if I were a stranger.

"I am trying to help," he said quietly. "Why can't any of you see that?"

I said, "Maybe some people don't want your help." It was an honest answer to his question. I stand by it even now.

"Maybe some people do," he said.

I was confused. "Who?" I asked.

He furrowed his brow, also confused, or so I thought. He pulled away, as if I had suddenly become someone different. Then he came back and put his head in my lap and he cried.

I held him for a while. I tried not to look at him—this grown man crying—but I couldn't help it. I looked, and it was awful. His face was blotchy and red and screwed up in a desperate, ugly way. It was one of the most awful nights of my life, not because I was heartbroken, but because he was. It is heartbreaking to watch a heartbroken person cry when there is nothing you can do to help him.

Then we made love again. He fell asleep immediately after.

I got up from the inflatable mattress then, and I looked out the window and into Cunt Itchen across Main. Barb was staring back at me, standing straight, held up by her strong spine, coffeepot held up by her strong sinewy forearm.

This is a kind of love, I mouthed to her.

No, it is not, she mouthed back, and went back to her tables.

16

The rest of February through late March blurred into a steady stream of income tax returns. I ordered the tiny problems of the people in this town at a rapidly increasing pace—mileage woes, home-office expenditures, rental property remodels, oppressive child support payments, which are neither taxable nor tax deductible. I solved them all with rules prescribed to me by the federal and state governments. I solved them from sun up to sundown and beyond.

It was a relief really. There was no time to think about Clive, or Hope, or hundreds of little packets of cold medicine. There was no time to contemplate which was a risk to the other, or the Vo-Ag teacher's part in all of it. Or perhaps I didn't want to think about it, as I have never enjoyed contemplating my life's failures, even the ones that drag on for years and years. I saw a bumper sticker on a foreign car at the bank once that said DENIAL AIN'T JUST A RIVER IN EGYPT. I have never been to Egypt, but I have been to denial.

The Vo-Ag teacher came by most evenings. From where I sat in my office, I could see him peek into my lobby window from the street to see whether I was occupied. Most of the time during these weeks I was, and so he would move away from the window and be gone. I was both nervous and grateful for his presence and then absence. Nervous because I didn't want to lose him, grateful because I had business to attend to, and there is no denying that business is business.

Most of my clients did not notice him peeking. Imagine your own income tax appointments and try to note the specifics of your tax preparer's environment. Such concerns are almost always secondary to your fears about what you stand to lose at the hands of the government.

But some of my clients noticed, because the town that I live in demands that my affairs be public knowledge at all times. Sylvia Vontrauer sat holding her breath during her appointment, her mouth a thin line that quavered in the corners, as if she had sewn it shut to keep from blurting out her disapproval of me but couldn't keep the seams tight. Dave Oppegaard, the head volunteer fireman, leaned back in the chair where my clients sit and winked repeatedly at me. He said, "Any good news on the home front, Tandy Caide?" to which I replied, "Nothing to write home about," to which he replied, "Well, who would be home to get it anyway?" to which I responded by handing him a pen with my name on it, to which he responded by tucking it behind his ear and winking again.

Howie Claus did not even come in. "He went to La Crosse to get his taxes done, he is so appalled by your behavior," Doc told me when he brought me the bean soup on Wednesday. "He's appalled by everyone's behavior," I said, to which Doc replied, "Touché."

The high school principal, Dieter Bierbrauer, noticed. He sat in my office mussing and smoothing his floppy white-blond combover and contemplating me more intensely than he had during any of his fifteen previous income tax appointments, even the very first one when he asked me twice how old I was. He sat at the edge of the chair and answered my questions with one-word answers and tracked my every movement with his eyes.

Finally, as I was printing his finished return, he said, "So what do you think of the new vocational agriculture teacher?"

"I think he is just fine," I said.

"So do the students," he said. "Others, not so much."

"Well, you can't please everyone."

"But you can please some of them."

"Do you have one of my pens?" I asked him, trying to change the subject.

"I have sixteen of them."

"Good," I said. "Give some to your friends then."

"All of my friends have them too."

"Maybe you should get some new friends."

"Like the Vo-Ag teacher? I just saw him peeking in your window."

"Doesn't he deserve friends? People who move to new areas for employment and develop strong social networks there tend to be better employees." This was something the Vo-Ag teacher had said to me once.

Dieter sighed the sigh of my people, the one that means both satisfaction and resignation. He said, "Well played, Tandy Caide."

One evening, after ten P.M., several hours after the Vo-Ag teacher had peeked through my window and then disappeared, I was turning off the lights when Hope walked in. She was wearing that baggy black hooded sweatshirt with the skulls, and sweatpants, and she carried that backpack with the skulls on it.

Her eyes darted around the lobby. "I haven't been here since I was twelve," she said. "It looks exactly the same." She walked around in a circle, taking it all in, until she stopped at the window and looked across the street right into Cunt Itchen, where her mother was pouring someone some decaf. Hope turned back to me quickly. "I need your help. Right now," she said. And so I invited her back to my desk.

She sat in that chair across from my desk and tried to be dignified in the way she perceived adults to be, but soon she was nervously fingering everything on the desk. She turned over the stapler. She held the letter opener in one hand and moved it across the palm of her other hand. She pulled the pens with my name on them out from their mug. She looked to the shelf behind me and said, "Nice trophy."

"It's not mine," I said. "It was my father's."

"People sure do love their fathers," she said. "Except my mother. Do you read all of those books?"

"I don't have to anymore," I said. "Now it comes in a computer program."

"That's easy," she said.

"I still update them by hand," I said, though I don't know why I said it, or even why I continue to do it.

She picked up her backpack and fiddled with its zippers, then she went back to fiddling with everything on my desk. She was paler than usual. She still looked just like Barb only thinner, more hollowed out. Her short black hair was spiked up in all directions and her eyes seemed larger. I could see the blue of her veins in the corners of her forehead and underneath her eyes. I noticed that in addition to the skulls on her backpack and skulls all over her black hooded sweatshirt, there were skulls dangling from her ears. "That's a lot of skulls," I said.

She did not reply or even acknowledge that I had spoken.

So I began to treat her like a customer. I said, "How can I help you?"

She pulled some papers from her backpack and slid them onto my desk. They were financial aid papers for college, and a little brochure for the University of Iowa that showed kids in black-and-gold sweatshirts hugging a giant Herky the Hawk.

Have you seen the face of Herky the Hawk? He has a menacing face. His eyebrows point down and he has a gigantic hooked beak with jagged teeth inside of it. If you saw him walking toward you on the street without knowing he was a college mascot, you would run for your life. And yet good-looking students of diverse racial backgrounds hug him and smile as if Herky is the greatest privilege afforded to them by their important, vibrant lives.

"She won't tell me what I need to know to fill out the forms," she said.

"Why not?" I asked.

"She doesn't want me to go."

"Why not?"

"I don't know. I have no idea."

I thought for a moment about what reason Barb could possibly have for not wanting Hope to go to college at the University of Iowa and then I remembered what my father had said about it. "There are hippies there, people from Chicago."

She looked at me, confused.

"Drugs," I said. "There are drugs there."

There was a long silence, and during it I could see something inside her rise to the top, something I had not seen in her before, not seen in anyone except her own mother. It was similar to what I had seen from her in the women's bathroom at the Valkyrie, but it was so much more. She held her breath, and from her shoulders to her neck to her cheeks to her forehead the color rose and watered her eyes, and then, finally, she sucked in hard. She bent over and let out a wail. "She doesn't like me!" she cried.

I did not know what to do then. I was not surprised that someone sitting in that chair was confessing something to me. People have always confessed things to me while sitting in that chair—difficult things they cannot say to other people. But no one had ever cried out in desperation, and no one had ever been a high school girl.

I was not a mother. I had never even had a mother. How does one comfort a sobbing teenage girl? I had no idea. A television mother like Bonnie Franklin as Ann Romano would have stood and taken the girl in her arms and soothed her with words that were kind and wise, but how could I do that? I was not her mother, and this was a place of business, and I had no wisdom, and again, I was not her mother and I had never had a mother of my own.

I sat at my desk and I tried not to stare at her. I found myself fiddling with those pens with my name on them. I found myself running the letter opener over my own palm, just to have something else to look at and consider. Finally she pulled herself together. She wiped her nose on her sleeve. She wiped away the black mascara running below her eyes with her fingertips. She took a few deep breaths. "I really don't know why she won't help me fill these out," she said. "I have made some really big mistakes, but I am still going to be the valedictorian. They told me so. I mean, haven't I done most everything right?"

I nodded, but only because I am used to providing calm reassurance to the people sitting in that chair. What did I know about what is right and what is wrong in the world? Particularly at that time, as a person making many mistakes at once, I was not qualified to answer.

"I just want..." She stopped, trying to find the words. "I just want to look out of a window at something other than that," she said, pointing behind her to the window facing Cunt Itchen. "I just want to worry about myself. Is that so wrong?"

And though part of me took great offense to her dismissal of my business, part of me understood her deeply, deeper than anyone else could ever understand her, even Barbie, and even the Vo-Ag teacher, though on certain days I might be inclined to agree that the Vo-Ag teacher had, in some ways, a surface understanding of her dilemma that correlated to my deeper one. In her folding in on herself I could see myself. I said, "I was just like you. I wanted to leave too. And I did, you know."

"Why did you *come back*? Were you pregnant or something?" A fair question, asked in an exhausted voice. I put it out there, and it was fair of her to take me up on it.

"Someone had to be the CPA in this town," I said.

She sighed the sigh of my people. "Everyone in this fucking town is a fucking CPA," she said.

"Actually," I said, "it's just me. I've got the market cornered."

She laughed at that. She let her shoulders down a bit and leaned back in her chair. She took a few even breaths. I felt a great relief. I had been witty. I thought perhaps we had rounded it.

Then she said, "Did you know my father?"

"A bit."

"Was he nice?" she asked.

I hesitated.

"Say yes," she said. "Please say yes."

"Yes." It was a kind of truth.

"What was his name?"

"I don't remember his last name but his first name was Cole."

"Like what you get in your stocking at Christmas if you're bad?"

"Yes," I said, but then decided that was a poor image to promote. "Also what you use to fire a train. Energy."

"Something that helps things go," she said too eagerly. This also was not an image I wanted to promote, so I said nothing more.

"She won't tell me anything about him, but I just have this feeling that he could help," she said.

"Help you what?"

"Help me fill these papers out. Help me leave."

I did not want to be cruel. Understand this. But there were things I felt she needed to face, dreams I felt she needed to know were unrealistic, so that she could set them aside and make space for more realistic dreams. There was no dream father. He would not be coming for her.

"He can't help you."

"Why not?" she said defiantly. Her lips quivered and then became very still.

"Because where is he?" I asked.

She did not like my answering a question with a question so she got up to leave.

"That is the end then," she said. "I have come to the end."

I did not like the sound of that, coming from a little high school girl I knew had promise, so I said, "Wait."

There are rules in my business about what you can and cannot do. One thing you cannot do is show a client's tax return to someone else, even if it is to that client's dependent, especially if you have an inkling that this would be against that client's wishes.

But it is not against the rules to walk out of the room to go to the bathroom and leave that dependent alone in the room, which is also the room where all your client files are, ordered alphabetically, in unlocked file cabinets.

People have to go to the bathroom. It's part of being a human being. I myself have to go to the bathroom several times a day. No one has ever disputed that I am a good businesswoman who respects and protects my clients and their wishes. True, I have done some things that make no sense to most people in this town, and probably make no sense to people like you, but no one has ever disputed my ability to be a good businesswoman.

If they did, they would be wrong.

She came back three days later. "They told me she makes too much money," she said.

"Technically, it's her land holdings, not her income. It's the farm that Huff gave her," I said. "And there is a legal agreement that prevents her from selling any of it until after his death."

Her eyes narrowed but she did not cry this time. After I said it, I could tell that it sounded callous, that I had behaved callously, even if it was technically true. I could have been kinder. I can see that now. I am learning.

"There are loans," I said, trying to redeem myself.

She nodded, or rather tilted her chin up and then down enough to convey to me that she had heard what I said, but not enough to indicate what it meant to her.

"I'll figure it out," she said.

This, in my mind, was worse than her assertion that she had come to the end of something. Coming to the end of something was the end for one person. Figuring something out meant she could take others down with her.

"How will you figure it out?" I asked with as much kindness as I could muster.

"I have friends," she said. "In high places."

A darkness came over both of us. The space over my desk between us became heavy and prickled.

"Like Clive?" I asked.

"Clive who?" she asked, answering a question with a question, lying in that stupid, petty way the little girls around here lie.

"Clive, the person who gave you hundreds of pills of cold medicine."

If there was a hitch in her confidence she did not display it. "Did the Vo-Ag teacher tell you that?" she asked. And when I did not reply she said, "Isn't it interesting what people will do to make themselves feel like your hero?"

"I have not had the good fortune to experience that," I said.

"Maybe someday," she said, as if I were a little girl, and then left.

Not long after that, Barb blew into my office while I was with Connie Euchre, one of the nurses up at the hospital. Barb ignored

Connie's presence entirely and threw a stack of papers at me. They flew around, landing all over Connie's tax items.

"She is not your problem!" Barb shouted. I did not understand what she was talking about until I picked up one of the papers and saw that it was a letter from the University of Iowa with a list of numbers and dates on it that would be key for someone starting college there in the fall.

"Stay out of our business!" Barb shouted.

Connie slowly backed out of my office.

"She asked for my help," I said. I was stunned. "I shouldn't have done it but—"

"Of course you shouldn't have done it! My tax returns are private! You have no right to interfere with my affairs this way!" Barb's voice was shaking, and it made me feel like comforting her, though I knew I had lost that privilege long ago. "What right do you have with my daughter anyway? What makes you think you get any say at all about what she does and doesn't do?"

"I have not been the kind of person I want to be," I said. I choked on the sentence. Hot tears flowed down my face.

"Are *you* going to take care of her, Tandy? You disappeared when the going got tough for me. Are you sure you're willing to clean up *her* messes?"

My shame was so great I could not speak.

"You don't know what it's like to be a mother in this town. You don't know what I'm staring down here."

"Of course not," I said, looking down at my feet. When I looked up, I saw her tears.

"If she leaves, what will I have left, Tandy? Answer me that."

I thought her question through, and though I did not want it to be true, I said what we both knew to be true at that time.

"You will have nothing."

17

It was from this place in my life, this low point in which I was a person who deserved nothing, that Too-Tall Travis called my office to tell me I was invited to break ground on the sod house.

I said no. I did not want to come between Barb and Hope, and Hope would most certainly be there. And I had other reasons. April 15 was less than two weeks away, and I had no time to do anything but work. But then the Vo-Ag teacher called. "They need your support," he said. "Your support means there is something here worth standing for."

And though the simple idea that there was something in this town worth standing for made me feel like I had just downed a Mexican sidecar for breakfast, I put on my big black coat and headed out to Mueller's. From the road in front of his wraparound porch I saw Mueller standing there, holding a cup of coffee. He raised his mug to me, grinning. I waved back, making as little eye contact as possible. I walked out across the black dirt and corn stubble of his eastern field toward Kennicott Creek and the patch of matted and melt-soaked tallgrass where the Vo-Ag students were working.

They had mowed a few areas down to the ground, then taken some string and some short stakes and, in one of the mowed areas, marked off the basic frame of a sod house. It was only sixteen feet by sixteen feet, about the size of a large bedroom. "This is pretty much as big as they got," Korn Phil said to me. "Can you believe it? Whole families. But they were all in it together." The Vo-Ag teacher stood nearby, beaming at Korn Phil's awakened awareness. He was passing out sharp spades and held one out to me.

"Thank you for coming, Tandy," the Vo-Ag teacher said as though he were standing behind a podium before a large audience.

"We appreciate all you have done for Vo-Ag and FFA." Hope stood by him, spade in hand, but moved away as I approached.

"I live to serve," I said, and took the spade.

We moved to about fifty yards away from where the sod house was marked off, to the second mowed-down area. As instructed by the Vo-Ag teacher, we stood in two lines, shoulder to shoulder, only a foot apart. The Vo-Ag teacher was at the end of my line. Hope was at the other end, in her baggy hooded skull sweatshirt and sweatpants and little moccasins with no socks. We all propped our spades up next to one another and prepared to slice downward.

But then the Vo-Ag teacher held up his hand. We all turned to listen. "I would like to say a few words. I know that you have not always felt proud of this community in which you live. I know that life has been hard and confusing in this economically depressed environment. I know you have lived without faith that this world has something to offer you."

"Word," said Too-Tall Travis.

"Truth," said Vampire Missy.

"I feel very close to you all right now," the Vo-Ag teacher said. This made me uncomfortable. Inside my coat, I began to sweat even more profusely. It was unlike any publicly displayed emotion I had ever witnessed, even in church. I imagined, perhaps, a group therapy session—though of course I had never actually been to one—and I did not like it. I am not proud of it, but I admit that I did not want the Vo-Ag teacher to be close to anyone but me.

The Vo-Ag students all smiled shyly at the Vo-Ag teacher's words. He went on. "I feel like I was put on this earth to help you discover your own beauty as individuals, as students of agrarian life, and as a group of exceptional young people." More blushing. More shy smiles.

Except for Hope. She leaned lazily on her spade, staring off into the distance. Out there in the field was Mueller's anhydrous ammonia tank sitting on a trailer, and beyond that a large building filled with hogs, and beyond that a sharp white-blue horizon and a few high and wispy clouds, and a line of faded old boxcars, and the outline of the grain elevator.

"On the count of three, we will all push our spades straight into the earth as far as they will take us. This sod will become our home. One. Two. Three."

And with that, we all experienced together for the first time what the Vo-Ag students would call the Sod House Experience. We worked all day, peeling the sod out of the ground in long rows and cutting them into bricks. The sod bricks were moist from new thaw. The roots of the tallgrass intertwined and were holding the sod together more than I had imagined they would. We carried the sod bricks gently, as if they were newborn puppies, over to the roped off area. Following the guide of the strings, we laid the bricks grass-side down, two at a time, so the walls would be two feet thick. We laid the next layer crosswise to make the walls strong. And so on. And so on.

As we worked, the Vo-Ag students struck up a song. It was about living in a small town, and being educated in a small town, and dying in a small town, and how that was good enough for them. The Vo-Ag teacher sang along too, loudly and lustily. And I must say, they all sounded pretty good together.

Hope did not sing. When pressed by the Vo-Ag teacher to do so, she told him she was not in the mood. Instead, she came to stand next to me, which was a surprise. I did not know what to do, so I let her. Then she asked, "Is that tank out there Mueller's?"

"Of course," I said.

"It's anhydrous ammonia. He fertilizes his fields with it," Dolphin Beth said.

"I know what it is," Hope said.

"We send our tanks back to the ag lot where we buy it because it's locked up there with a big electric fence," Dolphin Beth said. "People make meth out of anhydrous. You just need lithium from batteries and a whole lot of cold medicine."

"I live here. I know," Hope said.

The very next day, in the very early morning while we were out there again and before I had any appointments, the alarms went off again in town. We could hear them even out in Mueller's eastern field. And so we did what must be done by the people in our town—we got in our cars and trucks and followed it.

This time there were flames. The roof was mostly gone. All the windows were shattered and blown out into the street. Burned-up Mickey Mouse wallpaper curled off the walls in one of the upstairs bedrooms. Papers and furniture guts and dirty socks and underwear blew around in the street.

The house was next to the library, so the library was on fire too. Black smoke billowed out from its two front windows. Sophie Johnson, the librarian, sat in her car parked across the street. Her forehead was on the steering wheel and her back was shaking.

Dave Oppegaard came over in his big fireman boots and hat and said to me, "This is a big one. I figure someone from Channel 9 should be here soon."

"The news is going to be here?" Hope asked. The mention of the news made her suddenly more alive, popped out, like when she was Ms. Hannigan.

Oppegaard just stood there, smoking, as the house and the library went down. "How long do you think it'll take the news to get here?" he asked.

"Hour?" I said.

"That's what I was thinking," he said.

We all sat on the curb then and watched the library burn. Dusty drove up with his sirens blaring and again told us all to move downwind because the poisonous fumes from the chemicals in the house—anhydrous and lithium and cold medicine all mixed up on its way to becoming drugs—could kill us. Down the block by the Methodist church, Oppegaard put on a white plastic suit that made him look like an astronaut. But he didn't put on the helmet. He just stood around in the suit and smoked with some of the other volunteer firemen, none of whom were wearing suits, because our town can afford only one of them.

After an hour, a man in jeans and a sweatshirt carrying a big video camera showed up. He took some video of Oppegaard in the astronaut suit moving a large stack of books out of the burning library on a dolly. Oppegaard tried not to look at the camera but failed, so they had to do the whole thing again. The man wrote down a few notes and Oppegaard spelled his name for him a few times. Then Oppegaard and the other volunteer firemen put out the fire.

When the man from Channel 9 went back to his truck, Hope ran after him. Her little Indian moccasins flapped in the street. "Hey," she said. "Aren't you going to interview anyone? Because if you are, you should interview me."

The man looked at her in that up-and-down way men do to high school girls who almost aren't in high school anymore. He said, "If I was going to interview anyone around here, you'd be the one." Then he climbed into his news truck and drove away.

Hope started walking away from everyone. The Vo-Ag teacher chased after her like a cocker spaniel.

For a long time I stood in front of the empty shell of the library, alone. I went there often when I was a child, and snuggled up in the library's big cushiony furniture doing math puzzles and reading those magazines they make for kids that are all about exotic animals. I had fallen asleep there often during those dark winter days when my father would work through dinner and Suzy Jensen would have to wake me at close and drive me home through the cold.

Time kept on slipping, slipping, slipping into the future.

18

It was almost two weeks later when I saw Hope again. I remember the exact evening because it was the evening of April 15: Accountant's New Year. I was walking home late from the post office's extended hours, having filed the last of the income tax returns and just four extensions. I was feeling light and bouncy, as I always do after I file the last returns. I thought about running, like I did that first morning Gerald was gone. That had been a good feeling. And even though I was not wearing appropriate shoes for the task, and I had on my big black coat and it was almost 50 degrees, and I was still downtown and someone could have seen me doing it and thought, *Oh, look, Tandy Caide has taken up running now,* I started to run.

She was standing behind Prairie Lanes, just off Main Street, under a tree lit by the light from the Prairie Lanes sign. She didn't notice me in the dark in my big black coat, but that was less about the coat and more about the fact that she was bent over vomiting.

The rusty pickup I had seen before around town pulled up. But driving the truck was not the pock-faced man I had seen before. It was Clive.

Hope turned, and when she walked toward the truck, I got a glimpse of her backside. There was a thing in the way she walked—her hips tilted up behind her, her spine curved at her lower back, pulling her midsection forward even as the rest of her body refused. It was still early, but in this town, our many years of experience have taught us to recognize the thing quickly.

I ran around the block and down the street along the abandoned railroad yard and then back up again and right up to Cunt Itchen to tell Barb. But then I stopped and remembered what Barbie had said in my office only weeks before: how I had disappeared when she was pregnant, how I did not know what she was staring down here.

At that moment I saw what Barb was staring down. Barb already knew.

So I bowled. I bowled so badly Cindy gave me a free game. I bowled the three shittiest bowls of my adult life—147, 130, and 131.

I was holding my breath in my chest.

When everyone else left and all the lanes were dark, Cindy asked me if I wanted to sleep there.

I said, "There will be no sleeping tonight."

There was not.

Hope was pregnant, and most certainly by Clive—someone I had thrown away as a nobody, someone I saw as a harmless, common man. The rules are clear here: if you fuck with little girls, they send you to jail for up to fifteen years, and when you get out, you have to register with the government so that wherever you go for the rest of your life, everyone knows what you did. You can fuck with little girls in a lot of other nonsexual ways that the rules aren't clear on. This I know all too well. There are so many ways to fuck with little girls here, and so few ways to help them recover from it.

But you cannot fuck with little girls in a sexual way. The rules are clear. And everyone agrees on those particular rules. Maybe Clive didn't know about the rules, I thought. No. They were there on the Internet, everywhere. There is even a link to the rules on our school district's website. The information is prevalent and readily available. On the Internet it says that the longer the person who fucked with a little girl goes to jail, the more the little girl who got fucked loves him. That is the greatest irony of all, isn't it?

From the lobby of my office, I looked across the street and saw Barb in the window of Cunt Itchen, holding her pot of coffee up with that iron forearm. I stared at her. She stared right back.

I don't know what to do, I mouthed.

She shrugged her shoulders and disappeared.

But I could not let her go.

She was rolling silverware. Her hands were a blur, like she was trying to win a contest.

"You're not getting any coffee," she said. "I'm closing early tonight. It's my prerogative."

"Okay," I said. What else could I say? "Do you ever stop working?" I asked. I don't know if I was poking at her or if I wanted her to look at me so we could really talk, like we had talked so many years ago.

"No," she shot back, and I thought that was fair enough and I got up to leave. But then I sat back down. I could not leave. What could I do? There was no time left. It had slipped too far into the future. And so I began to talk. I told Barb everything—the Vo-Ag teacher and me, Clive and me, even the cold medicine, though I had promised the Vo-Ag teacher to keep that a secret.

She never stopped rolling silverware, wrapping the napkins around the silverware fast, tucking and folding and wrapping. She said almost nothing. At one point she asked, "Who do you think is the father?" and I said that all evidence pointed to Clive. I want you to know that I am an honest person, a good person. I am a person of integrity. I hope you can see this about me.

"I want to show you something," she said, and she went into the bathroom. As it has always been with Barbie, I followed her.

I didn't think it appropriate that we should be in a one-person bathroom together as we are two people, but finally she just said, "Get in," and so I got in and she closed the door behind us and locked it.

I felt very strange in there. I had never been in a bathroom with another woman.

She moved a little garbage can away from the wall, which was covered with green tiles. She took a pen out of her apron and lightly tapped a tile. It popped out a little, and she grabbed an edge and pulled it off. There was a hole behind the tile, and she reached into that hole and pulled out a pair of black leather gloves.

She sat down on the bathroom floor with her knees up to her chin and slipped them on. Then she touched her face with her hands.

"It was hot," she said. "It was summer, but he handed me these gloves in one of those purple bags that Crown Royal whiskey comes in. He said, 'I don't ever want my baby to be cold.' I said to him, 'It's not even winter!' and he said, 'It will be.'"

She said, "He looked like Chachi from *Happy Days*, remember?"

Of course I remembered. A boy who looked how Cole looked was impossible to forget. "Scott Baio," I said.

She said, "Are they the actors or their characters? I never know." We laughed about this for a bit.

She said, "He was so good-looking, like he should have been on television." She rubbed the gloves over her face. "Do you ever still wish our mothers would have stuck around, Tandy?"

"Yes," I said. "Almost every day."

"I know it seems dumb, but sometimes when I see mothers on television, I still pretend they are my mother."

"Like Ann Romano," I said.

"Like Bonnie Franklin," she said. We laughed again.

"Sometimes I pretend that Doris Mavin, that woman who bowled a perfect game at Prairie Lanes, is my mother," I said.

Her laughter burst out so hard it made her tip over and curl up onto the floor of the bathroom into a little ball. It was one of the loveliest things I have ever seen her do. It made me feel good about us. It made me have hope for our future.

"Oh, Tandy! We're just a couple of crazies," she said. She put the gloves to her cheeks again. "He did what all the beautiful people around here do. He left."

Sometimes at night, when the sun has gone down and I have not yet fallen asleep, and I am holding my soft pillow around my face, I think about the quality I love most in Barb. It is this: Barb *never* makes statements into questions. She says what she needs to say, which is always what needs to be said. The fact that you might not want to hear it means nothing to her.

For people like you, people who are used to answering questions that are really judgments delivered by judgmental people masquerading as pleasant friends, questions like "Are you sure you want another drink?" her directness may seem abrasive or cold. Know this about Barb and other people like her: You are wrong. Barb is far smarter and more loving than all the fake question-askers you've ever met in your whole life combined.

She is not without vice. But who is? Are you?

We sat there next to each other on the cold floor, our backs against the wall. Barbie started to cry, and I put my arm around her. Then she started to sob, and it wretched her whole body, and before I knew it she had crawled into my lap and I was rocking her back and forth, saying into her neck, again, "Shhh. Shhh. We will figure this out." But unlike the time in high school when she had crawled pregnant through my bedroom window, I was crying too.

19

He came as soon as I called. He touched every single item on my desk. He scratched at some scabs on his arms.

"What is this about, Tandy?" he asked. "I know you didn't call me here for a date."

"She's pregnant," I said.

"News flash," Clive said. "For a CPA, you sure can be clueless."

"What do you plan to do about it?"

He jumped up, reached across the desk, and pushed me hard on my chest. The wheels on my work chair rolled back and I fell off it, and some of the U.S. Tax Code fell off the shelf and onto me, as did the World's Greatest Accountant trophy.

He shouted, "It is none of your business what plans I have!"

I was shaking—that I could not help. I was lying on the floor, buried in volumes of the U.S. Tax Code, and they were heavy—that I could not help either. I said, "I'm sorry. I'm very sorry. I would like to help you. How can I help you?"

It was like that for a very long time, me buried, me offering to help him, him panting and clutching at his hair and pulling at it and sometimes screaming. Finally I climbed to my chair. He put his head in his hands and then he looked about the room and then he focused his gaze on me, very intensely, as if he was trying to figure out if I could be trusted with the very important information he had. He said, "I have a lot of things riding on this."

Neither of us said a thing for a long time. Then he shook his head, "I know you want to believe it's me, Tandy. But I'm not that dumb. I have other uses for her."

"Like what?" I asked, even as my temple throbbed and a lump began to grow there.

He narrowed his eyes and said, "You had your chance with me." Then he was gone.

I sat there, breathing hard, for a long time. Nothing like this had ever come from Clive before. It slowly dawned on me that the Vo-Ag teacher had been right about him. He was a dangerous person. And then logically it followed that perhaps the Vo-Ag teacher *did* know my people, at least a few of my people, better than I did.

I no longer knew what to believe. What I thought I believed was very quickly eroding beneath me.

20

When I boarded the bus the next day to chaperone the Vo-Ag students to the FFA regional competition, I hardly recognized them. There was still some blue mascara on Dolphin Beth, but it didn't look as bad as usual. This Beth actually looked human, and sweet. And Vampire Missy, who had hid behind the black bangs and the black eyeliner, had chopped the bangs off to almost her hairline so that they were just tinyspikes. The heavy black eyeliner was there, but suddenly so were her eyes.

The zombie shirts were gone, and in their places were white button-down shirts, and black pants and black skirts, and blue corduroy FFA jackets with the FFA eagle and owl and plow on their chests over their hearts, and their names embroidered on the other side of their chests, the non-heart side: Too-Tall *Travis*—still too tall but at least nicely dressed. *Missy*—the girl with the new eyes. *Beth*—no longer a dolphin. *Phil*—minus the Korn shirt.

Hope, whose jacket could not cover her belly.

And the Vo-Ag teacher's of course—*Mr. Tischer.*

Around each of their waists was a multicolored and beaded belt, just like the Vo-Ag teacher's.

"We're Team Yoruba," said Phil. "After the Yoruba people."

"Of course you are," I said. What else was there to say?

The Vo-Ag teacher was in the front row and he patted the place next to him. Hope was in the back row, as far from the Vo-Ag teacher as you could get, her beaded belt straining to hold together.

I sat by him. It was the place where I was to sit.

The Vo-Ag teacher beamed, as if he had fathered all the Vo-Ag kids himself.

I could not keep it in. I whispered to him the obvious: "Hope is pregnant." I can admit that I wanted him to be shocked and then outraged.

He patted my knee and said, "Let's not judge, okay?" I did not know what to do with that, and so I did nothing.

The bus gave a sound like a fart and then lurched forward and headed north out of town. The Vo-Ag teacher said to the students, "Let's have some music!"

They had their musical instruments with them, as the regional FFA competition also serves as opening act auditions at nationals. Team Yoruba had prepared some songs. The Vo-Ag teacher and I turned around in our seats to watch as Phil pulled out his banjo and started to play. Beth pulled out her fiddle and played too. And then Missy and Travis started singing, and then even Hope.

It was a song about losers and most of it was gobbledygook, but the refrain was loud and clear, because all the Vo-Ag students shouted it: *I'm a loser, baby! So why don't you kill me!*

The Vo-Ag teacher stood straight up in his seat when he heard this. "You sing a song about losers?! We are heading into a competition where your job is to *prove your worth by winning*, and you sing a song about *losers*?!"

"But... we *are* losers," Travis said. The snickering erupted all over the bus, like little toilets flushing.

"You are not losers!" the Vo-Ag teacher shouted. His face got red and his chest heaved up and down and he pounded the window of the bus and he screamed to Brody Fogle, Gerald's replacement, "Pull over! Pull over!"

Brody looked at me, as if I directed the actions of school bus drivers by virtue of my being married to one, even one currently living in a mental institution. I shrugged, and I guess that meant "pull over" because he did.

"You are not losers!" the Vo-Ag teacher shouted, so loud he bent over to shout. His face turned purple. He did that thing with his arms—his encompassing of all of us with his wingspan—and said, "*You* are killing you!"

They looked down, or out the bus windows. Even Hope.

"When you sing a song that says you are losers, *then you become losers*!" He banged the bus window, over and over again. "It doesn't have to be 'Eye of the Fucking Tiger'! Just sing a better song!"

At times, he was a very good teacher. I know that. This town never knew that, but the Vo-Ag kids and I know that. He cared. I think that is a good thing for teachers and all people to do, even if they go about it the wrong way.

The Vo-Ag students looked at each other. Then Phil started to pick something again, and Beth started to pull some very long notes from her fiddle. *There's a bright golden haze on the meadow,* Phil sang very quietly, timidly, eyeing the Vo-Ag teacher to see if he would stop him. *The corn is as high as an elephant's eye,* he sang, and then all of them, softly: *And it looks like it's climbing clear up to the sky*. And then louder, at the chorus, they sang: *Oh, what a beautiful mornin'! Oh, what a beautiful day!*

Do you know this song? It's from *Oklahoma!*, one of the longest, dullest musicals ever written. In addition to the fifteen-minute dance scene, during which the people in our town can always be heard snoring, the story is boring and, in the end, astoundingly inaccurate with regards to rural life. No farm girl I have ever met is as frivolous as Laurey. The song "I Cain't Say No," sung by the girl who wants to have sex all the time, is the only song with any truth in it.

But the way the Vo-Ag kids sang "Oh, What a Beautiful Mornin'," especially the part about all the sounds of the earth being like music, well, I could actually get behind it, in theory. They made it sound like they believed it. So I wanted to believe it too.

The Vo-Ag teacher sang along, and he held my hand. He sang, *I've got a wonderful feeling! Everything's going my way!* and he looked at me, pleading a little bit with his eyes, as if he really wanted me to believe it. With all of his heart, he wanted me to believe it.

I still think about that moment, about the way those Vo-Ag students and the Vo-Ag teacher sang, in harmony; about all that joy on that bus, barreling toward the river and my old college town, all that promise. Out the window, everything looked just as I remembered it: fields and rows of evergreen windbreaks and little farmhouses with porches and roofs intact and dogs with all four legs running out to greet us, running alongside our bus and then after us and then stopping because we could not be caught we flew so fast. And then suddenly Upper Prairie University in view—the low brick buildings, then the higher one, my old dorm, unchanged, just like out of the movie of my mind.

Fourteen miles and eighteen years and it all flew by in eighteen minutes, without a single house with windows blown out, or siding blackened with soot, or a yard blocked off by police tape, covered in dirty laundry.

I swear. He never even looked at her then. He was looking at me. He was thinking only of me, of how hard it must be for me to be on a school bus going back to school.

21

I was given my own dorm room. It wasn't exactly my old room, but it was close. I climbed to the top bunk where I surveyed all the things in the room—the desk, the sink, the closet, the radiator, the bulletin board, the chest of drawers—and in doing so a calm came over me, a reassurance that I had not missed anything. Even the woods were the same: dark and deep and cool.

I lay back on that top bunk and I felt like a happy, free-floating cloud. Maybe you will think this is odd, but despite what I knew about Hope, I was positively contented there. I could feel it in my cheek muscles, how they ached from smiling. I could feel it in my heart too, if hearts could smile, which they probably can't, though I don't know for sure. I know it sounds impossible, especially at this particular time, and maybe it was selfish of me, but I let myself enjoy that room. I let that room all the way into my heart and it was lovely.

There was a problem, though, with the Vo-Ag teacher. He knocked frantically on my door. I opened it and he ran in and wretched into the sink.

"I can't do it!" He winced. "I can't go to the 'Living to Serve' presentation."

"Why not?"

"I might shout something dumb," he said.

"Don't shout something dumb," I said.

"I might not be able to *not* shout something dumb." He held his stomach and groaned. "The judges. The audience. The whole thing with these people here. They will be judging me too! These are *your* people. You're the one they will accept. You're the one who can do this with grace."

So far in my lifetime this has been the only time I've been accused of being graceful.

"Just take notes," he said. "I know you'll deliver an unbiased account."

Throughout the room, sitting on folding chairs, were the teams of students and some of their families. There were only three "Living to Serve" projects up for judging. There aren't as many young people living to serve as you might hope.

I sat in the back with a yellow pad of paper and a pen. From the back, these various Vo-Ag students all looked the same, and I could hardly tell mine from the others, except for Hope, with her short-cropped hair, shorter than even the boys', and her spine curved away from the chair in that pregnancy way and her FFA jacket unbuttoned and her belly popping out.

Off to the side sat a panel of judges. One was a fat man with a big red face and nose, wearing a green jacket with the Pioneer Seed logo over his heart. One was another fat man, also with a big red face, wearing a black sweater with a Land O'Lakes logo over his heart. And one was a frowning woman with red-rimmed glasses that seemed to have the top halves cut off so that they were little half-glasses. She looked down at us through those glasses. There was an Ag Extension logo over her right breast, embroidered onto her red cardigan.

The first team was from Decorah: three ninth graders who fumbled their way to the small card table. They set up their trifold cardboard display on which were printed the words WHERE'S THE BLUEBIRDS?, which was grammatically incorrect, even I knew that. They also set onto the table a little wooden box with a hole drilled into it.

Then the team—two girls and a boy—stood in the corner and faced away from the audience. They put on some safari hats and started to prowl around the card table, squinting, with their hands pretending to shade their eyes. They said repeatedly, "Where's the bluebirds? Where's the bluebirds?"

Hope's back began to shake. Then came the repeated toilet flushing of her snickers.

The judges began to write furiously on their scorecards.

The presentation went on for about ten minutes—the gist of which was "Bluebirds will come back when we build houses for them."

When it was time for questions, the Land O'Lakes judge said, "So. It's kind of like a housing project for bluebirds." He and the Pioneer Seed judge looked at each other and smiled. The frowning half-glasses judge continued to frown and judge.

Hope raised her hand.

The judges looked at one another and then put their heads together and whispered and then sat back. "This competition doesn't allow for audience questions," said the Pioneer Seed judge.

"I was just going to ask how this project 'lives to serve,'" she said. Her hands were folded neatly in her lap and her legs were crossed at the ankles.

"Well, you're not allowed," the judge said again.

Hope shrugged. There was some shuffling from the judges, and then Half-Glasses asked the Bluebird Team, "How does this project 'live to serve'?"

A team member consulted a notebook. "Ummm," she said.

"I think, you know, because serving bluebirds is good for our community," said the boy.

"How so?"

"Ummmm... because they are endangered."

"So?"

"Endangered things are... super important... to our community."

"Because?"

"Oh, I know!" said the girl. "Because they're in our *ecosystem*."

Frowning, Half-Glasses scribbled furiously.

Pioneer Seed asked, "How do you know if there's a bluebird in that little box?"

The team looked at one another and fidgeted. One of the girls paged furiously through her notebook.

"Probably, you know, if we see some bluebirds," the boy said.

"But you can't see them in that little box."

The team had no response. They just stood there and shuffled their feet and grew red in their faces.

"Are a bluebird's eggs blue?" asked the Land O'Lakes judge.

The team had no response to that either.

"I think it would be cute if they were," he said.

Next up was a team from Jesup: two boys with huge cowboy hats and belt buckles. The belt buckles had long plastic horns made to look like the long horns of a steer, like on the front of Boss Hogg's car on *The Dukes of Hazzard*. It looked like there were giant mustaches growing out of the tops of their pants.

Theirs was a project to educate the community on Texas longhorn cattle. They would do this by making a traveling display that would be presented to elementary school children. Their cardboard display included a photo of the head of a Texas longhorn, and lists of facts written in tiny script that no one could read, so the boys read each of them out loud, alternating the task between them, and that's twenty minutes of my life I'll never get back.

"How does this project 'live to serve'?" asked Pioneer Seed.

"Because Texas longhorn are endangered," said one of the boys.

"But why should it matter? They aren't native to this area."

"Yes, but they are part of the *ecosystem*," said the other.

"Not *our* ecosystem," said Pioneer Seed.

"*Someone's* ecosystem."

"Well, whose ecosystem do we live to serve, kid?" Pioneer Seed sat smugly, arms crossed.

"Well," said the first boy, folding his hands gracefully in front of him while the other boy bowed a little and stepped back. "An ecosystem doesn't follow county, state, or even national boundaries. An ecosystem follows"—he paused, searching for the right words—"the natural circle of life."

Pioneer Seed nodded, and then he leaned forward. "Well, I can tell you this, son. If the Texas longhorn had followed the natural circle of life, *they wouldn't even exist*."

He is correct. I looked it up on the Internet when I got home. The Texas longhorn was created by ranchers who mixed American domestic cattle with feral Mexican ones in order to make a tougher breed.

The other judges nodded, and that's as far as that went, though the Land O'Lakes judge made a point to mention that he really appreciated the team's belts.

Then: Team Yoruba and the Sod House Experience.

Inside my chest there was a squeeze. There was a flip in my stomach.

"Ooh! More neat belts!" the Land O'Lakes judge said, clapping his hands.

Phil had made what looked like a blueprint of the sod house, but from all angles in a three-dimensional way, which showed how it would stand up structurally. It was glued to a cardboard display. Travis had made a tiny model of the sod house using brown modeling clay and that plastic grass people put in children's Easter baskets. He set it before the cardboard display. Beth had drawn detailed pictures of the projected finished sod house with charcoal pencil, and Missy had painted them with watercolor paints. These were pasted onto either side of the cardboard's two side panels. The drawing of the interior showed knotty wood paneling, a rocking chair, and a bed with a quilt. Across the top of the cardboard display were these glittery words: HOME SWEET HOME.

Before all of this, Hope placed a clump of shrunken head sod taken from Mueller's. She stood in front of the whole operation with her hands clasped serenely below her prominent, obviously pregnant belly. She waited as if she were about to receive communion, or a sub from Subway. She waited as if she were about to receive a wonderful gift.

There was that creeping tingling feeling in my fingers.

Travis said, "Ladies and gentlemen, we, Team Yoruba of FFA Chapter Fifty-Seven, present to you the only 'Living to Serve' project that *truly* lives to serve."

He bowed toward Hope. She looked down for a few moments as if deep in thought, and then looked up at the judges.

"You know," she said, "I sometimes wish I had never been born here."

Team Yoruba looked at one another nervously.

"Don't you ever feel that way?" Hope asked the judges.

"I don't," said the Pioneer Judge.

"I know *you* do," Hope said, pointing to the other judges who sat with faces unmoving like stone, and then she pointed to us in the audience, and, perhaps, me specifically. "I know you think to yourselves, *If I had just done a little better in school. If I had taken bigger risks when I was young, been friendlier, gotten to know people from bigger cities. If I had gone to college, if I had gone to a college in a place where there were more opportunities. If I had gone to grad school, married later, had fewer children.*"

She rubbed her belly for dramatic effect.

"Then I wouldn't be stuck here in this shithole."

There was noticeable and frequent coughing now. The Land O'Lakes judge nodded in agreement with his eyes closed in a way that showed he was not listening; Pioneer Seed and Half-Glasses alternated between being aghast and furiously writing.

Travis reached out and touched Hope's shoulder.

"I'm not done," she said. But she was aware then of losing her audience, I think, and she reined it in. She said, "These feelings are terrible. Believe me, I know. It hurts to walk around in your home place and feel like it has nothing to offer you. It hurts to know there is no way you will ever achieve the greatness your heart desires there."

She moved to stand among the other Vo-Ag students. They all linked arms to form a chain of humans behind their display.

"That's not what our pioneer ancestors were thinking when they came here, their precious belongings in tiny wagons, their bellies bloated from dysentery, their babies wailing from hunger, searching for a way out of their own suffering in order to be free."

Down the line, the Vo-Ag students each said their last names: *Gustafson, Joregenson, Mauer, Moeller, Huff.*

"To our ancestors, this was the promised land," Hope went on. "And when they got here and staked their claims and saw that there were no trees to make homes, they did not cower exposed under the stars and die in the open air. They dug down into the source of life here, *the sod*—teeming with billions of microorganisms. The dirt was alive. *They* were alive!"

Hope picked up the little model of the sod house and held it out to the judges.

"The Sod House Experience is about reclaiming that promise."

She held it out to us, the audience.

"It is about taking back that which is ours, reclaiming our land and our hearts. It is the promise of a shift from irresponsible poisoning and its inevitable decay to the return of our pioneer ingenuity. It is the return of the shared vision, *the shared life*."

It was straight from the horse's mouth.

There was a slow, tentative trickle of applause. Then came the question-and-answer.

"But how does this project 'live to serve'?" Half-Glasses asked Hope in a smug way that demonstrated her belief that she had just shot Hope up with her own medicine.

Hope did not flinch. She smiled back. "I've been waiting for you to ask that," she said. "It lives to serve because the soil lives to serve us—with its hundreds of billions of microbes. It pays homage to our *heritage*."

Half-Glasses raised her eyebrows and looked at the other judges. If the eyes could speak, I think they would have said, *This is the kind of answer I expect from a first-place team.*

Pioneer Seed spoke. "But sod houses were made from real prairie sod that was hundreds of years old. The roots in it were longer than my arm." He held up his arm, in case none of us knew how long an arm was. "You don't have *that* kind of sod."

Frankly, I thought his arm was small and stubby and fat, like a cocktail weenie.

Hope picked up the clump of sod. It barely held its shape. Its grassy hair had turned gray brown.

She showed it to all of us in the audience, and even encouraged some children to touch it—"Go ahead," she said. They did and said, "Ewww."

Hope dropped it in the Pioneer Seed's lap. His little cocktail weenie arms flapped up and the sod fell apart, crumbling into a pile of dirt in his crotch.

"Your house is going to fall apart!" he said.

I couldn't help it, I laughed—a little toilet flushing of my own. As if we didn't know this!

"Of course we know this," Hope said. She bent down and looked right into his fat face. "The rules of the 'Living to Serve' grant project specifically state that we must—and I quote—'use resources from within the community.'"

Pioneer Seed looked away.

"This is what we were given," Hope said, addressing the judges. She turned to address the whole room, her hands out to us in the audience. "And so we offer it in return. Like the original pioneers, we do what we can with what we have. We make what we can out of what we see before us in order to serve our own. Whether we like it or not, whether we have chosen it or not, whether we want to or not, this is what it means here to 'live to serve.'"

There was the shrugging of shoulders among the audience. There was the furrowing of brows. No one moved. It felt as if the whole room had one big breath caught in one big throat.

The applause began slowly and quietly, then turned fast and loud, and then became enthusastic and from a standing position. Half-Glasses wrote furiously on her score sheet. Pioneer Seed wiped sod crumbles from his lap onto the floor. Land O'Lakes clapped while he looked at his watch, as if it were perfectly natural to do both.

Hope bowed as far as the baby in her belly would allow while the rest of Team Yoruba gathered up the visuals. They followed her out the front door and away from us, heads high, while we in the audience remained standing, clapping like crazy.

22

I waited at Margie's while the Team Yoruba performers auditioned their songs.

I asked Hope to join me, as she was not one of the song performers, but she said no, she wanted to rest. I did not press. Think of me what you will, but I did not want her to join me. I wanted to enjoy my slice of pizza with white sauce alone. I wanted Margie's to be mine again.

The room was different—there were booths around the edges of the room, and it was painted in a bright white instead of the deep wine color I remembered. I ordered a Pepsi and a slice with the white sauce, and thankfully it was just as I remembered. For a moment, I felt that things might be okay.

When Team Yoruba walked in and saw me, they began to whoop and jump and clap. They had made it! They would perform at the FFA opening ceremonies at the national conference in Indianapolis in October.

They were so alive! There was loud, full-out laughter instead of snickering. A judge had said the harmonies of their group were tighter than the Eagles. When they said this, their faces seemed to be pushed up by a new and better kind of gravity.

I told them all to order the pizza with the white sauce even though it was more expensive. I told them I would pay for it.

"Who said there's no such thing a free lunch, Tandy Caide?!" Travis shouted. "Don't say I never taught you anything, Tandy Caide!" And when the check came and I took it, they all cheered for me.

That was by far the freest lunch I will ever eat in my lifetime. I certainly cannot, at this time, imagine anything more free.

They wanted to see a show. There was a show being put on by the Upper Prairie University drama department, and it started in less than an hour.

"It's a musical," Missy said. "No one loves the theater more than you, right, Tandy?"

The Vo-Ag teacher did not attend the show. He was still queasy, he said. His stomach was upset. But still, when I asked him where I could find him later, he whispered, "Room one-three-seven," to me.

It was of great relief to me that he told me where to find him later. It was also of great relief that he did not attend the show, considering what had happened at *Annie*. Between those two things lies the great complexity of my relationship with the Vo-Ag teacher.

None of us had ever been to a show that was not put on by our town's own high school. I was the Vo-Ag students' official chaperone, so I had to remain vigilant to their behavior, which fortunately absolved me from having to view the musical. I clenched my fists and sat down and became alert to them all around me, particularly Hope. She sat at the end of the row with her hands cradling her belly, her feet crossed daintily below her chair, saying nothing, modeling excellence.

The rest of Team Yoruba did not need help either. They talked in soft whispers. They did not draw attention to themselves, though occasionally the girls pointed out various FFA boys from other schools they thought would be worthy of looking for after the show. The boys simply tried to find places for their big feet.

I got nervous when I saw how easy it was going to be to chaperone. I told Missy to stop waving at someone she knew on the other side of the stage, though it wasn't hurting anyone.

The stage was one of those circle stages, where the seats are all around a long lane with several narrow lanes radiating through the audience, like a lollipop made from sunbeams. It was decorated to resemble a junkyard—not a real junkyard like out at the old rail yards in our town, where the boxcars are. This was more like, say, a junkyard you would see on *Sesame Street*. All the "junk" was a variation of the same color and looked nicely put together. It was *the idea* of a junkyard.

This is something you learn, I think, from shows—that the idea of something and the real something are different, yet the idea of the something can tell you a whole lot about the real something if you pay attention.

The lights went out. I expected the lights to come back up so that the stage would glow in that show-y kind of way. That did not happen. Instead, tiny lights on the sides of the sunbeams came on. They looked like little airplane runways. Then, from all around us, came Upper Prairie college students dressed in full-body leotards and furry manes, crawling on all fours, with whiskers painted on their faces and pink triangle sponges stuck to their noses.

They were acting like cats! They were doing their acting and that was to act like cats—*cats!*—coming right down the lane next to me at my eye level! One was so close I could touch him! He looked at me and hissed, and reached out with claws that even in my surprise I could see were made from those little flat knives old ladies cut cheese logs with!

I screamed. All the Vo-Ag kids screamed. Then we all went into a laughing fit together. And in that very strange and wonderful way that laughing with others makes you feel as if you are really living your life, I did.

By the time we fully recovered, it was intermission. Missy asked, "Is . . . this . . . it?" I had no answer.

Beth said, "But... I thought stuff like this was supposed to be *good*."

"They're *cats*!" Phil said. "We've got ten of them in our barn!"

It did get a little better during the second half. There was some good fighting, and some stuff about being happy. And that song "Memory" is pretty good. I had to cough a couple of times during it, and other people did too—all up and down the theater, people were coughing like crazy during "Memory." I think the people who wrote that particular song had something there.

There was more fun, though, when Magical Mr. Mistoffelees showed up. His costume was made from a black wrestling singlet, a black turtleneck, and black running tights to which someone had pinned bits of an old fur coat. And stuffed into his crotch area was what appeared to be a giant fake penis.

It got us all going again. Mr. Mistoffelees waved that furry wrestling-singlet-covered fake penis in front of our squealing faces. And when Missy whispered, singing along to the Mistoffelees song, *No was there never, ever, ever a magical mystical dick that big,* we squealed some more. A college boy dressed as a cat waving a fake penis in front of my face? Certainly you can understand the hilarity of that.

I've thought about this a lot since it happened, and I must say this: *Cats* was the dumbest piece of crap I have ever seen. I do not understand why you people think it is so great. All it did was make me cough a couple of times, and laugh so hard I nearly pissed myself—which I don't believe was the intent of the people who created the musical *Cats,* nor the cast and crew of Upper Prairie University's recent production.

Still, I lost myself a little in the show. I disappeared a little into it, especially the "Memory" part. And this is another important thing I have learned this past year: even when things are very bad, even when you cannot imagine how you will possibly go forward in your life, you can still lose yourself a little in a show, even a bad one.

When the lights went up, Hope was gone.

The Vo-Ag students all went back to their rooms. I did not.

I was running when I hit the elevator button. I was gasping as I ran to room 137. I was holding my breath when I knocked on the door.

No one would open the door. I pounded on it. "Let me in!" I cried. "Let me in!"

There were footsteps, and then the Vo-Ag teacher's voice. "You won't judge, will you, Tandy?"

"I won't judge," I said, though I can admit to you now that I was judging all up and down that particular river.

"You will try to understand this delicate situation?"

"Of course I will!"

"You will remember that we are all animals of the earth, that we are all fallible?"

"Yes. I will remember." Then, quietly, "Please. Please let me help you," I said, as I am in the habit of saying all of the time and doing at least some of the time.

The Vo-Ag teacher opened the door, and there he was, and there she was.

23

His skin was pale, not unlike that of a dead person. He was looking at the floor.

"I have made some mistakes," he said.

I did not understand. "Where is Clive?"

Hope rolled her eyes and shook her head. She was standing in the farthest corner of the room, the farthest you could get from him. She was calm, her hands clasped beneath her belly. "You don't want to know," Hope said.

"Where is Clive?" I asked again. "Are you hiding him?"

"I wanted her to live up to her name, Tandy. I wanted her to believe. It went too far." He was still looking at the floor.

"Where is Clive?!" I demanded.

"Don't you know that Clive bears no responsibility here, Tandy?" he said.

"Don't you know you should never answer a question with a question?" I said.

The Vo-Ag teacher paused. He took a few deep breaths. "I have no idea where Clive is. It doesn't matter. Everyone that matters is already in this room."

In the end, it was she who told me. She is like her mother in that way. She is not afraid to say what needs to be said, even if you do not want to hear it. The rest was a ringing in my ears. He gathered his things. He said, "This doesn't change what happened between us, Tandy. They'll be looking for me. I know that no one in this room wants them to find me."

She said, "Don't tell my mom."

It wasn't until they were gone that I found my voice and was able to speak. It was small and thin and barely audible, and it didn't matter anyway because no one was there to hear it, but I know I said it because I heard myself say it. I said, "She's just a little girl."

24

Team Yoruba did not get first place for their "Living to Serve" presentation. They were by far the best, everyone knows that, but the judges gave them second place and the Texas longhorn boys first. Team Yoruba would have to get first or second at the state competition in Des Moines in May in order to advance to nationals in Indianapolis in October.

It wasn't their belts. There was no belt specification.

It was her belly. Hope's jacket was not zipped up, and therefore she was not dressed to regulation.

The rules were clear, the judges had written in their evaluations. There was a rulebook, and in the rulebook the rules were clear.

The temperature rose to above 60 degrees but I kept my coat on during the bus ride home. Sweat dripped down my temples and through my blouse and down between my breasts.

Neither Hope nor the Vo-Ag teacher got on the bus. Brody Fogle looked at me to see what he should do. I just shrugged, so he closed the door and pulled away. The Vo-Ag kids did not ask me where Hope was. It was somehow expected that she would be gone. Or maybe they assumed correctly that I did not know, so what would be the point of asking?

But they did ask me where the Vo-Ag teacher was. I said, "He did what all the beautiful people around here do. He left."

The Vo-Ag kids were silent. Finally, Phil said, "You don't really mean that, do you, Tandy?"

And though I *did* really mean it, I didn't want to mean it, so I said, "Of course not. Never."

They are going to find a place where the sun still shines, those Vo-Ag students. I'm not clairvoyant or anything, nor have I run their numbers in a spreadsheet I've created to simulate outcomes for various life scenarios, which I could easily do, but to what end? Life is essentially unknowable in the middle parts. Only the very beginning and very end are certain: We are born. We die. All we know of the middle part is to pay our taxes.

But I do have a strong feeling that they will be all right, they will find their place in the sun. And there is some tangible evidence to this. Consider the song "Tomorrow," from the musical *Annie*. Consider the word "tomorrow." It's what I will see written on their sheet cakes at their graduation parties, and in the cards the people in this town give to them, and in the letters of recommendation this town will write about them to help them gain entrance to the various colleges in your towns closer to the river. It's what I will hear said when they walk across the stage to get their diplomas, what will be shouted out of car windows while those cars peel out of the Subway parking lot late at night.

They will bet their bottom dollar, if they have one, and find a place where the sun will come out for them. And when they smile at the old days, it won't be because life was so beautiful then. It was not. It will be because they have transcended their ugliness and thought of a new life that is more beautiful than anyone ever imagined, much more beautiful than yours—in your big cities where life's pleasures are open to you like a twenty-four-hour supermarket.

I have faith that this will happen to them, even to Hope. You in your big cities, I know how you do it. You wait for them to show up because they are relatively smart and overly dependable. You hire them and they do all the work you ask of them, and they do it well. They keep your businesses alive and profitable and moving forward while you sniff at them with your fancy skepticism even as you show spreadsheets they make to the people *you* must serve, at meetings where you all eat shrimp cocktail.

Wherever you are, they are coming. And they are strong.

Clear away the cobwebs and the sorrow, Vo-Ag students. Soon it will be morning.

Long live Team Yoruba.

25

As soon as we made it back to town that day, I went to the Kum & Go and I picked up a pack of Mike's Hard Lemonade. I waited there for about a half an hour, drinking three of the Mike's in a dark spot between the dumpster and the free air for tires, so that if the Vo-Ag teacher went to my office he wouldn't find me. It was there on the curb, surrounded by crushed plastic Mountain Dew bottles and cigarette butts and oil stains and exhaust, that I did the approximate math. As far along as she was, she had likely become pregnant before Thanksgiving, right around the time the Vo-Ag teacher first began coming to my office.

I walked home, drinking another Mike's on the way. And when I got home, I fell facedown into my bed and cried and cried and cried and stayed there.

Of course I could have done something more! Of course I could have turned him in! Of course I could have called my lawyer Huff, my doctor Doc, the high school principal, the school board, the cops! Of course I could have protected myself! My father's best friends! My best friend! My best friend's daughter! My customers! The baby! I really have tried to understand this delicate situation and my position and my actions in it.

It is why I tell you this story.

I wish the Vo-Ag teacher could know how hard I have tried. I wish that all of you could know how hard I have tried. By the time I became scared of losing him he was already gone. Let that be a lesson to all of us. Even people like you.

When I woke the next morning, I went directly to my office. I placed a call to someone I know in Dubuque, a very smart accountant I knew who worked for a big accounting firm there. I didn't expect him to come to the phone, but when his secretary told him my name, he took my call.

I inquired of this accountant—very tactfully, as I am a prudent businesswoman—about opportunities that might be had at that big accounting firm in Dubuque for someone with my skill set, someone willing to learn new things, someone who may also be interested in changing her geographic location. And to reinforce our personal connection, I asked that accountant if he still wore a shark's tooth on a leather strap around his neck, and he laughed, and he said, "Tandy Caide, you strange bird, after all these years nothing would please me more than to eat lunch with you on a regular basis here in Dubuque."

Perhaps you understand this. Perhaps you do not.

Perhaps people like you do not understand people like me. Perhaps you *can't* understand me. Perhaps no amount of concrete evidence surrounding why it is that I do certain things and not other things, no amount of explaining myself with touchy-feely heart-to-heart talking about my Very Important Feelings, will ever make someone like you understand someone like me.

That is not my problem.

And even if it were my problem, I wouldn't do anything about it anyway, because obviously I have much bigger problems than you.

26

First came Dieter, the high school principal. He sat in the chair in my office and smoked a cigarette and did not say anything for a long time.

"He isn't insubordinate yet," Dieter finally said. "He's still got a few days to show up. And anyway, there's no way to prove he's the baby's father."

"I suppose there isn't," I said, which was another way of saying nothing.

"What do you think? You're close with him." Dieter was pulling another cigarette out of his pack.

I shrugged. I did not know what "close" meant.

"What I mean is that your opinion of him is valuable to me and to the school board," Dieter said.

"He enjoys the students," I said. It was the truth, was it not?

Dieter looked at me for a long time, almost the whole time it took for him to smoke that second cigarette, which he did so slowly that the end of it was wet and covered with his spit by the time he was done. "He sure does," he finally said.

"He believes he can change things," I said.

"Oh," Dieter said. "Then he *is* dumb."

But Dieter wasn't done. "I don't want you to be intimidated or alarmed by this, but the school board has requested a statement from you regarding the situation," he said.

"I am neither intimidated or alarmed," I said. That may or may not have been the truth.

"It appears there are some discrepancies with the FFA accounting," Dieter said.

Big problems—problems with a wingspan that covered my office and the building it was in and my cottage on the go-around and all the way out to the cold, cold hot tub.

Then came Mary Ellen from the Powerhaus to tell me that she and Doc and Eddie from the kitchen had just carried Huff out of the Powerhaus and onto the bed of Eddie's truck and rushed him up to the hospital. He had passed out in a booth and begun to choke on his own vomit, and now Doc was extracting the alcohol from him via a pump they make just for that purpose. Even bigger problems, reaching all the way to Cunt Itchen and Mueller's farm and the grave of my dead father.

Then came Huff, lying facedown on a hospital bed, his face almost the same green color as his hospital gown. Doc said to him: "You've got to do something about this."

"Maybe I should go to that place Gerald went." His big lawyer voice was small and dry and raspy. He lifted his face to look over at me. "Is it good there, Tandy? Has it been good for him?"

"Oh, it's been very good for him," I said, though I had not spoken to Gerald in months, nor had I thought about him in months, and I had no idea just *how* good it had been for him.

"Well," Huff said. "If it's good enough for Gerald, it must not be too big a piece of shit to swallow." He closed his eyes and turned his face away from us.

"I'm going to get your things now," Doc said.

"No. I'm not ready. I don't want them to see me like this." His head was buried in his pillow. His voice was muffled like it was coming from a faraway place in his head.

"They see people way worse than you," Doc said. "People get better there. People die here."

Huff did not move. "Please. Let me go with my dignity," he said, still facedown.

And so Doc promised him a few days to gather up what was left of his dignity.

Huff turned to me then and said, "She went off with him, didn't she?" He paused. "Tandy, how come nobody ever did that to you? What did your father do right that I keep doing wrong?"

"This is not your problem," I said. It was not exactly true. It was a problem that belonged to each one of us in a slightly different way. But it was a nice thing to say.

Then came Barb. I called over to Cunt Itchen and told her that Huff had gotten his stomach pumped. I asked her if she would go to see him. She said, "No. I have to work."

"Do you understand the severity of the situation?" I asked.

"Yes. I was there the last time," she said.

Before I hung up, she asked me if I knew where she was. I said no, and then I asked if Barb believed me. She said, "Yes, Tandy. I believe you are always telling me the truth, even when you know I don't want to hear it. You're good like that."

Then came Doc with bean soup on Wednesday. He sat and smoked and said, over and over again, "Jesus H. Christ, little girl, Jesus H. Christ," lighting each new cigarette with the tip of the old one, trying to smoke each one before it became too soggy with his tears. Then came a postcard from the Minnesota Valley National Wildlife Refuge Interpretive Center in Bloomington. The refuge comprises eleven thousand acres running right along the river for more than thirty miles. Some of those acres are native prairie. On the postcard was a mallard rising from the water and flying away. On the back, where on most sent postcards there is a handwritten note about what the sender is up to, there was no note. Even my office address had been printed on a label and then stuck to the postcard. There was no evidence of a human hand on that postcard anywhere.

Team Yoruba came next. By this time, Huff had tried to get the county police and the state patrol to search for Hope, the same way he had done so many years ago for Barbie. They were no longer at his disposal. Hope was eighteen. She was not what they considered a "vulnerable adult." There are rules about what cops can and cannot do now.

But Team Yoruba was not worried about Hope. My guess is that they knew Hope to be one of their own. They knew what she could do, which was take care of herself. They were worried about themselves. The Vo-Ag teacher had failed to show up in his classroom for a full week. He had missed the deadline to confirm their performance and participation in the FFA state competition in Des Moines. They pleaded with me to tell them where he was.

"I have no idea," I said, though I was staring at the Internet when I said it, at the website of that native prairie refuge in the middle of a Minneapolis suburb.

"Is there anything you can do to help us?" they cried.

"No," I said.

I'm not perfect. Show me someone who is and I'll show you a righteous asshole who needs to be knocked down a few notches.

Then came Team Yoruba again.

"Some of our money is gone," Phil said. They were standing before my desk in my office. "We used to have thirty-one thousand dollars and now we only have twenty-one thousand." They showed me their bank statement.

"It looks like there was a withdrawal two weeks ago," I said.

"No shit," Phil said.

"Was it you?" Missy asked. "You're authorized as a cosigner." It was not me. We all got very silent, since we all knew who the other two signers on the account were. And when we all walked over to the bank and asked to see a copy of the withdrawal, that is exactly what we found on the cashier's check: On the payee line, *Hope Barbara Huff, secretary of FFA,* in a tight and upright scrawl. On the signature line, the same.

And, as the account requires two signatures, there was another signature on the signature line: *Kenny Tischer*, pulling up and away from the line, loopy and airborne.

27

I am a good person. I am a person of integrity. I do my best to protect the people I love. I will not stop doing it either, even if the circumstances become difficult. I went to the bowling alley. Even though Cindy had just locked the doors, she let me in. I drank four Mike's and I bowled a 267 with my straight-pin bowling as Cindy went about her closing-up business. I looked at that picture of Doris Mavin for a long time, and while I was looking at it, Cindy said it again, "You could really be something if you just loosened up a little, rolled a curve once in a while," and I smiled and I nodded, like business as usual, in the businesswoman's way.

But as I walked up the hill to the go-around and I looked in everyone's windows, I saw all the things I had seen a hundred times before—babies, and counters being wiped, and family photos and paintings done on saws, and deer heads and silk flowers and all these things I had seen over and over and over again thousands of times, thousands of the same things—and I thought about the boy Barbie had loved, and how good-looking he was, and I thought about the Vo-Ag teacher, and how silky was his ponytail, and I thought about him and Hope, gone to who knows where together, and about my mother and father, gone to who knows where together, and I thought about me stuck here alone, and how I couldn't throw a bowling ball curve to save my goddamn life. And I tell you, everything looked really shitty then. I wish I had words to describe to you how shitty it looked. It looked like the shittiest place on Earth. It looked like my whole life was a giant piece of shit, and that the only place to go now was down the drain and into some sort of muck pen, some sort of shit pond full of excrement that, in the end, would just seep me farther down into the deep underworld of hell. I thought about the plot in the cemetery right next to my father's, the plot that he was prudent enough to purchase before he drove his car off that bridge, the cemetery plot that I knew he had purchased on my eighteenth birthday, just as I was beginning to imagine what life might be like for me, because he cared enough to leave the receipt right on top of the mail, where I would find it on my way to do my duty at the post office.

TANDY CAIDE, CPA, it is etched on the headstone. It is as unmovable and unchanging as death itself.

I was so drunk, and this was all so depressing, that when I lay in my bed that night under my white eyelet comforter, the room spun around. I began to believe Cindy. I began to think that maybe I *could* be something special if I just had the guts to throw a curve. I began to think that perhaps I had some control in the matter, and so all was not lost exactly.

Why did I go there in my thoughts? Maybe because when a person is that low she grasps at something good that someone said to her once, as petty and insignificant as that might be. Maybe this is how people get what is called "resilient"—by remembering that even when things are very bad, there is always a possibility of some kind of improvement. There is always a little promise somewhere around the bend.

So even though it was deep into the night, I got up and walked all the way out to the sod house. I wanted to see my promise and believe it and attach to it and become it.

It was cold out there and it was drizzling. A car drove by very slowly, with the lights off, and then peeled away into the darkness. And though the Vo-Ag kids had marked it off with string and little posts in the ground, and though bricks of sod had been layered into a U shape up to my waist, as far as I could tell, the Sod House Experience was just a muddy hole in the ground.

28

When I drove up the go-around after my last day of my first semester of college, my father came out and got in the car. "We're going to the Chamber luncheon meeting," he said.

They had never included me before.

And despite all that first semester of college was, and that wonderful room I lived in, and what had happened with Karl, and what had happened with Barbie—despite all of that, I felt like I was being awarded a prize. It felt bigger than that time they let me drive them home from the riverboat when I was thirteen because they were so drunk. It felt bigger than that time they took me out for a steak dinner up in Decorah after I realized Mueller was overpaying his employees' Social Security contributions.

They brought me the bean soup, and they told me up front they would be paying for it. They made a big deal about it with Mary Ellen. My father said, "We think she can stomach her own bowl! Fill it to the brim!" Everyone was happy, including me.

And then Doc said, "We think you are ready to join the Chamber."

I did not expect that. Back then, there were more than just myself and Doc and Huff and Howie Claus in the Chamber. There was the jeweler, Arnie Cunningham, and the manager from the plastics plant, Don Wingert, and even some suits the railroad was keeping around, though those guys had long stopped attending meetings.

I was just a college student, you see. All I could say was "Oh."

"You do most of the same work as your father," Doc said. "It was his idea."

I looked to my father. He raised his eyebrows and lifted a whiskey to his mouth, but he was looking at his drink and not at me.

You see, then, what he really wanted?

"What does this require of me?" I asked, though I already knew.

My father said nothing.

Huff said, "It requires your celibacy."

Doc slammed his fist on the table and said, "She is not your problem!"

My father rubbed his face. He said, "She is *my* problem," and then we all sat silent until finally I got up the guts to say, "I don't understand. Am I a problem or a solution?"

No one answered my question. Instead, Doc said, "What Chamber membership requires is for you to attend regular meetings and maintain a positive business presence in this town. You may have to lead some development efforts and help plan budgets and things. To start. This is all to start."

"You would have to belong to the Order of the Pessimists," Huff said, "but that's not much of a selling point."

My father continued to look at his drink. "It would be best if you lived here," he said. "You would spend your time on the current clients here, the ones who know you and are comfortable with you. That would free me up for larger clients. Out-of-town clients."

"You'll go far in this town," Doc said.

A way out occurred to me. I said, "Perhaps I could be the one to solicit the out-of-town clients. I am already at Upper Prairie half the day."

"Don't be stupid," my father said. "You're just a kid."

"No thanks then," I said. "I'm going back to college."

They stopped. It was clear they had not considered that I might say no.

"You can finish it by correspondence," my father said.

"Studies have shown that students learn better in the classroom," I said, though I had seen no such studies.

"You already have what those students are trying to get," my father said.

"He is right," Doc said.

And I suppose he was. The only person I knew of for whom it might not have been true was Karl, but even smart, dedicated Karl had no real accounting experience.

This was something, you see. This was something special about me. And yes, I suppose my father gave me this. I am capable of gratitude.

But still I said, "There are things I need to learn there."

My father ordered a third drink. "What 'things' could you possibly need to learn at a piss-ant, piece-of-shit college like that?"

Huff shouted, "It's a boy, isn't it?! Oh Christ, a boy! Fuck all those boys! Just go fuck 'em, then!"

Doc sighed and closed his eyes.

The bean soup came, warm and bubbly and smelling of carrots and onions. I remember Mary Ellen said, "I don't have a candle for it. You should pretend there's a candle in there," and so I did. I blew out an imaginary celebration candle, sinking into a very real bowl of bean soup.

Of course it wasn't a boy, but I didn't deny it. I didn't know how to deny it because I had no language for that little window near the ceiling of that little dorm room, and that place that sold pizza by the slice, and that view of a woods as seen in the movies.

"I am going to go out to see Barbie then," I said.

No one looked up from his soup. "Wait until Christmas," Huff said. "Give her some time." I didn't know what she needed time for, but I didn't ask. At least I would have Barbie at some point, I thought. At least he didn't say no outright.

It didn't matter anyway. The week before Christmas, my father finally hit that deer he was chasing—drank himself so far into that deer that when it jumped off Kennicott Bridge out on County Road 8, he did too. And I was identifying his truck, the Bronco, and the clothes he was wearing—blood-soaked shirt, bloody shoes—and screaming at Doc to show me his body and Doc was saying no, I was too young, even though I was legally old enough, because he had previously given my father his word. And then Barbie was sending word that she couldn't come to the funeral, she didn't want to take the baby out, it was too cold, but I knew it was an excuse. And then I was taping together Doc's cigarette and pledging to go far in this town.

I did what I said I would do. And look where it got me.

IV.
DUBUQUE

29

When you drive to Dubuque in the very early morning of a late spring, and the sun rises up over the horizon before you, there are many green things to look at. There are greening buds on branches that were bare just a few weeks before, growing from a warmth that will make you shed your big winter coat. There is green grass in yards, and rows of little green shoots of soybeans pushing out of the black dirt in fields, and rolling green hills of varying sizes and undulations. From all that green and from the dirt comes that sharp smell of freshness, that promising sagy smell of wet new things that are inexplicably both old and new, from before and only of right now.

And when you reach the top of the bluff just outside of Dubuque and the big blue river appears below you against all that new green—that deep blue river, fat and flowing, alive and ready for you to dip your toes into, with Dubuque wrapped around it, so many buildings of so many stories high, so many coffee shops and businesses and restaurants and galleries with arts and crafts, so many nice brick homes, Colonials even, and kinds with unique rooflines and interesting plants in the yards, and those multiple college campuses with orderly grounds in the shape of squares, and America-colored riverboats parked along the river's edge with bells and whistles and blinking lights, and hawks and herons flying high above, even a great blue heron swooping down, having her pick of a wide diversity of meals—well, it's something to see, for sure.

You might even hear that Carole King song on the radio, about how great it is to be a woman who is too big too ignore. Your royal-blue blouse with the bow at the neck might bring out the blue in your eyes and the blue sections of the multicolored beaded belt you're wearing and even the blue of that big river.

All of it is enough to make a big woman feel pretty full of herself.

The firm was downtown in a turn-of-the-century building that had once been a bank. It had recently been saved by a preservation ordinance, which the good citizens of Dubuque are known for voting in favor of. I walked through the front door and a woman wearing a cardigan sweater and jeans greeted me. I thought she was dressed too casually, but I was also aware that the rules are different in different places of business. Part of being a businesswoman is seeing beyond the obvious.

"Tandy Caide!" she said before I even had the chance to introduce myself, and she smiled a big smile and shook my hand with both of hers wrapped around mine, as if to thank me for my long and illustrious career about which she somehow knew everything. I liked it. It was a nice touch.

I sat in a large brown leather chair. I sunk so far into it my knees touched my stomach. The lobby was five times the size of my own and filled with other overstuffed leather furniture. It smelled rich, and it smelled green too, from the many houseplants the woman in the cardigan sweater was watering. I was deep in the chair, but I felt as if I was in good hands. There were huge windows that faced the street, with full-sized screens in them, so I had the most pleasurable feeling of being inside and outside at the same time. I could smell fresh bread and newly roasted coffee and the moving water of the river. I watched people walk by, none of whom I knew, and none who knew me.

The joy in my heart—you could have filled an auditorium with it.

Then some elevator doors opened and there stood Karl. He wore a blue shirt, the kind they call "chambray." He was a little heavier than I remembered, and he had jowls, and his arms were hairier. But his eyes were the same and so was his hair, light brown and curly and a little longer in the back.

I stood up. He was smiling and laughing a little, and he was blushing too. I suppose I was doing the same. When he moved toward me I saw that he still had that thigh bounce. He too shook my hand by putting it between both of his. This time it was even nicer. It was him. It was Karl. From college.

He said, "My God." And stared at me.

He said, "My, my, my, *my*."

No one had ever looked at me like this, not even the Vo-Ag teacher. But then again, no one but Karl had known me and then not known me and then had the pleasure of knowing me again. It was thrilling in a very interesting way. It was like he desired me but had also missed me, and so was nostalgic for me too. I was not disappointed by this. I am not ashamed to say that. It is not an unsatisfying thing to see a man look at you this way.

He took a deep breath and looked at the floor. Then he said, "This is business!" We got into the elevator and stood as far apart as we could, because the space between us was filled with electric energy. It was like the elevator was a giant battery and we were the dangerous ends of jumper cables. I held on to the handrail and stared at the numbers as we rose. He did the same, though periodically I heard him giggle, and certainly he heard me too. It was spilling out of me. I couldn't help it.

"Tandy has owned her own firm for almost twenty years," Karl said to the four other men in the conference room. They were all dressed exactly as Karl.

"You don't seem that old," one of them replied. They were alternating between squinting at me from behind their bifocals and squinting at my résumé, which was composed of one page on which was printed five lines, including my name.

"I feel that old," I said, and they all chuckled, though I did not mean it as a joke.

The table was black and shiny. The chairs were those kind of high-backed office chairs you see in movies, the kind CEOs and corporate lawyers use to lean back away from tables to put their fingertips together below their chins in little triangles as they mull over some complex business dilemma.

The four men did this. It was straight out of the movies!

"Who are your clients?" they asked.

I told them about Mueller and the school and the church and the personal income taxes.

"And who manages things at your office?" they asked.

I relayed to them my extremely competent skills at self-managing all aspects of my own business, practiced since the day I was born.

"Who manages you?" they asked.

I considered responding with "The world's biggest assholes" but did not. It may have been my first and only job interview, but I wasn't stupid. I said, "My customers manage me. As a small-business owner, I must remain service-oriented. I serve the needs of my customers."

"That's interesting," said one of the men, removing his glasses and squinting at me. "Here we also serve the needs of our customers."

"We have something in common then," I said.

I don't know much about job interviewing, but I imagine that a shared concern for the needs of customers would be a promotable aspect about yourself.

"We also serve the needs of our shareholders," he said.

"I can share," I said, and this made all four of them laugh and look at one another as if I had made a very interesting joke, though I had not.

"Your clients, would you be able to share them? Would you bring your clients with you?"

I had not thought of that. *Those clients are mine,* I thought.

I panicked. Briefly. But then I remembered that this is business.

"Certainly a deal could be made there," I said.

They looked at one another and then back at me. Some of them smiled.

I never promised anything. I know business. It's the one thing I know.

Karl said in the elevator, "I think that went really well."

"Really?" I said, and then silently cursed myself for answering a question with a question.

"It's obvious that you can be trusted to know what you can and can't do in this business," he said.

I said nothing.

"Don't worry," he went on. "They'll take my word on you. I just have to say the word and you are here."

"Well," I said, "here I am."

"Here you are," he echoed, looking at me and smiling. And then he reached out and touched my arm lightly with his fingertips, and then he rubbed it with the palm of his hand, and then he rushed toward me and grabbed me and pressed his body against mine.

It was a little softer than I remembered but a very nice fit overall.

He buried his nose in my neck and inhaled. He whispered into my neck, "It's so *good* to see you."

I patted him on the back, and, yes, I smelled his neck as well. It was pungent and spicy in a good way, a way that made the back of my mouth water a little.

"It's so good to see you too," I said.

There were twenty different restaurants we could have walked to, but he chose one that served pizza by the slice. "Not as good as Margie's, of course. That white sauce! You remember?" he asked.

"Who could forget?" I said.

"Did you know I'd never had white sauce before Margie's?" he said. "I'd never had any sauce that didn't come from a can."

I said, "I'd never even had pizza by the slice. I thought the prices on the menu were for a whole pizza."

He doubled over laughing as he walked, bouncing himself forward on his powerful thighs to keep himself from falling over. He said, "Oh, we were such *rubes*, Tandy!"

I didn't know what a rube was. I had to look it up later. It means: "an unsophisticated person from a rural area; a hick."

The restaurant was like a school cafeteria for professionals and executives, with metal silverware and ceramic plates in all sorts of vibrant colors and a sunny room filled with tables with smooth stone tops. You didn't order from a waitress but rather you picked up a tray and walked along a path and examined various hot and cold salads spread out before you. You chose them based on your tastes or whims at that moment. Everything had some kind of special seasoning on the end of its name, like *with rosemary* or *with chives*, even the most everyday of dishes, like macaroni and cheese. *Macaroni and cheese with sour cream and chives,* it said in excellent handwriting on a little card before it.

Karl whispered into my ear, "The firm is paying for it, so load up as much as you want."

His breath was warm and smelled like mint. I took nothing until the pizza with white sauce. It was six dollars a slice so I took only one. Karl laughed at me. "This is a free lunch, Tandy! You should enjoy it!"

I put a Diet Coke on my tray next to the pizza. Karl put his arm around me and squeezed my shoulder and whispered into my ear, "I've missed you."

I wanted to sit at a table by the window, to watch all the people walking by, but Karl wanted a table in the back—"For privacy," he said—so we went to the back. He ate nothing though he had two slices of pizza with white sauce and a brownie and a Diet Coke on his tray. He just stared at me with his hands clasped in front of his mouth.

"Aren't you hungry?" I asked.

"I'm just too happy to see you, I think," he said. But then he leaned in and said, "Can you believe it? I drive a BMW, Tandy! That's a foreign car!" He leaned in farther, his eyes wide open, as wide as eyes can open, and he said with that tone people on television use at the most dramatic moments, when something so incredible happens to them they can barely believe it: "Tandy—I live in Dubuque!"

The way he said it really made me want to live in Dubuque too.

I said, "Tell me about your life now." He talked about his family then. His parents, who had sold their farm five years ago and moved into a condo near the home where he and his wife and children live. His home, a Colonial with cedar shingles and a two-car attached garage that is heated. ("A heated garage, Tandy!" he said.) His two children, who were hilarious little miracles and also giant pains in the ass and expensive Catholic school attendees, but it was all worth it for the values, he said. His Catholic wife, who does not work anymore but does yoga, and plans outdoor community arts events, whom he met at an accounting conference in Chicago. His wife, who had gone to the University of Iowa and was originally from a suburb of Chicago, who loved to decorate, especially at

Christmas, when they would open up their home to strangers who paid to see her holiday decorations so she could give the money to charity, which for her was the Dubuque Symphony Orchestra, which he said was amazing.

"You would love the Dubuque Symphony Orchestra," he said.

I didn't even know what a "symphony orchestra" was.

He said, "She loves the Cubs. You wouldn't believe a woman could love a sports team so much, especially a sucky one." He paused. "During the Christmas tour, she hides the clutter under the living room couches. No one knows that.

"She's a lot like you," he said. "She's not very—I don't know—girly. I mean, she is... but she isn't. But she's not as...large as you, or something. Not as solid. She has"—he searched for the words—*"bad moments."*

"I have bad moments," I said. Obviously it was a gross understatement, but certainly you can understand that I was trying to get a job.

"Oh, I doubt that," he said. "I doubt you have any bad moments at all."

"Is that a compliment?" I asked, and then got stuck on this in my head.

Everyone in the world has bad moments. The Vo-Ag teacher, Barbie and Hope, Clive, and, of course, Doc and Huff. And suddenly I found myself thinking about how much I hated them for their bad moments, and how maybe that hatred was irrational if everyone does indeed have bad moments. I thought about Gerald and our many years of moments that were neither bad nor good but rather completely insignificant to me. I thought that perhaps if we had had a moment or two that could have been described as either "good" or "bad," then at least I would have had a greater reason to sit or not sit with him in the hot tub.

"Yes, it's a compliment," Karl said, and he reached out under the table and touched my knee.

There was a quick whoosh inside my chest. It was so familiar and warm, the weight of his hand—it was as it had been eighteen years before.

There I was with a beautiful boy I had already made love to several times in my life, who had become a man who works for the Dubuque branch of a national CPA firm, where I had just interviewed for a job that I had then been told was mine if he gives the word, and his hand was on my knee at a fancy executive deli where hundreds of meal options were laid out before me, all for my choosing, and all for free! I ran the top of my foot along the muscle of his calf. He put his hands back into his lap.

"Where are they putting you up?" he asked.

"The Hilton. Right on the river."

"I love it there."

I swallowed. "Why don't you join me?"

He shook his head and looked at the food on his plate.

"My family is expecting me."

I nodded and looked at that single slice of six-dollar pizza. "All families expect something," I said.

I imagined that when he went home to his family, they would all be standing in the doorway of his beautiful cedar-shingled Colonial, clapping for him and his breadwinner-ness, holding out their arms to him in a welcoming way, with appreciation and generosity and kindness. Later, they would all go to a concert together, outdoors, on a blanket. They would drink coffee from a disposable cup, with a little cardboard sleeve that goes around the cup so you don't burn your hand when you hold it. His parents rubbing his shoulders, patting his back, so struck by his success, by the bounty of Dubuque, so proud. His wife, so yoga-ed.

I had no beautiful cedar-shingled Colonial in Dubuque. I had no adoring parents or spouse. My town could provide no outdoor performance event.

This made me angry. It was all downhill from there.

He said, "You'd bring a lot to the firm."

I'd bring a lot to a lot of places, I wanted to say.

"Would you like that?" I asked him.

"Very few people understand me here, Tandy. They don't understand people like us."

I believed that wholeheartedly. I still do. I believe there are people like Karl and me, people from places so far away from the river that no one knows the names, or the names of the people living there, or what the people living there do with their lives and why they do them. People like you who live closer to the river do not really understand people like me who live far away from it.

Don't feel bad about it. It's probably not your fault. But don't pretend it's not true either.

"I want you to be here," he said. "We could... We could make something special between us." He was not specific about what that might be.

"It would be... a special deal that you and I could make." That was a little more specific.

"No one would have to know." And that is as specific as it gets.

He brought his hand back to my knee and gave it a little squeeze under the table. He said, "I'll make sure they're not expecting me next time."

"Of course," I said, knowing I would not be returning.

This wasn't business. This was something else, something I already had, and in far greater quantity than I could handle.

He left then.

They all do.

30

It was a very nice room: a queen bed with mauve sheets and puffy beige bedding, and a thinner deep-red blanket folded on top. There were five pillows, more than I had ever seen on a bed. There were two layers of regular pillows in striped beige pillowcases, and another pillow shaped like a tube that was deep red and patterned with beige diamonds. I don't know how someone is supposed to lay his or her head comfortably on a tube-shaped pillow. I actually tried it, and I can tell you with certainty that those tubular pillows are not suitable for use when sleeping.

There was a big sitting chair that was a deep burgundy, and a desk that was stained a dark color but also glowed gold. On it was a coffeemaker, along with some coffee samples, and two coffee cups and two water glasses and an ice bucket, which was empty. And there was some creamer that was flavored French vanilla, and different kinds of sweeteners—any kind you could want. At the Hilton on the river in Dubuque, you can put twenty-seven packets of five different varieties of sweeteners into your coffee, if you so desire.

The whole room smelled fresh. Not summer-breeze fresh, but new-car fresh, if a new car could be a room. It smelled new-room fresh.

And strangely enough, the wallpaper was striped nearly exactly like the wallpaper in my own bedroom in my own little cottage in my own little town far away from the river. It was a slightly different beige, but the pattern—thick, thick, thin, thick, thick, thin, thick, thin—was exactly the same. How Doc and Huff would have loved the irony, I thought.

I sat on the bed, and for a long time I just looked out the window at the Dubuque riverfront, and the bridge over the Mississippi River, and that riverboat casino and the river itself. It was very beautiful, the river. It was right before dusk and the sun was going down on the other side of the hotel, and its position in the sky made everything glow. The green leaves of the trees and the pink purple of the sky and the blue black of the river and the reds and blues of all the cars crossing the river and the lights of the riverboat all looked so nice. It all looked vibrant and clean and clear and alive.

I had never seen the river look so perfect.

For a long time I watched the movement of those little red and blue cars on the bridge, going from one place to another. All those cars, all those people in those cars, I imagined what their lives must be like, what their homes must be like, what they look like in their homes when they are just doing the normal things that I know that everyone does, like drink coffee and hold babies and vacuum and read and watch television and fall asleep on couches and in big chairs with their feet up.

I was not afraid. It is important to me that you understand this. It was just that I had never imagined living in a place like this, like where you live. And the more I thought about it, the more I thought about what it might really be like, maybe, to live right in that very room.

Perhaps you find this naive, or rube-like, that I would think of living in a Hilton hotel room in Dubuque. But frankly, I don't really care what you think. I was excited by the thought of living in that room. There was no kitchen, true, but I could eat in restaurants. Dubuque has many fine restaurants. I could make coffee every morning with the little coffeemaker, or I could pay a visit to one of the many coffee shops along the river, and order my coffee in one of those disposable cups with the cardboard sleeves, and nod politely to the person who made the coffee and not have her know my entire life story. And every night after I came home from my job working with some of Dubuque's brightest accounting minds, talking with them about complicated tax matters and how best to help our customers solve those complicated tax matters, I could sit in front of this window with a cup of decaf, and I could look out onto the river and watch the movement of all those people I didn't know but could meet if I wanted to. All those interesting people from interesting places going to and coming from other interesting places, and all around us and between us that river that flows all the time, slipping from one interesting place to another without ever stopping or slowing down or worrying about whether it was the right thing to do or what people might think about it.

Maybe I was thinking about the Vo-Ag teacher too. You might ask: There was Karl, right before me, and I was thinking about the Vo-Ag teacher, who had gotten the high school daughter of my best friend pregnant? Yes. I was thinking about the Vo-Ag teacher, despite all the things that had happened between us and what had happened between himself and Hope. I was thinking about him in that room with me, but just visiting sometimes, not living there with me, maybe taking a walk down along the river with me and then coming back up to the room to talk about what we had seen. He would have liked Dubuque, I think. He would have had a lot to say about commerce, and how living near a river changes people. I would have liked to listen to him talk about these things while he stood by the window of my room with a cup of coffee in his hand, laughing his big horselaugh and poking at me with his long finger.

There were two coffee cups, after all. Certainly when a hotel employee puts down two coffee cups, the expectation is that there will be more than one guest in the room. Naturally, a hotel guest who is alone where two such coffee mugs sit side by side will imagine whom the other cup might be for.

I would have slept in the chair if that is what he would have preferred.

I don't know why I laid awake nearly all night despite the very comfortable bed, and I don't know why, when I finally fell asleep, Doris Mavin, the woman who bowled the 300 at Prairie Lanes, came to me in my dream. She was an old lady in it. She waved me down a corridor, and I followed her through a room filled with old furniture and white floor-to-ceiling bookshelves and framed black-and-white photos of the bodies of naked women—soft and round and fuzzy on the edges—all hung under those special lights owned by people who know what they're doing with art. The carpet was dark blue, and padding across it were several cats. I followed her to a sunroom where a little table was set for two, with coffee cups painted with strawberries on saucers also painted with strawberries. She poured coffee into my cup, slowly and carefully. Her pouring hand was extra large—it was her bowling hand. It was powerful and strong. She did not spill a drop. I swallowed hard. "You may have known my father," I said in my dream.

She scrunched up her nose and shook her head.

"My mother?"

She shook her head again. She looked out the window at her garden. It was blooming with cherry tomatoes and different colors of lilies. "It just wasn't for me," she said. Then she put down her coffee and looked right at me and said, "You're good." And then she said it loud, and with force: "You're good!"

I cried out in bed, waking myself up.

When I fell asleep again, I dreamed I was Cybill Shepherd as Maddie from *Moonlighting*, and that I wore dresses from the Victorian era and was stunningly beautiful and also known for my tremendous intellect. And I wore hats. In fact, my beauty and intellect required two hats, one on top of the other, upon my golden locks of hair. It was something I accepted about myself, Cybill Shepherd, Maddie from *Moonlighting*, with a mixture of pride and pragmatism. You might say I was smug about it. You might say I was the opposite of a rube about it.

In my dream, I sat on a couch in an empty room, smiling, waiting for Bruce Willis. He was going to be there any moment.

On my way out of Dubuque, I stepped into one of those little shops that sells arts and crafts down by the river. There were belts there, colorful woven belts with tiny shells sewn onto them, hundreds of these belts, exactly like the Vo-Ag teacher's.

All the tags said MADE IN TAIWAN.

31

Gerald was in a big room, like a lobby at a funeral home but with a linoleum floor. He was sitting at a card table, in jeans and a white T-shirt, across from a woman wearing the same thing. They were playing the board game *Sorry!* The woman had long brown hair, straight, with no bangs, and she was very short. Her toes barely touched the floor as she sat in the folding chair. She had big eyes, though, and long lashes. She had a plastic straw that she kept taking in and out of her mouth like she was smoking it.

It was not shocking to see him with another woman. I could have guessed as much, and there was the Vo-Ag teacher to balance things out. What was shocking was Gerald himself.

I recognized him from the shape of his head, but that was all. It was not the Gerald I knew. I had to stand in the doorway for a few moments just to make sure that, yes, he was wearing jeans that did not have elastic in the waist.

He was a normal-sized man!

"Oh!" he said. "Oh! There you are!"

"Here I am," I said.

"This is Ginny," he said. She waved her little chewed-up fake cigarette at me.

"I didn't know you had a girlfriend," I said to Gerald.

The two of them looked at each other and shrugged. Then they laughed.

"I don't like labels," he said to me, but he was looking at her when he said it.

"Is that so?" I asked.

He did look at me then, and this time he smiled. It was a gentle smile, the kind of pity smile you would get from a teacher who knew you had no mother.

His face! It was so thin! It was like the face of a younger man! It was just like the way he had been in middle school, just a little more saggy in the skin and neck. It was like he had lost years and gained years at the same time and come out the other end a reordered person!

The woman, Ginny, got up. She pulled the straw out of her mouth and said, "Nice to meet you. I've heard so much about you."

"Yes," I said. What was I supposed to say?

"See you this afternoon," she said to Gerald, and he moved his thin face toward hers and she kissed it.

If my heart could have changed into a different kind of material, it would have turned into a stone and fallen through my ribs and out my belly button. We went up to his room. It was on the third floor. Gerald walked the three flights of steps so easily, right next to me the whole time. Our feet took each step in unison.

He was wearing a new pair of shoes, a pair of Converse All Stars, which is a kind of shoe he had not been able to fit his feet into since 1992. I could not believe those were his feet!

We reached a hallway and turned right, and then he stopped at a door and opened it with a key from his pocket.

It was like a hospital room but nicer. There was a hospital bed but a big armchair too, a white one with a jump rope on it. And there was a whole row of floor-to-ceiling windows. It was very sunny in that room. There was a ficus plant by the bed, and some ivy hanging down from a macramé basket that was attached to the ceiling.

It smelled clean, like Lysol. And it smelled a little like Gerald too, like Zest soap and Suave shampoo and that special Gerald smell that was just his.

"I keep it pretty clean," he said. "At first I didn't. But then it just got to be mine. I started to care about it. And then I wanted to take care of it.

"Sit down," he said.

I picked up the jump rope and sat down in the armchair. I held the jump rope in my lap. It was one of those expensive jump ropes, leather with wooden handles, not a plastic one that you buy at Walmart, more like what I imagine a professional boxer would use.

He sat down on the bed. He said, "I have a routine. When I wake up in the morning, I make my bed as soon as I get out of it. Then I wash my face and my hands. Then I clean all surfaces with a rag and soapy water."

There was a white radiator that ran along the wall behind my chair. It sighed a little. I saw that the top of the radiator was indeed dust-free.

"If it is a Wednesday, I also clean the floor. They only clean the floors on Saturdays."

I looked out the window. "That's great," I said. What do you say to someone who has become an efficient and tidy person?

"Then I get dressed. Then I go downstairs and I eat a banana and drink one cup of black coffee. Then I walk up and down the three flights of stairs four times. Then I come back to my room and I jump rope."

"Great," I said. I continued to look out the window. I wondered what he looked like jumping rope, now that he was a normal-sized man. I had seen Gerald jump rope once before, back when he was in the eighth grade. He was wearing cutoff jeans and no shirt in his mother's backyard. There was a ring of fat around his middle.

"When I first got here I used to jump rope for one or two minutes, then I would go back to bed. Now I jump rope for fifteen minutes and then I do fifty sit-ups and fifty push-ups. By the time I'm done it's about eight thirty and it's just an hour until group."

"How handy," I said. He went to group therapy. I had always been curious about group therapy. Perhaps that was where he met that woman, Ginny. Perhaps men and women meet each other at group therapy.

"I take a shower. If the weather is nice, I take a walk. If it's not, I read the Bible," he said.

There were plenty of things to look at out that window, but I could only see him jumping rope in his mother's backyard and me, my long legs tired as I rode by on my bike to my father's office.

It went on like that for some time, both of us looking out the window.

"Why wouldn't you ever kiss me?" he said suddenly.

I thought about it so long I was aware that my silence said more than my words. But he didn't jump in with his words, or a joke, like he would have before.

Eventually I said, "Because every time we kissed you took your pants off."

"And what is wrong with that? A man wanting to make love to his wife?" he asked.

I did not know the answer to that question. I suppose that is a question for the ages.

"Is it because I was so fat? I'm thinner now. I've lost seventy pounds."

I wanted to say no, that it wasn't because he was fat, but I had no real explanation to fill the gap. I should have, maybe. Maybe you would have had an answer. But I had no answer. Fatness was just the easy answer.

"Maybe," I said.

"What else could it have been?" He was trying to look me in the eye. I got up to leave.

"Maybe it's because you never really loved me!" he said.

"That's not true," I said. But maybe it was. I didn't know. I still don't.

He smiled at me, with his mouth and with his eyes, with that kindness again. And it seemed so, I don't know, so inappropriate. Intimate, but in a totally inappropriate way.

"Are you on some kind of happy pills that make you stupid?" I asked.

"Oh, Tandy," he said, and did not answer the question. He laid his head down on the pillow and put his feet up on the bed and then folded his hands over his much-flatter stomach. The weight of the skin on his face fell down to the sides and he looked even younger. He looked like a young man, a new man, but not *so* new. He looked like a man I recognized, like a part of myself from years past but with something new in it, like the boy I knew from before, but new and improved, more alive, more possible. He looked like a better twin, like someone who had surpassed me.

My mouth went dry. My hands and arms tingled. I began to feel crazy, like I should check into the room next door.

"Do I look good?" he asked. "There is a lot of extra skin on me."

"You look younger."

He chuckled. "I'll take it," he said. "Thanks."

He said, "You look the same, but you smell like smoke."

"It's the coat," I said.

"Oh, it's all right. You can smoke. It's not illegal unless you do it in my clean room."

Then he said, "Do I look good enough to kiss?"

To answer the question now, I suppose maybe. Certainly he was a different man. It seemed like he was a good man. But then again, he had never been a bad man.

He was smiling a kind smile. It still felt inappropriate, but not like he was out to hurt me.

We had had our moments.

But I said no.

Maybe it was just because I was holding his jump rope. Maybe I just wasn't that good. Gerald sighed. The radiator sighed and then gave a few knocks and then stopped making any sound at all. He said, "The food here is terrible. I didn't lose this weight willingly."

"I bet not," I said.

He laughed. "You know me so well. Did you know that I have learned to love now, Tandy?"

"Does she take the straw out of her mouth beforehand?" I asked.

It was a stupid thing to say. It was something Doc and Huff would have said. I tried to think of something better.

I said, "The grass isn't always greener on the other side."

"I would laugh if that didn't hurt my feelings," he said. "If I didn't already know about you and your own special friend."

I just sat there. There was nothing I could do or say to improve it.

"And besides," he said, "one thing I've learned this year is that the grass is green everywhere."

He must have checked out of that place a few days later. Lydia down at the bank saw them come through town—Gerald and that woman, Ginny—in a foreign car. They gassed up at the Kum & Go and then came into the bank. Gerald went to Lydia's window and took half the money from our savings account while that woman, Ginny, sat in the chair by the door and flipped through a *Country Living* magazine while chewing on a straw. Then they walked over to Cunt Itchen and had lunch for an hour while the car stayed parked at the bank, even though you're not supposed to stay parked at the bank if you're no longer at the bank.

Barb took their order. That woman, Ginny, had a Reuben but with turkey instead. She called it a Rachel. When she ate, that woman, Ginny, wedged the straw in an ashtray like it was an actual cigarette even though everyone could see that it was not.

Gerald had a salad, no meat, no cheese, with dressing on the side.

32

The day I found out about them coming through here, I walked home early from my office and I waved to no one and I didn't care. I drank three Mike's on the front steps of my cottage on the go-around. I sang at the top of my lungs, hoping Doc and Huff would come out of Huff's house. *Seagram's Golden Wine Coolers! It's wet and it's dry! My, my, my, my!*

Over and over I sang it. Huff's house stayed dark.

I was in a state, the kind of state that drunk people get into: drunkenness. I'm sure people like you know what I'm talking about.

I don't remember doing it, but apparently I walked to the bowling alley and I threw some money at Cindy and I put on some bowling shoes and I started to throw. Cindy told me that I screamed at her to leave me alone when she told me she was closing. And so she turned off all the lights but the one on my lane and left me there alone.

I bowled and bowled and bowled, game after game after game. *That* I remember. I bowled my straight bowling, I bowled wild throws that landed in other lanes. I walked right down to the end of the lane, slipping and falling on my ass halfway there, and then crawling the rest of the way to where the pins were, and then I rolled the bowling ball all around them while on my belly until all the pins fell. Somewhere in there, near the end, I bowled a 300. It wasn't a true bowl, though. It will not be recorded in the newspaper. And, thankfully, no one was there to witness it but me.

Another house blew up that night. I heard the sirens coming from the other part of town as I stumbled back up the hill to the go-around, tripping on the cracks in the sidewalk I should have known were there, falling, skinning my knees, crawling at some points, losing my shirt somewhere along the way. I didn't care. I knew that Doc and Huff were at this latest blown-up house in their golf cart, scowling and scoffing and being smug, and the cops and the firemen were there, sharing their white spaceman suit, trying to scrub anhydrous ammonia out of people's kitchen sinks, out of people's skin, out of children's skin, out of their own.

If I had understood how they were doing it then, known the basic chemistry that makes lithium, anhydrous, and pseudoephedrine into a bomb that blows your roof off and a drug that blows your brains out, I would have done it to myself that night. I even thought about looking up how to do it on the Internet, but by the time I thought of it, I was already to my shabby little cottage on the go-around, and I didn't have the Internet there. And besides, all I really know is how to account for things. And even at that I am mostly a terrible failure.

It was so hot. Steaming. There were no birds chirping, no crickets. I opened another Mike's and I took it to the backyard, where I rolled off the heavy top of Gerald's hot tub. The water was green and there was a white scum floating on top. It smelled like human turds. I took off the rest of my clothes, including my bra and underwear, and I climbed up the stepstool naked with that Mike's in my hand and I descended into that cold, shit-smelling water and I stood there, naked, submerged from the waste down, boobs hanging out, my skinned knees stinging in that scummy water. I looked up at the stars and I chugged my drink.

I thought: *What will that granite headstone with my name on it do besides collect bird crap and snowdrifts? If I died tonight, will I have left no trace of me on this earth? Or will there be a little something left of me, a little patch of me, still holding on somewhere around here, like that bit of grass in a ditch the mower always misses because it's in such a tough corner, at such an odd angle, that most people in the world can't and won't ever reach it?*

I moved to the edge of the hot tub, and then I leaned that Mike's over the edge and offered it to the night. I suppose I was drunk enough to think that a shaggy dog might come around and lick delicious drops of malt liquor off the top of the bottle.

No dog came. No shaggy dog will ever come here to lick any bottle of mine, no matter what I rub on it.

V.

THIS IS BUSINESS

33

From their living room windows, their gas pumps at Kum & Go, their tables at Cunt Itchen; from the backs of their push lawn mowers and the tops of their riding ones; from their cars as they drove slowly by and from the sidewalk as they walked slowly by, the people of this town watched. They watched me walk from the go-around all the way down the hill to the high school. Doc and Huff watched as they passed me in their golf cart. Huff laughed and raised his drink to me. I wished for my coat but there was nothing my coat could do for me now. Every crack in the sidewalk had been there since I could remember. Every car in town was in the high school parking lot or waiting in line to get there.

The auditorium was packed front to back. The members of the school board—Howie Claus, Elmer Griggs from the golf course, Silvia Vontrauer, Dave Oppegaard, and, of course, Dieter—all sat behind a long table on the stage, each with a microphone. Near the front, directly before the stage, stood a lone microphone, around which sat all the Vo-Ag kids—Team Yoruba, minus Hope—in their FFA uniforms and colorful beaded belts. In Des Moines, the FFA State Competition was about to start. But here they were, trapped like the rest of us.

I sat down in an empty seat next to Mueller. He was halfway down the aisle, on the end, next to one of the last seats left. He had saved it for me. "You're the star," he said.

Dieter called the meeting to order with his characteristic lack of grace. "Uhhhh, here is the situation: the Vo-Ag teacher hasn't been to work in two weeks," he said.

Marlys Harmon from the bank, sitting behind me, said, "Of course he hasn't."

Ronald Clayton said, "Why aren't the police after him? Didn't he kidnap that little black-haired girl?"

Dieter sighed. "She is eighteen," he said. "She legally cannot be kidnapped."

"That doesn't seem right," Marlys Harmon whispered under her breath.

Dieter stared into his microphone as if there might be an answer of some kind inside it. There was not. He went on anyway. "As you may or may not be aware, no additional high school students have signed up for Vo-Ag next year. After this year's seniors graduate, there will only be two students in the class. That's not enough to justify a full-time Vo-Ag teacher, even if that person was to be the FFA adviser too."

There was a sound from the crowd, that sigh we do around here, but collective, from all of them at once. It was the saddest sigh I have ever heard. "Well," Ronald Clayton said, "what are you going to do." He was not asking a question.

"We'll be deciding what to do in the next few days," Dieter said.

Mueller raised his hand then, though he did not wait to be called on. "What are the options?" he asked.

Dieter fumbled around a bit and then started in on his chicken pecking, bobbing his head up and down. He looked to the other school board members to help him answer the question. Oppegaard and Elmer Griggs shrugged their shoulders. Howie Claus crossed his arms and frowned. Silvia Vontrauer held her piano scarf up to her face and cried a little.

Finally Dieter spoke. "Well, we may vote to run the classes out through the school year with a substitute teacher. We may cut the class and give students credit for an independent project to finish out the year. We may consolidate Vo-Ag and FFA with another school district, though that poses a busing problem. We can't host students from other school districts here. None of the school districts we've approached are, uh, happy with our classroom," he said, referring to the temporary construction trailer behind the school.

Behind me, Jessica Henderschott shouted, "Where *is* that Vo-Ag teacher anyway?"

"Yeah," Ronald Clayton shouted. "I've got a few things I'd like to say directly to his ugly face." Though of course he never would have.

"We don't know," Dieter said. "He has not made contact."

Howie Claus leaned toward his microphone then and said in a very amplified manner: "I bet Tandy Caide knows where he is."

Everyone turned to look at me, including the Vo-Ag kids.

"I bet Tandy knows where all the money is too!" Howie Claus went on.

"Do you?" Dieter asked me, into his microphone.

"Say no," Mueller whispered.

Missy was crying. Her mascara was running down her cheeks. It looked like someone had drawn lines on her face with a blue ball-point pen. Phil's head hung low as if all there was left to do was consider the nature of his crotch.

"I think the Vo-Ag teacher is in Minneapolis," I said.

"What?" Dieter said.

"Go to the microphone," Mueller whispered. I was not about to go to the microphone.

"Minneapolis," I said a little louder, "I think he is in Minneapolis, though I can't confirm that."

The faces of those Vo-Ag kids, individually and collectively, fell down.

"Has he tried to contact you?" Dieter asked.

Though it hurt me to say it, I did. "No."

"Good answer," Mueller whispered.

Dieter looked over to Howie Claus, as if to say, *See?* but Howie Claus looked back at him like there was more to be taken from me.

Dieter turned back to the microphone and closed his eyes. "Do you know where the missing money is?"

Mueller in my ear: "Say no."

"No." It was the truth.

"Do you know if the Vo-Ag teacher is with Hope?"

Mueller in my ear: "Tell the exact truth."

"No," I said.

"Do you know if he has run off with the money from the FFA account?"

Mueller in my ear: "You don't have to answer that."

"I don't have to answer that," I said. "If I did, no one in this room would ever come to me for tax services again."

Dieter looked to Howie as if to say, *See?* Behind me, I could hear the erratic breathing and snorting of Huff's laughter and him saying, "Oh, she is *just* like her father!" Then, from the same general area, I heard a scuffle. Huff had climbed atop his chair and was weaving back and forth. Doc was trying to pull him down. "Is it Hope's everlasting soul you're concerned about, Howie?" Huff cried. "Well, tell Jesus not to worry his pretty little head! She's a confirmed slut! They're both sluts!" Huff pointed his finger at me.

Doc couldn't get him down so Mueller ran back and pulled him down. "You can't trust sluts!" Huff screamed as Doc dragged him out. There was a feeling in the room, then, of defeat, like our whole town had been pinned to the mat. Or maybe it was just me. These feelings—you know, whose are whose? I cannot always tell.

"What about her mother? Why isn't her mother here?" Dieter asked.

The answer to that question was as long as the U.S. Tax Code. I summed it up into the shortest truth I could: "She's working."

"Well. The whereabouts of all the rest of them aren't the big deal here," Dieter said. "The Vo-Ag teacher has been fired already. We're really here to inform the community of that and to gather comments for next steps. Please note that the only comments we can officially accept are those that are addressed to us in front of a microphone."

In one motion—like they were all hanging on to the same rope the way the pioneers would do during a big blizzard—the Vo-Ag students stood up and moved toward the microphone. Phil set up an easel and Missy placed a poster-sized piece of cardboard onto it. They looked at one another for a moment and then Phil said, "We can't control who the school board hires to instruct us. Nor can we control who provides volunteer or financial support to us. What we can control is our money."

At that point, he pulled a checkbook out from his back pocket.

"This morning we went to First National. Even with the unfortunate events of the past month, we have, as of today..." He opened the checkbook and looked at the register and read the number: "$21,470.47."

I knew it to be true. It was congruent with my records. Someone in the back shouted, "Woooo!"

"Thank you," Phil said. "This money belongs to the FFA Chapter Fifty-Seven, a 501(c)3 organization. It sits outside of any school jurisdiction. So when we say 'we' have $21,470.47, we literally mean 'we.'" He spread his arms out as Hope had done at the regional competition. Around him, the other Vo-Ag kids moved closer together. They grabbed one another's hands.

"If you vote to eliminate vocational agriculture and Future Farmers of America both," Phil said, "we will use this money to throw a massive keg party."

Missy flipped the cardboard around, revealing a pie chart of how the funds would be allocated for the proposed keg party. They had figured it out: 48 percent of their budget—that is, about $10,500—had been allocated toward beer and marijuana equally. "That's five hundred twenty cases of Coors Light, and six and a half pounds of marijuana, though one pound of the marijuana will be used to pay for security detail performed by the Mason City chapter of the Hell's Angels," Phil said. He pointed to a dotted line that represented this.

"They have already agreed," Travis added.

Nine percent of their budget would go toward sanitation and cleanup, with the majority of that for porta potties, and some going to Boy Scout scholarships for the Decorah Boy Scouts in return for volunteer garbage duty the morning after, leaving 43 percent, or roughly $9,250, to hire a band.

"We're currently in contract talks with some of the original cast members of *Rent*," Travis said.

People began to look around at one another.

"It's a musical from New York City about AIDS," Travis said.

That really got everyone. A low buzz of questions and protest rose from the crowd. Mueller's face turned red and his back started to shake. Then he began to snort.

"It's far less than their usual asking fee, but none of them have performed for people like you before," Travis said.

No one said a word after that. The Vo-Ag kids stood before us, holding hands, unmoving.

Marlys Harmon whispered, "Can they do that?" Elmer Griggs looked to Dieter and appeared to mouth the same thing.

Dieter nodded into his microphone—the old pecking-chicken routine—and wiped his face with his hands. He looked lost. Then he looked at me as if my presence reminded him of how to work.

He asked, "Has it occurred to you that neither your FFA adviser nor your FFA secretary is around to write the check?"

"Yes," Phil said. "That has occurred to us. But there is a third person authorized to write our checks."

Well, certainly you know who that is.

Dieter looked at me with his mouth open and his eyebrow skin pulled into wrinkles in the center of his forehead. He looked like those 520 cases of Coors Light had suddenly dropped from the sky at my command.

He said, "Would you do that, Tandy?"

The line of Vo-Ag kids could have looked at me then, pleading somehow. But they didn't.

They didn't have to.

"Yes," I said from my seat.

Mueller in my ear: "Go up to the microphone." He gave me a little push. I didn't budge.

Howie Claus began to squirm in his seat. He was waving his hands around and sliding back and forth in his chair. "But, Tandy, really?" he asked. "Really? You would do such a thing, such an obviously terrible, obviously wrong thing?"

Everyone stared at me, as if everything that ever mattered to anyone hinged on my answer. As if I was the only one accountable, as if all the things we are supposed to do that are right or wrong, good or bad, in the world are all in my own rights and wrongs.

Mueller in my ear—"Go. To. The. Microphone."—and then he stood up and he yanked my arm and before I knew what I was doing I was walking down the aisle with him.

I have learned in my many years as both a businesswoman and a human being that the scariest things that happen to you—the defining things, the snapping-branch things—actually happen very quickly. They take up only seconds of your real life.

It is in your brain later that they happen slowly, and over and over again. When your best friend crawls through your bedroom window pregnant and cries in your lap. When you make love to someone you love for the very first time. When you see your husband with another woman. When you learn your father has driven off a bridge. When you walk up to the microphone to defend all that you are in the world, before the people who have raised you and known you all of your life, who also happen to be the customers who decide if you will continue to be clothed and fed.

These snapping-branch things get analyzed and reanalyzed and rehashed and replayed, like pivotal plays in football games watched on television, or grainy videos of crimes at convenience stores committed by desperate people upon other desperate people. These moments are played over so slowly. In times of distress or questioning they provide you answers. In times of extreme joy they anchor you to reality. In times of boredom or quiet they remind you that once upon a time you were very much alive.

I have spent hours replaying that moment at the microphone, but really, it was only seconds that I was there. Dieter saying to me, "Would you really? Would you sign their checks?" And me saying very loudly and clearly and directly into that microphone, "Yes, I would." And Dieter, truly stunned, saying, "But why, Tandy? Why?" And my reply coming from my mouth solid and straightforward, not so that I could protect the Vo-Ag teacher or Hope, and not so that the people of this town would think I was special, and not so that this town's local chapter of FFA would be spared for at least one more year, which was the consequence of my reply, but rather because it was the real truth about me, their very own little girl, their hometown girl, Tandy Caide, their very own certified public accountant.

I said, "Because it is my business."

34

Mueller whisked me out of the auditorium immediately and drove me away in his dirty little pickup. He was afraid of people harassing me all the way back to the go-around if I were on foot.

"No one would do that," I told him as he jammed the pickup into reverse and peeled out of the lot, but he said, "You're my CPA. You're a valuable business asset to me. I'm not taking any chances."

He drove fast, and on side roads. He whipped corners on two wheels and the force slammed my body against the truck's door, which popped open once, and for a moment I was suspended over the streets of this town flying faster than I could walk or run, the road whizzing by underneath me, and I screamed, and Mueller reached over and pulled me back in, and then I was laughing, my head on the dash, laughing so hard tears dripped onto my shoes.

We rounded Old Airport Road and then turned onto Cherry Lane, then up the little hill to the driveway to Mueller's big white house with the big wraparound Bruce Willis porch.

My hands were numb. I told Mueller this, and he said it was stress. It happened to him all the time in the 1980s.

As we walked up to the house, me shaking my hands, I realized that in all my years of knowing Mueller, all my years of doing his payroll and taxes and even an audit once, which resulted in a discrepancy that came to within $2,000 so we were both safe, and all those years of walking by the house in early mornings and late evenings, going over things in my head, and even the recent times when I was out there with the Vo-Ag teacher, I had never once been inside. I had never even stood on that porch, which had somehow come to be more than a porch to me.

There I was, stepping onto Mueller's porch.

The paint on the steps and floorboards was chipped. They creaked when I walked on them. The railings had different ridges on them and different widths, not exactly matching but sort of similar in a pleasing way. It looked like Mueller had hewn them himself. There was a bend in the porch that was rounded, not an angle. It was a half-circle splayed out in front of my feet, equal in all directions.

It was dusk. The sun was real low. The sky was orange and purple. Before us was the road, and just beyond it the western field where Mueller had just planted beans. The soil was dark and black like a giant lake of dirt. Beyond it, a chain of abandoned railroad cars, all faded oranges and greens, and they lay like a necklace. There was a breeze. Mueller lit some citronella candles to keep the mosquitos away. The smell was sharp, like lime and wax and spice.

Mueller brought me a cold Coors Light. I gulped it and the fizz tingled my nose. He unfolded some folding chairs and set them at the porch's bend so we could survey what lay before us.

So this is what Bruce Willis would have seen, I thought. *Not too shabby.*

Mueller told me later that my shoulders fell down a little, that I looked relaxed for the first time in months. And I do remember the feeling, I suppose, of letting down some. I mean, really, sitting on a farm porch with a man I had known all of my life, whose net worth was significant, a net worth I was at least tangentially a part of building, drinking his beer? You would have felt like things were going to be okay too.

I let out a big sigh. "Jesus Christ," I said to Mueller.

"Exactly," he said.

I gulped some more of my beer, and then I started laughing, and together we laughed for a long time. Mueller said, "You sure got a way about you, Tandy Caide."

I asked him to clarify and he said, "Just the way you are. The way you think. Your father, he wasn't as cut-and-dry as you. You're a straight arrow."

I suddenly got very curious. No one had ever talked about my father in great detail to me. There was a buildup in the back of my throat, like something was going to poke out of it. "I don't understand," I said.

Mueller tipped his lawn chair back on two legs. "Oh, you know," he said. "Your dad was always twisted up about something. Everything was a sign of disaster. Even the good things that happened to him meant disaster, because to him it meant that he was going to get something twice as bad later."

This disappointed me. I already knew it.

"But you," he said. "You're solid. You're what my mother would have called 'righteous.' It's not the arrogant kind of righteous. It's more like you're doing the right thing, and you know you're doing the right thing, and you really don't care who else knows it either."

I didn't know what to say after that, because I could not believe someone could be so completely wrong about me. Should I have contradicted him? Should I have smiled and shook his hand, the way that's good for business? Should I have rubbed my foot along the muscle of his calf? What does a businesswoman do when someone mistakes her for something greater than she really is? It seemed irrational to accept his incorrect perception of me. It seemed irrational to not.

I chugged my beer, and then I looked at it. The "Coors" part was red and in cursive. Behind it was a mountain range. Coors comes from Colorado. All I knew of Colorado was from *Mork and Mindy*. Mindy drove a Jeep and taught music. Mork picked daisies and ate them and wore rainbow-colored suspenders.

"Have you ever been to Colorado?" I asked.

"No," he said.

"We are alike in that way," I said. "I too have never been to Colorado."

He would not let up. "All I'm saying is that you're competent. You seem to know that you're doing the right thing," Mueller said.

"But I'm not always doing the right thing," I told him. My voice came out sounding like it was wrapped in tinfoil. "Certainly you're aware of my relationship with the vocational agriculture teacher."

Mueller nodded. "I don't think you should get your undies in a bunch about that. Everyone fucks a fool at least once in their life."

It's strange how other people's wrongdoings can make you feel better about your own. It doesn't excuse your wrongdoings. I know that. I'm not a fool. I'm also not foolish enough to ask my biggest client about all the various fools he's fucked in his life, no matter how much I wonder if I know any of those fools personally.

"What I mean is, you just don't let anyone get to you. You just do your thing, and then you let others do their thing. And you don't take to others judging you. You just let their judgments lie. I admire this quality in you," Mueller said.

"Thank you," I said. It was all I could think to say.

He told a story about me then, one I will never forget: "Once, when you were a little girl, maybe you were seven or eight, I came to the office. Your dad was passed out on the couch in the lobby. He had been out drinking all night with Huff. It was a bad time; it was the early eighties, and things were bad. The kind of bad that makes your hands go numb.

"Your dad and Huff, they were very busy with some shitty-ass business, bankruptcies and suicides and fathers leaving their families and such. I myself was going under, and if my own father hadn't died and left me an additional one hundred fifty acres, I would have been getting one of those visits myself.

"Tweedle Dead and Tweedle Deader we called your dad and Huff, down at the co-op. It wasn't about them personally; it was just their jobs.

"I was trying to wake your old man there on that little green love seat in your lobby, to tell him that my own old man had passed and that I had these acres coming to me. You came out from that little back room and said, 'Come with me.' You sat me down in the chair in front of his desk. You were wearing these messed-up pigtails, one was way higher on your head than the other one. I could tell you had made those pigtails yourself. No one helped you. And you were wearing a puffy brown winter coat, a boy's coat, probably from the thrift store.

"You opened up his desk drawer and you said, 'Care for a smoke?' and you held a pack of cigarettes out to me."

I didn't remember any of this, but it was interesting to me. It could have been me. It sounded like me.

"I said, 'No thanks.' And you said, 'He'll be with you in a moment.' And then you left. Well, I sat there for a while, and when he didn't show, I got up and I looked out to the lobby. There, I saw you. You were holding a glass of water to his lips while he drank it."

Mueller stopped then. "That's what I'm talking about," he said.

"I didn't know any better," I said.

"But you would do the same thing today. You would. That quality is still in you."

"I wouldn't call that anything special," I said. "I would just call that customer service."

Mueller shook his head. "No. No. It's a way of caring about people. I don't know where it comes from..." He trailed off for a little bit, thinking, and then he picked it up again. "Maybe it comes from being around losers all the time. Maybe when people like you grow up, you become the kind who just accept the losing nature in everyone. It's not defeat, really, or negativity; it's just, I don't know, a solidness, I guess, a stand-up-straightness. A way of loving—you know—from the ground up."

I let him have the last word then, partly because what he was saying made me uncomfortable, I can admit that, but mostly because I couldn't argue it. When you boil it down, really it's just his perception. And perceptions aren't true. They change all the time. You can't count on them. And really, as I think about it now, all this talk about the way I love, it probably had nothing to do with me anyway.

When the mosquitos got too bad, Mueller suggested we go inside and watch a little television. As my husband was gone and the Vo-Ag teacher was gone and I was on my second beer and I had never been in the house of my biggest client, I said yes.

The sink was filled with dirty dishes. The kitchen table was covered with oily rags and parts from various machines, including what appeared to be the disembodied handlebars of a motorcycle. The dining room had a plow attachment for a pickup truck where a dining room table should have been. In the living room there was a love seat with an Iowa Hawkeye blanket draped over it, just like in every other living room I'd ever been in. And there was a coffee table covered with dirty bowls crusted with Cheerios.

There was a very nice La-Z-Boy, though, I'll give him that. It's the best one Dean Schletter sells down at the furniture store, and you have to special order it. It has beverage holders in both arms, and a little recessed box in the right arm where you put your remote control so you never lose it in the cushions. Mueller sat in that chair, pulled the lever so that his feet popped up, and almost immediately began snoring.

My father always said those kinds of chairs were for trust-fund dickheads or the frivolous wives of dumb people.

It was a nice chair, that's all. It was a very nice chair.

I didn't know what to do so I left.

35

Of course I wonder if he has ever regretted falling asleep that night, just as I wonder if he regrets that he has never married, and if he has plans to marry, and, if he does have plans to marry, if he has someone particular in mind.

That night I thought about what he had said about my righteousness and the way it relates to the special way I love. And as I walked down Old Railroad Road, with the air crisp but mild and the black dirt smelling deep and wet and rich, well, for a few minutes I believed these things he had said about me were possible.

Of course, I had also consumed two Coors Lights. As you probably know, that's just enough to make you believe the good things people say about you. But the more I walked, and the more I thought about it, the more I knew these things he had said were not true.

The evidence of this was clear. For instance, I carry around in my chest the things that people say about me, and for a long time too. And though I didn't want to, I felt in my heart that the Vo-Ag teacher—though certainly a fool—was not exactly a mistake.

Then, as I walked, I began to think that maybe what Mueller said about me was true in some ways and not true in others. Clearly what I present to people like Mueller, to my clients in this town, and even to other powerful people is an image of a person who really has it together. That's a good thing for a businesswoman to demonstrate—the appearance from the outside that you are a decent person. You know it's working when the clients you want to think nice things about you actually do.

So isn't it a truth, of sorts, when someone like Mueller thinks nice things about someone like me?

Yes, I decided. It is. But it is a truth I created. So how "true" can that really be?

But then again, Mueller is different. I didn't exactly create that truth for Mueller. Mueller has known me since before I knew myself.

Then I got angry. I got angry that the rest of them didn't know me as well as Mueller did. Why does Mueller think these nice things about me, but Huff and Doc and Barbie and Gerald and the school board and other people don't?

Especially Doc and Huff, who were most certainly looking out their windows with binoculars at that very moment, scheming to ruin me some more. They were the men who had pledged to take care of me, and they had never seen the things in me that Mueller had seen. Or at least they had never cared to mention them to me directly. Wouldn't someone who had pledged to take care of you mention such things to you directly at least once?

I very quickly began to second-guess my goodness. I thought that perhaps it is a detriment for a person to be righteous within herself and nonjudgmental with others, to be someone who goes about her business like a happy little elf, like one of the dwarfs in Snow White, "Worky" dwarf or something, doing things for all the other dwarfs and taking care of their tiny dwarf problems and protecting them from their dumb dwarf actions.

That made me sad.

Then I wondered if I could ever think of myself in that good way that Mueller thinks of me, with the perception that loving in a way that is both righteous and nonjudgmental comes from a special person.

I *wanted* to think of myself in that way.

Then I thought: Honestly, if I had that perception of myself, wouldn't that mean I was actually *not* that kind of person? Wouldn't having that idea of myself negate the whole effect, because what kind of righteous-yet-nonjudgmental person actually believes in his or her own specialness? It has always been my experience that anyone who goes about advertising his or her own special way of loving is most certainly a very special asshole.

And then I thought, in light of all the events that had come to fruition by that point of the year, that perhaps it *is* possible to both feel good about yourself and still be a righteous and nonjudgmental person. I thought that perhaps the ability to do this is what keeps people keeping on in their life, despite life's overwhelming burdens. And maybe this *is* something special about me. And so I was back to believing that what Mueller said could be partially true, and so both true and not true. And then, as it could be partially true and not true, and as my burdens were currently overwhelming, I decided to believe Mueller. And I decided to believe all the good things the Vo-Ag teacher had said to me too, and all the things I had felt with him. I decided to believe it all.

And then a good feeling came into my heart, and I could smell the new green grasses and the sage in the ditches. I felt lifted up, like maybe how a hot-air balloon feels when it gets filled with all that warm and energetic air. I started running, and I felt like I was a good runner, even though this was only the second time I had run since puberty. I felt light and bouncy, as if I had been flying like a deer down Old Airport Road all of my life. Right at the bend, it smelled like cat pee. And as Mueller had already treated that field with anhydrous in October, a late spring evening at that exact field was the exact wrong time to smell cat pee.

36

Down the road, stretched as far as I could see in the darkness, were cars and trucks I didn't recognize, with idling engines and no lights. They were all empty. I walked along them for a while, looking into them, until a face peered at me from the back of a station wagon. It was a little girl, about six years old. Her strawberry-colored hair was cropped short like a boy's, but she had the chubby cheeks and heart-shaped mouth of a girl.

I tapped on the window, just to ask her if she needed any help.

She screamed so high it vibrated my eardrums. I nearly peed my pants. It's a figure of speech some people use, I know that, but I am not using it in that way. When she screamed, a little trickle of pee came out of me.

She scrambled to the other side of the car, opened the door, and took off running across Mueller's eastern field.

She ran fast, way faster than me. One of her shoes flew off in the dirt and still she kept running, running as if she had not dropped her shoe, running as if I were trying to hurt her.

She ran toward two points of light off in the distance, across that great dark expanse of dirt. There was a point of light to the right of her, out there where I knew the sod house was squatting, half completed, and there was a point of light to the left of her, out there where Mueller kept a tank of anhydrous.

She veered right, and I veered right, and we both ran right up to a long line of people waiting to get into the incomplete sod house.

I was confused. The house wasn't even done, and it was almost midnight. What could they possibly be doing? Some wore stocking caps pulled down low so their eyes were almost covered. Some wore giant tinted work goggles. Some wore face masks. I didn't recognize any of them. They were zombies, or aliens from another planet, trying to fit in by hiding themselves in our Earth clothes. Each had a small propane tank between his or her legs, the kind that goes with a gas grill. Each stared at me and did not move.

The little blond girl hid behind a man in a hooded sweatshirt and dark sunglasses. He had tied the hood tight around his head. "You need to wait in line like everyone else," he said.

"I helped build this sod house," I said. "And this is my client's land. I don't have to wait."

Another man stepped forward. He was wearing dark ski goggles and a stocking cap. There were scabs all around his mouth. He said in a raspy voice, "Are you Tandy Caide? The CPA?"

"Of course I am," I said. "Who are you?"

He turned to the rest of the line and said, "It's Tandy! It's Tandy!" And all along the line the people picked up their empty propane tanks and ran.

I walked right up into the waist-high, U-shaped bunker that the sod house had progressed into. There was Hope with her massive belly, sitting behind a card table. Before her: a metal cashbox, open, filled with cash, and a Red Wing shoe box filled with cold medicine. Behind her: a red suitcase, the kind with wheels, on its side and open and filled with cash. Also behind her: Clive, pointing a gun at me.

Hope stood up. She calmly shut the cashbox. She picked it up with its little metal handle, and she turned around and closed the suitcase and grabbed that handle. She left the shoe box filled with cold medicine. She walked around me with the cashbox and the suitcase, without looking at me or touching me. Then she took off running.

Just beyond the sod house among the corn seedlings, she tripped and fell to her hands and knees. She grabbed the suitcase and cashbox again, but the suitcase flew open, and as she broke into a run again, bundles of twenties dropped behind her like a trail of bread crumbs.

I started to go after her, but Clive said, "That money's not yours, Tandy."

He was not breathing hard. He was not wild-eyed. He was not shaking. He was not scratching at himself. He was not doing anything out of the ordinary at all. He stood before me as if we were at my office and he was telling me about his day and his dreams, except he was pointing a gun at me.

It is so clear in my mind now, so calm and reasonable. I said, "What are you doing?"

He said, "I deserve something."

I said, "No, you don't. Nobody does."

He said, "Yes, I do."

Then he shot me.

I woke up flat on my back on the ground. My side burned just below my rib cage, like someone had stuck me there with a hot poker. The walls of the sod house were collapsing around me and onto me.

Then: the sound of footsteps running away, a car engine firing, tires screeching.

Silence. I was alone. Above me: a billion stars. Around me: a billion micro-things in the sod, hundreds of billions of micro-things teeming with life, living and breathing and coming into me. I did not have my coat with me but I wasn't cold. I was—how can I describe this to you?—I was peaceful. I felt more peaceful than I have in all of my life.

I felt close to them—my mother and my father. My father closest, but my mother too, even though I had never known her. I felt her there with me. I felt them under me, above me, all around me.

I had hit my deer. It had poked me in the rib cage with one of its antlers. And though it may surprise you, I was not afraid. I was ready.

I waited for them. For my mother so that I could finally look at her face, and my father so that I could tell him I was sorry for all that I had done wrong to him and to myself and to others. I waited for them to come and carry me to the river.

37

I woke up in the cab of Mueller's truck with my cheek pressed to the window. The sun was just coming up over the horizon. The window was dirty and the view blurry, fading to white like a photo that's gotten wet and then dried out. I was sad. Or maybe a better word would be "disappointed."

Judy Skody's face was hovering over mine. "Bad aim," she said. "It didn't screw with your insides so Doc just picked out the bullet and sewed you up. You'll be sore and you'll have a scar, but otherwise you'll be fine. Good thing too. It could have got your spine."

I laughed. Judy asked what was so funny. I told her I was pleased someone could confirm the existence of my spine.

I woke up with Mueller standing by my bed with his hat in his hands saying, "That was some excitement, Tandy Caide. No one's ever been shot on my property before."

"I live to serve," I said.

That made him laugh. He laughed so hard he coughed, and his back shook, and he had to wipe tears from his eyes. It is always good to make your biggest client laugh. My father taught me that. It was one good thing he taught me.

"The money!" I said, remembering all that bundled cash pouring out of that red suitcase on wheels.

"She came to the hospital with a bundle of twenties in the waistband of her sweatpants," Mueller said. "The rest of them picked the fields clean. They even took all of that cold medicine. Believe me, I checked."

Later, I woke up to her screaming, and Judy Skody giving me some pills in a little cup, saying, "It's too early, but Doc is going to do it anyway because her water broke and she's already too far gone to get anywhere else."

And just like that, in the very room next to mine, Faith Madeline came into this world. Faith Madeline: someone Bruce Willis could love. I'd say that this is how things happen around here, but I'm not dumb. This is how things happen everywhere. Maybe most mothers don't start labor while running through a recently planted cornfield covered in thousands of dollars from selling stolen anhydrous ammonia inside a half-built sod house. Maybe most mothers don't walk three miles through a dead town while in labor, with their waters breaking somewhere between the bowling alley and the burned-out shell of a library.

But certainly the world's babies come in other unbelievable ways. Come hell or high water, they come. Over hill, over dale, they come. Over the river and through the woods, they come. You cannot stop them. Even if you tried, you cannot stop the babies from coming. And for this, Hope should know that she bears no responsibility, only so much as to feel a sense of pride, or a sense of accomplishment, because a baby was ready to come and she was there to push the baby through.

I woke up to Doc sitting next to my bed. He rubbed his face with his hand, just like my father would have done. He sighed. He said, "Faith is an ambitious name for that one, Candy Cane. But then again, I've seen sicker ones than her live."

Doc and Judy had packed Faith Maddie's tiny body into a special plastic see-through egg on wheels and rolled her into a helicopter that flew her to La Crosse.

I woke up and it was dark. Doc was still sitting next to my bed, smoking a cigarette. Huff was sitting on the other side, drinking Wild Turkey from that mallard glass. Judy Skody came in and said they couldn't smoke or drink in the hospital, and they of all people should know that. Doc told her to go fuck herself, so Judy said, "After a night like this one, I'm looking forward to it. I'll see you tomorrow."

I woke up and it was light outside. Doc and Huff were both asleep in their chairs on either side of my bed, their chins on their chests and their hands in their laps.

I woke up and they were watching the Cubs lose to the Expos on my hospital television. Barb and Hope appeared in the doorway to my room. Barb was in her Cunt Itchen uniform. Hope was in her hospital gown and that pair of ratty black sweatpants. Despite living within five miles of each other since Hope was a baby herself, it was the first non-Christmas occasion we were all in the same room together. Barb said, "Do any of you want to drive up to La Crosse to see the baby?"

And though it seemed impossible that we would look to Hope for her approval on any matters whatsoever, we did. We all looked to Hope, who looked down at the floor and said, "I would."

And what did we do?

We all said, "Yes! Yes! We would love to!" And we all got in cars, Barb and Hope in Barb's little Pontiac Sunfire, Doc and Huff and I in the Tempo, and we drove in a line up to La Crosse.

In the Tempo, Doc smoked, Huff drank, and I spread out across the backseat so my bandage wouldn't pucker. I watched the bright yellow sun disappear and reappear behind the white-blue clouds, and I thought about how wonderful the whole world was. My family was all together and we were going to visit a baby.

38

The Franciscan Skemp hospital in La Crosse merged with the Mayo Clinic in 1995. Here is what it says about them on the Internet: "Based on our Christian heritage and our belief in human dignity, Franciscan Skemp commits to putting the needs of our patients first and to collaborate in improving the health of individuals and the communities we serve."

Only the best for Faith Maddie.

We sat in the lobby. There were hundreds of magazines spread around the tables, nice ones about decorating and architecture and fancy ways to paint old things. There was a basket filled with toys and books for children. There was a giant tropical fish tank with fish of all different colors and a fake volcano that shot up bubbles. There was even a lionfish, the striped kind with the crazy fins, prowling through the tank.

There was a coffee shop where you could buy the kind of coffee I know people like you are used to, and shiny balloons with messages on them, and teddy bears with hearts stitched on their fur near the area of their bodies where their hearts would be if teddy bears had hearts.

I kept wishing I had a camera so I could record it all for Faith Maddie.

A doctor with a big mustache came out and said to Hope: "She's small but everything is there. We are helping her breathe." Then the doctor looked around at all of us and asked, "Who are you?"

Barb said, "I am her grandmother." Doc said, "I am her doctor." Huff said, "I am her great-grandfather and her lawyer," and then I didn't quite know what to say so I settled on the thing I knew to be the most true. I said, "I am her CPA."

The doctor said, "Well, she's covered then. No worries about this one."

She was in a glass room, inside a glass box. She was wearing no diaper, just a cotton ball where a diaper should be, but she was wearing a little pink cap.

She was splayed out on her back and she looked like a baby piglet, pink but with long spindly and wrinkly limbs. And she had a flat and round face, with a tiny turned-up nose, and there were tubes in her nose that went out to a plastic bone that covered the bottom part of her face, and there was also a tube at her mouth. And there was a machine that tracked her weight. It said she weighed 3.7 pounds.

I thought about Doc's words, how Faith was an ambitious name.

Then she opened her eyes and looked right at me! And it was like opening your own eyes from a bad dream and looking straight into the eyes of someone saying it will be okay! A sound came out of my mouth—not even a word—just a sound. She was so beautiful! How do I even tell you this? I can't. I can't. These things, they are impossible to tell. You can only live them. Good luck to you.

We went back to the lobby and the doctor said, "You are lucky with this one. Some of these babies are missing parts of their limbs, or they are born with their intestines on the outside of their bodies."

Huff fell down then, and Doc helped him up. The doctor called for a wheelchair and they put Huff in it.

Huff said to Doc, "I don't like it here."

The doctor said, "I think you should stick around."

Doc said, "He has a condition," and then Doc wheeled Huff away.

"The condition is drunkenness," Barb said to the doctor.

"Yup," said the doctor.

I went downstairs and bought one of those balloons, pink and shiny, and one of those teddy bears with hearts, and one of those fancy coffees that come with whipped cream and chocolate shavings. The coffee was too sweet. I gave it to Hope. She drank the whole thing and thought it was delicious. She asked where Huff was and we told her, and she shrugged and read a magazine that came from Minneapolis that told her of the fifty best restaurants to eat in when she got there.

According to the Mayo Clinic website: "The Child Advocate Team is a multidisciplinary committee which meets quarterly or as needed to review policy and procedures for mandatory child abuse and neglect reporting."

One of the women had a clipboard and a soft voice; she was a social worker. She took us to a private room that was the idea of a living room.

Another woman came in. She was round and had shorter hair. She was a child advocacy specialist. Then another woman came in. She had a long braid and she was wearing a police uniform.

"Is this your signature?" the round woman asked Hope, pointing right to the spot on a clipboard where it was clear to all of us that Doc's shaky hand had written Hope's name.

Hope said, "Yup."

The three women looked at one another, and then the round woman and the policewoman left.

Then the woman with the soft voice and clipboard said, "I need to ask you, Hope: Can you provide this child with a good home?"

Hope was quiet. Then she took a deep breath and looked right into the face of the soft-voiced woman and said no.

It was an act of love. Do you understand this? It was an act of love far greater than most you could perform.

The soft-voiced woman checked a box on the paper on her clipboard, and then turned to Barb and said, "Can you?"

"I can't say for certain the home will be 'good,'" Barbie said.

"She means yes," I said very quickly.

"Of course I do!" Barb said.

The soft-voiced woman checked another box. And that is how we do things around here.

When Barb and Hope and I drove back to our town from the Mayo Clinic in La Crosse, no one said much, though Hope did ask, "When will she be able to wear clothes?"

Barb said, "I don't know, I've never seen ones that small." And Hope asked, "Can we call when we get home to check on her?" and Barb said, "Yup."

The two of them dropped me off at the cottage on the go-around. The Tempo and the golf cart were both in Doc and Huff's driveway. All was in order.

I went inside and took off my shirt and took off the bandage on my belly and I stared at the place where Clive had shot me.

It was a little red tear in my side, a little frown with three stiches in it.

It reminded me of Gerald's neck wound from the mathematical compass, of Faith Maddie's mouth minus the tubes and things.

I popped one of the happy pills Judy Skody had given me and I popped open a Mike's and I sat on my bed and I let the wound breathe.

39

There are special things about these babies. The woman with the soft voice told Barbie and I all about it.

When she spoke, the words floated out in white letters and hovered in the air in front of her mouth and then scrolled down slowly so that each word burned permanently into my brain.

These babies are very fussy.

They are uncomfortable in their bodies.

They have loud, piercing cries.

They are irritable.

They do not tolerate a lot of touch and light.

They tend toward excessive moodiness.

As they grow, these babies might have a hard time expressing themselves verbally.

They may have unprovoked rage.

They may act out.

These babies need calm environments.

They need caregivers attentive to their body language.

They need consistency and routine.

There are no longitudinal studies.

Each baby is different.

There is no way to know anything for sure except to live with her and watch and do what you can.

Now I send a message to Faith Maddie with my mind whenever I think of it. I say: *I too have a hard time expressing myself, Faith Maddie, but I will talk to you as best and as often as I can. It is hard to express oneself, Faith Maddie, but I have learned that the more you do it, the easier it becomes.*

I was there with her at the end of June, on her first night home from the hospital, out at Barb's farm with Hope and Barb. Even though I knew in my head they were mother and daughter, I had never actually seen it, never felt it in my heart. They leaned over the baby and laughed together. They moved about the kitchen helping each other do things. Barbie told stories to Hope about what she was like when she was a baby, and Hope hung on every word. They sat on the couch next to each other with their shoulders touching, staring at Faith Maddie, and at one point, Hope even laid her head on Barbie's shoulder, and Barbie laid her head over Hope's head, and I thought my heart would explode.

Barbie had done it. Even though she had never had one, she had become a mother. And finally I was there to see it and to be a part of it. Finally I was sitting in a room with Barbie and her baby, with my sister and her daughter.

And every time Barbie's baby's baby—that tiny Faith Maddie—moved or made a noise, we all jumped up to check her spunky yet innocent and completely and utterly precious little body. And when she wouldn't stop crying, Barbie picked her up and put her in my arms and I held her, and she breathed and grew quiet, and it was such a tremendous privilege to get to do that. I thank whoever made that possible: God, the universe, the Vo-Ag teacher, Clive, Huff, Doc, Hope, Barbie, whoever and everyone and all of you, I thank you.

VI.
Faith

40

Right before high school graduation, Huff drove his golf cart on County Road 8 out to the bridge over Kennicott Creek where my father had hit his deer more than seventeen years earlier.

Then Huff drove right off it.

This time I got there before Doc, and Vern and Dusty let me identify the body. He was gray and his lips were thin and he was small, so much smaller than he was in my head, but it was him.

When Doc came and insisted that he too identify the body, I stepped aside. I was present as he sat next to Huff's body and wept. And I was present when he stood up after and said, "I am ready now."

And I was present with Doc as he sat on the steps of my cottage on the go-around all night long. He held my hand and smoked. "He finally hit his deer," he kept saying. I was present to hear it.

In the morning, we called Barbie.

She said, "All right, then," and hung up the phone.

That doesn't have to make sense to you but I hope that it does.

A few days later we buried him out at the cemetery in the plot on the other side of my father, so that the headstones go like this: LESLEY HUFF, ROBERT CAIDE, TANDY CAIDE. It was just me and Doc and Gary and Mueller and the mortician, Buddy Kleinfeld, present. How ironic for a "people" person to have so few actual people at his funeral. Huff would have laughed with glee.

Gary sobbed the whole time. "Please make sure that more people come to mine, Tandy!" he said to me between sobs. And though I could promise no such thing, I said, "I will."

My stone looked nice, missing an end date like that.

Barbie and Hope were not in attendance. Barbie had to work and Hope had to be home with Faith Maddie, who was too little to leave the house.

Howie Claus did not officiate. We did not ask him to.

"That's what he would have wanted," Barbie said later when we sat in her booth at Cunt Itchen. "Nothing."

Neither Doc nor I could argue with her. Or would. And for not arguing, she put a hand on both our shoulders and kissed each of us on the tops of our heads.

She was thin and her eyes were sunken into her face. Faith Maddie was a terrible sleeper, and Barbie was afraid always that she would not live through the night.

But she did. Every night, Faith Maddie lived.

And there was something new in Barbie too. Even though she was tired, a light that had not been there before shone on her face when she looked at those of us around her. I could speculate that the death of Huff was good for her. And I will.

But Hope—a light had gone out in her. Perhaps it was because of the difficulty of the baby. Perhaps it was because all the teachers had voted against allowing her to give the valedictorian speech. She said she didn't feel bad about it, but none of us believed her.

It didn't feel right to go to commencement. Instead I sat out at the farm with Barbie and Hope and Faith Maddie. We ate one of those ice-cream cakes from Dairy Queen—the Oreo one—to celebrate. Later, Cindy down at the bowling alley told me that Travis from Vo-Ag and FFA gave the speech instead.

The title of the speech was "There Is No Free Lunch in the Free World."

41

All summer, instead of doing my summer bowling, I skipped lunch so I could close up my office at 4:30 and walk out to Barbie's farm in time to give Faith Maddie her 5:30 bottle.

I had to walk fast because it was five miles. And the heat was oppressive. June was bad and then July got worse, blindingly sunny and sticky and smelly. My blouses stuck to me in hot wet sheets. I felt like a mummy in a Scooby-Doo cartoon.

Finally I couldn't stand it anymore. On Hope's recommendation I bought several cotton T-shirts with V-shaped necks off eBay, all in different colors—flashy ones, hot pink and deep purple and a bright sunshiny yellow, Doris Mavin colors. Hope recommended V-necks because they are cooler, and also more attractive for bottom-heavy women.

I can tell you from experience that they are cooler, but I cannot say for certain if they make you more attractive. I have yet to ask anyone specifically about this, and unfortunately no one has yet said anything to me to confirm it.

I bought the V-neck T-shirts from another tall woman, named comeonirene. She had recently had a breast augmentation and so her shirts, though long enough, no longer fit her in the chest. As I have not had my breasts augmented and have no plans to do so, the shirts fit me perfectly. And as they were all used, I did not have to worry about them shrinking.

I also bought on eBay something called a sports bra.

I don't participate in any sports, so I would never have known to buy a sports bra, but again, Hope recommended it, especially after I showed her and Barbie the rash that had developed under my breasts where my bra had rubbed against my sweaty skin.

Apparently it is common practice for women who don't play sports to wear sports bras. Maybe even you do this. Barbie even wears one when she gardens.

Like the big black sleeping bag of a coat I wore all winter, this sports bra and these cotton V-neck T-shirts have greatly improved my life. I still wear my same pants, as I must always remain professional, even if I am walking somewhere after work on my own personal time. But no one can see my bra. And Hope told me if I wore some jewelry, I would "dress up" the T-shirt so that it would approach professional business attire. I ordered a necklace off of eBay for just this purpose. It says *FAITH* in silver cursive letters, all in one piece, on a silver chain that is just the right length so that the name sits on my skin just below my clavicle, framed by the V of my T-shirts.

I wear this necklace every day.

There was a baby shower right before the Fourth of July.

This is a special kind of party where the friends and family of a baby bring gifts they think the baby might need. You probably already know all about these events, but I had never been to one. I can tell you that from now on I am going to try to get invited to as many as I can.

The Vo-Ag kids organized it and they all came. The boys brought a little John Deere wagon they had pitched in to pay for, and the girls brought outfits they had picked out from Walmart. Each outfit came with its own baby socks. The Vo-Ag kids had invited Mueller and so he came too, though he only stood in the corner of the kitchen and drank a beer while Phil talked to him about the sod house. He looked at Faith Maddie from a long distance and said, "Looks good."

He brought one of those fancy electric baby swings, the kind that has several speeds and a seat that changes positions as the baby grows. He got it at Sears over in Cedar Falls. It would be hard to take back, he said, but if it didn't work out for any reason, he would.

Faith Maddie hates it but we still have high hopes.

Doc came too, driving Huff's Tempo. He did not bring anything. He sat on the couch and held Faith Maddie while his back shook, and the rest of us tried to not pay too much attention. He left early, but before he left he asked every single Vo-Ag kid his or her name, and then he told them what the weather was like on the day that he delivered them. He patted everyone's hand, including my own. It felt nice.

I brought Faith Maddie a Series EE savings bond. In about twelve years it will be worth $1,000.

Then it got even hotter. For weeks it was that muggy hot, the kind that feels like you're wrapped inside an electric blanket from the time you wake up, and things go downhill from there. By midafternoon you're sitting in your office with your pants at your ankles and a fan between your legs.

One evening, after we had all eaten a bowl of ice cream with strawberries out on the lawn, Barbie and Hope and I talked about going to the county fair. I wanted to take Faith Maddie. "She won't even remember it," Barbie said. But even if she cried in the car on the way there, I knew it would excite Faith Maddie once she got there—to see all those colors, to watch all those moving parts, to hear all that music. Plus, I had just purchased one of those devices that allows you to wear a baby on your chest. On a video I watched online, the baby's legs are free to wiggle around with excitement. I wanted Faith Maddie to do this.

Barbie said okay, but she wanted to go in the morning, before it got too hot.

"You love the fair," Barbie said to Hope. "Remember?"

Hope did not remember. Hope had not left the farm since she had signed the papers at the Mayo Clinic.

When I returned to Barbie's in the morning, Barbie was rocking in a chair with her feet drawn up around her and tears streaking down her red blotchy cheeks. Faith Maddie was rocking in her fancy swing, cheeks blotchy red too, wailing at the top of her lungs.

Hope was gone. Some of her clothes and her backpack were gone. And something else was gone. How can I describe it? There was a hole somewhere in the middle of the house. She took something with her we couldn't see. She would have walked at least a mile through corn nearly double the height of her head, but I know she was not afraid. She is the corn's own children. It's one of the things she could trust. The corn had done a very good job hiding her for eighteen years.

The rooms have gotten stuffy. Breathing is more difficult now that she is gone, and I have come to believe that it will be difficult for many more years.

When you meet her, say hello from me.

You will know her when you see her.

42

Before the senior Vo-Ag students left for college, they went out to Mueller's, dug around in the tall corn until they found that muddy hole in the ground, and in just three days they built that sod up into a house. The FFA "Living to Serve" judges had said it couldn't be done, but they were wrong. The sod house stood up, and with some two-by-fours Mueller donated to help reinforce the walls from the inside, it stayed up. The Vo-Ag students put a grass roof on top of it and a wooden roof inside of it. They put in a rocking chair and hung cross-stitched art inside it, just like the "Living to Serve: The Sod House Experience" presentation showed.

For your information, it is very pleasant to sit in a sod house and rock a baby and look out the open door and be surrounded by all that tallgrass prairie. I have done this myself, late in the evening, encircled by the smells of so many kinds of grasses and living things, and the sounds of crickets and the dancing of fireflies, which make for a beautiful, musical show. All of these things can fill my heart with joy and my eyes with tears, though sometimes Faith Maddie screams the whole time and so I am good and distracted. Sometimes she looks just like the Vo-Ag teacher. Something in the way her eyes move, the way her mouth moves, especially when she screams or laughs. It is a nice reminder that at least in one small way the Vo-Ag teacher and I are family.

And since the grand opening in September, ten people per day have visited the Sod House Experience!

You can check it out yourself. If you're coming from Minneapolis, there's a little sign on Highway 150 just south of Decorah. If you're coming from Des Moines, there's a sign right after the Walmart in Independence.

It's not that hard to find now that Mueller has harvested the corn, but if you aren't used to the vast distances people like me put between things, you might want to give me a call. Plus, Mueller can be kind of an asshole about strangers on his property. You would be well served to let me grease his wheel of fortune for you before you get here.

43

During that *Annie* year, twelve houses and the public library blew up or burned down, forty-seven of my clients died, forty-two of my clients failed to pay for their personal income tax services, Mueller bilked me out of $5,000 for the sod house (though he spent about that much on new locks for his anhydrous ammonia tanks), and Clive went to federal prison in Fort Dodge on aggravated assault and drug convictions. That was some bad business, trying to sell stolen methamphetamine ingredients. For Hope, that one night would have bought her a whole year of college, if it had worked out. For Clive, he would have needed ninety-five nights like that to buy the farm he always wanted, and two nights a month to keep it running. He will be eligible for parole in six years. Maybe things around here will be different then, but probably not.

From those numbers, it looks like it was a bad year for business all around.

But consider this: during that school year, Mueller purchased the co-op in Winthrop, plus several apartment buildings in this town and in nearby ones, and 150 acres from the estate of Florence Nagle, one of the forty-seven clients of mine who died. Now I manage several rentals and the co-op payroll in addition to Mueller's business and farm payroll, all of which have grown significantly larger.

Bet your bottom dollar there'll be sun.

It's about to get even better, as Mueller was just named the new FFA adviser.

It was an emergency decision so that the students who had earned the right to perform their songs at the national competition in Indianapolis could still attend with a competent chaperone who knows at least a little something about farming.

For reasons that I imagine are obvious from all I have told you, it was a controversial decision. The school board believed Mueller possessed the necessary knowledge of horticulture and floriculture, and could use and maintain shop and landscaping equipment in a safe manner, and that he possessed the necessary abilities in problem solving, patience, reasoning, and judgment. What concerned them was his lack of interpersonal skills. Dieter even called me to ask if Mueller had ever, in my presence, demonstrated anything resembling interpersonal skills.

I told him, "Mueller has that special ability to be righteous while remaining nonjudgmental."

The school board got around the rule about an FFA adviser needing a four-year college degree by canceling the Vo-Ag class altogether. Beth and Missy will be Mueller's FFA advisees next year, but they won't be able to take any publicly funded Vo-Ag class in this town. Any students who want to take Vo-Ag for high school credit now have to drive to Fayette.

What Missy and Beth—and Phil and Travis and Hope—will be able to do, though, is cash out the remaining FFA funds after their trip to Indianapolis. They'll split about $19,000 five ways to partially fund their college.

Hope's share will be waiting for her here in my office whenever she comes home.

Also, said Dieter as he sat smoking in my office, "Mueller is from this town, and though that doesn't count for shit anywhere else, it counts for something here."

Still, the school board required Mueller to purchase the Vo-Ag trailer from the school, and pay to move it off school property and onto his own, so it didn't count for everything. The cost of that came to what I lost in income from the sod house deal. Mueller's only requirement was that he would not have to use the word "ecosystem."

"Now we're even," he said to me recently at Cunt Itchen, as he popped an onion ring into his mouth.

I just nodded and smiled in that way that is good for business and fingered the ends of my colorful belt.

There is nothing in this town resembling musical or acting talent whatsoever this year, not counting the two remaining Vo-Ag students. Therefore, the high school has chosen to do *Oklahoma!* Dee Dee Scarsdale will play Laurey, and she will most likely be pretty good. It may, in fact, be the role she was born to play because she has a good strong church voice but no spunk—exactly what the role requires.

By far my favorite part will be Ado Annie's song. Ado Annie will be played by Missy, who was inspired to try out for the musical after singing harmony with the Vo-Ag students and seeing *Cats* at Upper Prairie University. "If that's all it takes, it must not be that hard," she told me.

When she sings, *Every time I lose a wrestling match, I have a funny feeling that I won!* I will laugh louder than anyone else has ever laughed at any of our high school musicals, so hard I will almost certainly fall out of my chair. No one will wonder who it is doing that laughing either, because I doubled my contribution to the Theater Boosters for this upcoming school year. I will have the privilege of sitting front row, dead center.

I thought Sylvia Vontrauer was going to wrap her piano scarf around my waist and kiss me when I gave her the check.

No one loves the theater more than Tandy Caide, CPA.

Shortly after Silvia Vontrauer got her check, I received a letter from the Vo-Ag teacher in the mail. It was written on white paper with blue lines, ripped out of a spiral-bound notebook like the ones the Vo-Ag kids use. It was in a plain white envelope and it said this:

> *Tandy,*
>
> *I'm writing to you from the wet crotch that is Florida. It's hot and moist and sticky. I cursed that prairie winter, but Florida's fall? Wow. It's in my mouth, my nose, my ears, everywhere. But in so many ways I am in love with it. It's not like that endless icy sky and all that broken corn on the ground.*

The dirt is so wet it is sometimes sludge. The heat keeps me humble.

You would hate it here.

I'm working alongside Mexican migrant workers, fruit pickers, all undocumented, and we will move north up the coast soon. We are picking tomatoes, at least for the next few weeks. This means I sleep in a tent with my migrant worker comrades, or my car if it is raining or I need to be alone. I am up before the sun makes the heat unbearable, walking behind a flatbed truck plucking green tomatoes from tied-up vines and then carefully placing them in bins on the trucks so that they do not bruise.

As I reach for these green tomatoes and gently place them into the bins, my shoulders and hands get sore, my legs get sore, my whole body gets sore. And the more I feel physically exhausted, the more other things shake loose in me. Sometimes I am cutting and dropping tomatoes and sobbing all at the same time. Sometimes it feels like each one of these tomatoes is a flaw in me that I need to shed, but gently, with forgiveness. The Mexicans who work alongside me pat me on the back sometimes and say, "El Dios quitará todos sus pecados," *which means, "God will take away all of your sins."*

I have never met such warm, loving people. They know how to make a community. I feel a reciprocal bond to them, like my destiny is to help them become freer, more dignified workers, and their destiny is to free me from my own mistakes and fears.

Tandy, do not feel guilty about what happened between us, or what happened between Hope and me. The latter is not your responsibility. And the former, well, you owe me nothing. I do want you to know that I am in pain every day over what happened, but I am working through this pain. I am taking care of myself in the ways I know have worked for me in the past, and in new ways I am open to learning. I will be okay. I know you will be okay too. You're a strange bird, Tandy Caide, but you stand tall. It is the quality I most admire in you.

Kenny

Of course I had to laugh at that letter. And then I had to rip it up.

And then, of course, I had to admit to myself that I was happy to receive a letter. It is always nice to get a letter in the mail.

But then I had to throw it in the garbage. Then I had to take it out of the garbage and walk it down the hill to the burnt hole that used to be the public library. Then I had to light it on fire and throw it behind the chain-link fence that keeps kids from picking through the rubble and then I had to watch it burn. Then I had to walk back up the hill to my cottage on the go-around, pour four entire Mike's into one giant German beer stein I bought off eBay specifically for such a purpose, and sit on the hot cement of the back steps in front of the drained and empty hot tub and drink myself so drunk I couldn't see the mug anymore.

The next morning I slumped into a booth at Cunt Itchen before the sun was up. Barbie brought coffee, took a good look at me, and said, "How nice of you to join us here today."

Soon, Doc and Gary joined me, and Gary said, "We think you should know: the Order of the Pessimists has decided to disband."

"But why?" I asked. I was surprised. It had been so important to them, to us.

Doc smiled. "We see no future in the organization," he said.

Now, instead, the three of us, plus Mueller, meet at Cunt Itchen every other Wednesday afternoon, alternating with the Powerhaus because we don't want Mary Ellen to lose too much of our business. Doc doesn't say much, just listens to Mueller pontificate about wind turbines and the viability of going completely off the grid, but he always nods in agreement when Mueller looks at him or asks his opinion. Doc, apparently, is attracted to the idea of shedding the grid.

Gary just blinks. The bright lights of Cunt Itchen stun him. "It's like a foreign country in here!" he says.

We try to ignore the fact that Country Kitchen is a corporate chain of restaurants, with headquarters in Madison, Wisconsin, which is also home to thousands of organic-farming hippies and communists. Like her farm, and the farmhouse on it, and Huff's house and Huff's sizable estate that was willed to her, and like Faith Maddie who lives with her and is cared for by her, we pretend Cunt Itchen belongs to and has always belonged to Barbie.

One night, after I walked out to Barbie's farm and ate dinner with her and rocked Faith Maddie to sleep in the rocking chair while Barbie surfed one hundred channels of cable television, the wind picked up. The trees whipped around. There was electricity in the air. The scar just below my rib cage itched.

I looked out the window to the sky and saw dark clouds gathering, moving fast and strong over us. They looked so large, so uncontrollable, I felt small and scared for all the things that might harm us.

For the first time in my life it was I who cried in front of Barbie. She said, "Jesus, Tandy, what the hell is wrong with you?"

I said, "I don't know," but the truth is that I didn't want to go home to the cottage on the go-around. I wanted to stay out there forever, with Barbie and Faith Maddie—my family.

So I asked. I said, "Can I live out here with you and the baby? I will help you with the baby. I will do whatever I can to protect you."

"Protect me from what? What else could possibly go wrong here?" Barbie asked. She was laughing when she said it. She was being ironic. Then she sighed and shook her head and started flipping the channels on the television again. "This isn't my first baby rodeo," Barbie said. "I love you, Tandy Caide, but I know what I'm doing here. And I would just walk all over you anyway."

This made me cry even harder because it felt like a rejection from the only family I have left, and also because I knew it to be true, and also because no one in my family had ever said out loud that they loved me.

Even after all that had happened to me, I didn't know I could have so many emotions at once.

Barbie said, "Oh hell, now I have two babies!" and so she called Mueller.

He was there in ten minutes.

I didn't want to leave her and Faith Maddie alone, but she said, "I've been alone for a long time. I know where to find you if I need you."

So I kissed Faith Maddie's forehead and I ran from Barbie's warm kitchen through a terrible rain and into the cab of Mueller's truck, sobbing and snotting through it all. I felt like I was running through the ghosts of my failures. And when I got into the warm cab of his truck, and he patted my knee, I knew I would not be going home.

But it took Mueller hours to get it done. It thundered and rained and the lightning lit up the sky and the cab of the truck, but still Mueller drove me all around the county, mostly in silence. The wheels hydroplaned in low areas. We almost hit a fallen tree on the road. He drove me all the way to Elkader and back, and around all the back roads that we both knew, and over the bridge of County Road 8 where my people had hit their deer, and across County Road 14 again, and out to Upper Prairie University and back, and over and over that winding, swollen, angry thing that is Kennicott Creek.

It was almost midnight when he finally said, "Why don't you sleep at my place tonight, just until you get your shit together."

I opened my mouth to say yes, and also to ask him why it took him so goddamn long, but before any sound could come out, he said, "Just business, of course."

The next day I got Gary and his out-of-work friends to pack up a few things from the little cottage on the go-around and board up the doors and the windows until the day I was ready to examine the ghosts. I put my work clothes in Mueller's truck, and I moved out to Mueller's farmhouse.

My room is in the corner turret that hangs over the wraparound porch. It faces out to the road and Mueller's western field. Mueller had to move a lot of tractor parts out of the room, but as he did, we found a big brass bed that no one had slept in since his mother had gone to assisted living. Mueller washed all the bedding for me, and made the bed for me, and that first night once the bedding was dry and I had fallen asleep on the couch, Mueller even tried to carry me up the stairs. I was too big, though, and he dropped me halfway there. He ended up just pushing me up the stairs while I half crawled. Both of us laughed like little kids. He sat me on the bed and took off my shoes, and then he pointed my body gently down toward the pillow. He covered me in blankets and turned out the lights, but not before I was able to note my favorite aspect of the room: no wallpaper—just a nice white paint and three floor-to-ceiling windows, good and solid and double-paned with prairie restoration money, framed with heavy velvet drapes in a color like wine.

And now I wake up every morning here in that room, and I open the drapes to the sunlight. I walk downstairs in my nightgown and out the screen door and onto Mueller's big wraparound porch. I look out toward Mueller's many acres, and the big red sun rising out of his eastern field, and the corn and the beans pushing up to meet that sun, corn and beans that grow a little each day, slowly, but definitely growing. It is a beautiful scene, framed by Mueller's hand-hewn banisters, and Mueller himself, standing there at the rounded corner of that porch, fresh from morning chores, in overalls and short sleeves, with a cup of coffee in his hand.

He hands that coffee to me. He pretends like he is Curly, the good-looking young farmer boy from *Oklahoma!*, and he says, "Oh, what a beautiful morning, Tandy Caide! Oh, what a beautiful day!"

I laugh. I raise that coffee. I say, "Everything's going my way." And I drink that coffee, and aside from the coffee Barbie serves, it is the most delicious coffee I have ever had in my entire life.

You can't get coffee that good in Dubuque, or all of your other places like Dubuque and bigger. You might believe your coffee is that good, but I know for a fact it is not. Coffee that good you can only get from my best client, Mueller, out on the edge of the particular town where I live, and from my best friend, Barbie, at Cunt Itchen in that same town. And even then, I'm not sure our coffee is a taste that you people closer to the river are built for, or can even understand, though I have done my best here to help you.

You can talk to us. You can try to understand us. We would love to have you over to see our sod house or try our delicious coffee, even if it is just so that you can tell your cosmopolitan friends that you have had the experience.

But do not mess with us.

Do not mess with us. Ever.

ACKNOWLEDGMENTS

Books are a business done with big love. Many thanks to my agent, Danielle Svetcov of Levine Greenberg Rostan, who fell hard for Tandy Caide and shaped her and kept a candle burning for her. Many thanks to Chris Heiser and Olivia Smith of Unnamed Press, who also fell for Tandy. Chris and Olivia are *those* kind of people—the kind who seek interesting books and know how to make them shine. Thanks to those who know Tandy from way back: mentors at Hamline University (namely Sheila O'Connor and Patricia Francisco) and friends, including David Oppegaard, Brady Bergeson, Susan Montag, Sam Osterhout, and Desta Klein. Thanks to the kids who made the *Electric Arc Radio* show and all the kids who showed up for it, and to the women who sang in Goth Mother. Thanks to the literary communities of Minneapolis/St. Paul and Saint Peter/Mankato, particularly David Unowsky of Subtext Books, Pamela Klinger-Horn of Excelsior Bay Books, and the creative writing faculty of Minnesota State University, Mankato. Thanks to writers Mary Mack, Jason Good, John Jodzio, Dennis Cass, and Lesley Nneka Arimah who have inspired me in new ways the past three years. Thanks to the people of Oelwein, West Union, Hawkeye, and Iowa City, Iowa. Thanks to my immediate and extended family, who accept me as an eccentric with a lot of crazy ideas. Thanks to my children, Christian and Charlie, for the meaning and urgency to fulfill some of those ideas. And always, always, thanks to Geoff.

PHOTO BY CAITLIN ABRAMS

ABOUT THE AUTHOR

STEPHANIE WILBUR ASH is a former editor at *Mpls.St.Paul Magazine* who now works for Gustavus Adolphus College, a small, rural liberal arts college founded by Lutheran Swedes. She lives in Minneapolis and Mankato, Minnesota, and is originally from rural Iowa. This is her first novel.